LITTLE, BROWN AND COMPANY

Dear Reader,

In the wee hours of a Sunday morning, in the financial district of Shanghai, a young American woman is found unconscious on the sidewalk, critically injured by a hit-and-run driver. This is the setup for my seventh novel, *Rabbit Moon*.

Lindsey Litvak is twenty-two, a college dropout who finds work teaching English in China. Estranged from her parents, she has built a new life in Shanghai, fleeing a complicated past. For her American family, the accident sets off a chain of shocking events. Stranded at summer camp in New Hampshire, her little sister, Grace—adopted as an infant from an orphanage in China—reckons with questions about her own history. At the hospital in Shanghai, their parents come face to face for the first time since their acrimonious divorce.

Writing this book was itself an accident, a confluence of fortunate events. In the summer of 2016, I traveled to China on a writing fellowship. It was the opportunity of a lifetime, to spend a season living and working in Shanghai. I planned to finish a novel I'd started back home in Boston, but this proved impossible. Shanghai demanded my full attention. I didn't want to be anywhere else.

Shanghai was an astonishment—a vast, vibrant megacity that overwhelmed my senses and lit up my brain. I was instantly captivated. I was also lonely. Unable to speak the language, I could only observe the life around me, the comings and goings of the other tenants in the apartment building where I lived. Unlike anything else I've ever written, *Rabbit Moon* was composed entirely in public spaces—parks, tea houses, bars, and restaurants. Everywhere I looked, I saw stories. At a neighborhood café, I began to recognize certain faces. A particular couple came there often, a young Chinese man and a Western woman with long red hair. They spoke in Chinese—animatedly, over giant lattes. Over the course of many mornings, they found their way into *Rabbit Moon.*

Writing a novel involves the collision of multiple fascinations. *Rabbit Moon* is an outsider's snapshot of Shanghai at a singular moment—a thrilling, newly prosperous city of the future, changing at a whirlwind pace. The novel is rooted in my longtime interest in international adoption, the thousands of mostly female Chinese babies adopted by American families in the early 2000s. In writing Grace's story, I drew on the experience of close friends and family members and their adopted Chinese daughters, who generously shared their insights.

I hope you enjoy *Rabbit Moon.*

With all good wishes,
Jennifer Haigh

Praise for Jennifer Haigh

"Ms. Haigh is an expertly nuanced storyteller long overdue for major attention. Her work is gripping, real, and totally immersive, akin to that of writers as different as Richard Price, Richard Ford, and Richard Russo." —*New York Times*

"A gifted chronicler of the human condition." —Chris Bohjalian, *Washington Post Book World*

"Has Jennifer Haigh's moment arrived? For years Haigh has been peering deep into the heart of lost America...A superb unsung novelist hovering just under the radar." —*New York Times*

"Haigh has been a brilliant witness to the struggles of ordinary people." —Ron Charles, *Washington Post*

"One of America's finest novelists." —Ron Rash, bestselling author of *Serena*

"Jennifer Haigh is a young master of this form." —Richard Ford

RABBIT
MOON

ALSO BY JENNIFER HAIGH

Mercy Street

Heat and Light

News from Heaven

Faith

The Condition

Baker Towers

Mrs. Kimble

RABBIT MOON

A Novel

JENNIFER HAIGH

LITTLE, BROWN AND COMPANY
New York Boston London

Copyright © 2025 by Jennifer Haigh

Hachette Book Group supports the right to free expression and the value of copyright. The purpose of copyright is to encourage writers and artists to produce the creative works that enrich our culture.

The scanning, uploading, and distribution of this book without permission is a theft of the author's intellectual property. If you would like permission to use material from the book (other than for review purposes), please contact permissions@hbgusa.com. Thank you for your support of the author's rights.

Little, Brown and Company
Hachette Book Group
1290 Avenue of the Americas, New York, NY 10104

littlebrown.com

First Edition: April 2025

Little, Brown and Company is a division of Hachette Book Group, Inc. The Little, Brown name and logo are trademarks of Hachette Book Group, Inc.

The publisher is not responsible for websites (or their content) that are not owned by the publisher.

The Hachette Speakers Bureau provides a wide range of authors for speaking events. To find out more, go to hachettespeakersbureau.com or email hachettespeakers@hbgusa.com.

Little, Brown and Company books may be purchased in bulk for business, educational, or promotional use. For information, please contact your local bookseller or the Hachette Book Group Special Markets Department at special.markets@hbgusa.com.

Print book interior design by Taylor Navis

ISBN 978-0-316-57713-7

LCCN [tk]

Printing 1, 2024

LSC-C

Printed in the United States of America

For Josh

Chance is a word devoid of sense; nothing can exist without a cause.

—Voltaire

2016

I

Modern Universe

It could happen anywhere.

A red-haired girl stands on a street corner staring at a cell phone, music streaming through her earbuds. Stands, crucially, with her back to the street.

It could happen anywhere, but it happens in Shanghai, miracle city of modern China, on a Sunday morning just before dawn. Lujiazui, the financial district, is quiet as a graveyard—a ghostly proscenium studded with skyscrapers, a gleaming diorama of poured concrete. The buildings are sleek and fantastically shaped—a perfume bottle, a hypodermic needle, strategically lit like sculptures in a gallery. The streetlamps wear Mickey Mouse ears. The lampposts are decorated with colorful flags, printed in both Chinese and English: THE MAGIC BEGINS.

The street is silent. Except for the girl, there is no sign of life here. Traffic signals change ironically: green, yellow, red. For a brief, surreal moment, she feels that she is watching a light show, timed to the music feeding into her head—a pop song she remembers from childhood, sung by a girl with a scratch in her voice.

I'm like a bird, I'll only fly away

She nods to the music, a rhythmic self-soothing, and taps out a text message to a friend. **Waiting 4 dd**

And then, because she needs to tell someone: **Disaster night! Kill me now**

5

Six blocks to the south and one block west, a driver steers one-handed. The other hand covers his left eye, to stabilize his vision. He is nineteen and full of rice wine. His girlfriend screams at him through a Bluetooth earpiece.

I'm like a bird, I'll only fly away

The red-haired girl taps out another message, this one to her little sister. It's late afternoon in New Hampshire, where Grace has been sent, unhappily, to summer camp.

Good luck in the talent show!
Send pix!

On the long empty blocks the driver guns the engine, racing through green lights, testing himself. He feels that he is inside a video game: Lujiazui emptied out for his own amusement, the white Mercedes—his father's—his on-screen avatar. Green light, green light, green light. His luck is supernatural, his skill epic. He cannot be stopped.

Finally he encounters a yellow light, a sign his luck is turning. He makes a sharp left and hears a dull thud. With the firm conviction of the very intoxicated, he believes that he has struck a lamppost. With a puff of exhaust, the car squeals off, generating a sulfurous breeze.

The red-haired girl—her name is Lindsey—is thrown two and a half meters. Her purse and shoes go flying, her mobile phone skates along the pavement. She lands neatly, flat on her back, as though stretched out for a nap on the sidewalk. Her breathing is shallow. Beneath her head is a spreading pool of blood.

Above her the sky lightens. At dawn a street sweeper finds her. He calls the police on his old Nokia, then slips her iPhone into his pocket.

Johnny Du waits for the ferry, dressed in his Sunday clothes. His parents live on an island east of the city. One Sunday each month he joins them for the noonday meal, lavishly prepared by his mother: pork bone soup, seaweed salad, tripe dumplings, an entire steamed fish. Johnny takes the smallest servings possible, knowing his parents will stretch the leftovers to last the week.

On Sunday evening the ferry terminal is crowded—young couples mostly, dutiful adult children returning to their real lives in Shanghai. Johnny, the only single, studies his reflection in a smudged plate-glass window. In his good-son costume, wool trousers and a cardigan sweater, he's still himself, only less *niang*—no earrings or eyeliner, his hair combed flat. To a careful observer he's still plenty *niang*, but his parents aren't careful observers. Like most people, they see what they wish to see.

The boat boards slowly. As he climbs the stairs to the upper deck, he feels a man watching him, an employee of the ferry company. Such men are everywhere, in cafés and bars and, on summer afternoons, a secluded rock garden in People's Park. Usually the attention excites him. Today he feels slightly offended. He wants to ask: *Why me, Uncle?* In his good-son costume he feels above such notice.

When the uncle turns away, Johnny snaps his photo and sends it to Lindsey: **Dashu cruzin me on the boat.**

They text the way they speak, in both languages, toggling back and forth. His English is exactly as good as her Chinese. The symmetry makes for harmonious conversation. He's neither ashamed of his errors nor impatient with hers.

She doesn't respond to his message, a fact he'll remember later. They text at all hours, twenty or thirty times a day. Her last text was sent early that morning. **Disaster night! Kill me now**

Johnny wonders briefly about the nature of the disaster—a word she uses often, a word she taught him. A disaster, for Lindsey, might be anything or nothing: run in the stockings, lost wallet. Missed train, broken heel.

He finds a seat on the upper deck and settles in. The uncle is not unhandsome. He wears a nylon windbreaker like one Johnny's father owns. Johnny has nothing against older lovers—he prefers them—but Chinese men don't tempt him. Friends tease him about this. Potato eater, they call him. Only to Lindsey has he explained it: Chinese men are too beautiful. He needs to be the pretty one.

At his parents' house, the Sunday meal begins at noon. Today, because it was his mother's birthday, the entire family gathered: Johnny, his parents, both sets of grandparents. His father's parents are quiet and slender, his mother's talkative and round. Johnny is, officially, an only grandchild, the only child of only children. Seven people sat around the table, six lives that have culminated in his.

The visits unfold according to a template. Because the family expects it, he talks about his job at China Mobile. The job is imaginary, a fabrication of long standing. For three years he has worked as a hairstylist in Shanghai. At the Young Phoenix Salon he's known for spiky cuts and fanciful color, style with a streetwise edge. His imaginary self is an office flunky, known for nothing—an underpaid *diaosi* who sells mobile phone contracts, a job of such low status that no one would lie about doing it. His story thus has the ring of truth.

At each visit, Johnny's mother asks the same question. "Jun, is there any news from Lin?"

A year ago he gave his imaginary self an imaginary girlfriend. Like that of his job at China Mobile, the story of Lin has grown increasingly elaborate, an intricate tapestry embroidered over time. The story begins with a chance meeting, Lin coming into the store to buy a SIM card. Johnny gave her a widowed mother in a faraway province and, when his parents hinted that they'd like to meet his friend, a two-year scholarship at Wesleyan University in America. He wishes, now, that he'd made the scholarship longer. The first year passed too quickly. Soon he'll have to invent another story.

His given name, Jun, means "to be truthful." Each time it passes his mother's lips, Johnny hears it as a reproach.

She is a lonely woman. Johnny feels responsible for her unhappiness. His parents' marriage was inauspicious. His mother is sensitive and hungers for conversation. His father is an anchovy fisherman with a grade-school education. What is there to talk about?

Lin is a gift to his parents, a generous fiction, something to tell the neighbors. Lin brings peace and comfort to all concerned, even if they know she's a fantasy. Certainly his mother knows. What his father knows or doesn't, Johnny is less sure.

In this family, truth is selective. Many stories go untold. His slender, quiet father drinks and gambles. His round, talkative mother takes painkillers her body doesn't need. To Johnny she surrenders her secrets. She never wanted a son, not truly. She wanted, still wants, the daughter she gave up, her firstborn. The child she sent away.

Johnny isn't supposed to know he has a sister. At the table this fact isn't mentioned. His mother speaks of it only later, when she and Johnny are alone in the kitchen, after she's taken her pills.

"I had no choice," she often tells him. Her husband's parents wouldn't have forgiven her, their one chance for a grandchild wasted on a girl.

The story changes slightly with each telling. Johnny's sister is now twenty-five years old, adopted by rich Westerners and taken sometimes to England, sometimes to America. (To his mother they are interchangeable, different names for the same distant place.) Hearing the story for the first time, he understood that a mistake had been made. He saw himself with new eyes, the victim of a cosmic mix-up. *He* should have been the girl sent to England or America, not the dutiful Chinese son.

He's seen photos of Lindsey's little sister, the beloved round-faced child adopted from China. Her name, Grace, is tattooed on Lindsey's shoulder. Grace is fourteen years younger than his own lost sister, yet in his mind they've become the same girl. It's why he's fallen a little in love with Lindsey, a pure love that has nothing to do with the hungry uncles in People's Park. He loves her because they share a sister, the Chinese girl in America who is also, in some way he can't explain, his own true self.

Monday morning in the city. The subway trains are so crowded that Johnny commutes on foot. The stagnant air is moist and heavy, thick with industrial exhaust, the hot breath of coal-fired plants to the north, south and west. He wears a surgical mask of black silk, embroidered with tiny red flowers. A lover told him, once, that it made him look mysterious, like a harem girl's veil.

He crosses the street to avoid a building under construction. Long ago, it was the Gate of a Hundred Pleasures — at the time, the largest dance hall in Shanghai. Now the place is getting yet another facelift. A foreman in a lawn chair sits on the sidewalk in front of it, smoking. His head and shoulders are covered with white dust, as though he's been dipped in flour. Behind him the building's front doors are propped open. There is a terrific racket, the sounds of a demolition in progress: jackhammer, sledgehammer, shattering concrete.

The man in the lawn chair is brave but foolish. Sitting with his back to the work site is asking for trouble. It's common knowledge that an unquiet spirit inhabits the building. Workers have been killed here — two known electrocutions, a fall from a fourth-floor window. Last month a crossbeam collapsed on a carpenter, crushing his skull like a melon.

Johnny breezes past the cell phone store where his imaginary self — the dutiful *diaosi* — has already reported to work, neatly dressed in his blue China Mobile polo shirt. All day long, while Johnny shampoos and blow-dries, his imaginary self will sell phone contracts.

Pinned to his imaginary polo shirt is an imaginary name tag, printed with the real name his parents gave him: DU JUN.

Two blocks east of China Mobile, he crosses the street to the Wang Building, a nondescript tower nineteen stories tall. The doorman, a sullen thug with a shaved head, pointedly averts his gaze. This is their daily routine, a kind of silent conversation. In the three years Johnny has worked in the Wang Building, they've never exchanged a word.

In the elevator, a half-dozen strangers wait in silence, each staring at a cell phone. The elevator doors close and open. A well-dressed woman gets off at the second floor, which houses a karate school and the So Elegant Nail Salon. A pregnant woman gets off at the third floor, occupied by a travel agency and the Abundant Health Foot Massage Club.

There is no fourth floor.

No one gets off at the fifth floor, where ballroom dancing lessons are given, or the sixth, whose function is unknown. The elevator empties out on floors seven through twelve, which are occupied by the World Peace Guest House. The topmost floors, thirteen through nineteen, are home to the Modern Universe Service Apartments and a few small offices: a driving school, the New Me Acupuncture clinic, and Johnny's workplace, the Young Phoenix Style Salon.

The salon's door is propped open for ventilation. One of the stylists has an early appointment. Johnny recognizes the distinctive burnt-sulfur odor of a permanent wave.

The morning is busy. Young Phoenix is shorthanded, his colleague Anqi at home with a fever. Johnny works on her customers in addition to his own. Anqi is his mother's age; her clients, grandmothers with thinning hair and no imagination, don't interest him. Their tastes are conservative, their wishes predictable. They wish for the hair they had forty years ago, a miracle not even Johnny can perform.

At ten o'clock, he goes down the hall to Lindsey's apartment. As he does each morning, he knocks softly at the door.

"Girlfriend," he calls. "Are you sleeping?"

He remembers the last text message she sent him. **Disaster night! Kill me now**

He has a bad feeling.

Johnny waits and waits, but no one comes to the door.

* * *

He can recall clearly the first time he saw her—last summer, in this very hallway. He was taking a cigarette break, reading a *danmei* on his phone—erotic fan fiction about Sherlock Holmes, a character played by Curly Fu. The nickname was invented by the celebrity magazines. The actor's real name, Cumberbatch, is packed with consonants, nearly impossible to pronounce.

He was smoking and reading when Sun, the property manager, stepped off the elevator with a very tall Western girl. At the Wang Building, the presence of a foreigner was unremarkable. The World Peace Guest House attracted travelers from all over the world: European hippies loaded down with rucksacks; spry gray-haired tourists in matching tracksuits; Turkish women with more children than seemed physically possible, their tiny daughters already swathed in veils. The Modern Universe Service Apartments were occupied by long-term tenants—businessmen mostly, from Japan and Korea. They worked long hours and returned after dark, carrying takeaway bags—fried chicken to eat in front of the television, packs of cigarettes, and liters of beer.

Johnny smoked and studied the girl. His interest was professional. Her hair hung in loose waves halfway down her back. The color was extraordinary, brighter than auburn—the flaming red hair of a cartoon heroine, a shade he'd never seen on an actual person. Her hair reminded him of Princess Ariel in *The Little Mermaid,* a film he'd seen literally hundreds of times. Throughout his childhood, the DVD had played on a continuous loop.

Sun led her down the hallway to the corner apartment, delivering a speech Johnny had heard before. Rent was to be paid each Saturday. Electricity, water and internet were included in the weekly rate. They were halfway down the corridor before Johnny registered a surprising fact: Sun had spoken, and the Western girl had responded, in ordinary, correct Mandarin.

For weeks he saw her everywhere: buying dried jujubes at the corner market, hunched over a bowl of noodles in the shop across the street. Her red hair was impossible to miss.

One morning she came into the salon to ask about a haircut. A brief but heated competition ensued. Anqi held the girl's hair up to the light, like a length of fabric she might purchase. Incredibly, the color was natural. Even a master colorist couldn't achieve that red.

"She's mine," Johnny said, waving Lindsey into his chair. "I saw her first."

On the third floor of Xiehe Hospital, the girl lies motionless. A port in her left hand receives a dose of sedatives; the right hand, anticonvulsants. Another tube fills her lungs with air. Her shoes and clothing have been bagged as evidence. The satin pumps, with heels thin as chopsticks, were found two meters from her body. Her lace dress is the color oxblood, a shade darker than her hair.

Who is she, and where did she come from? The patient isn't talking. Her body speaks for her. Her height is measured at 183 centimeters; her weight, 62 kilograms. A female police officer photographs the Chinese character tattooed on her shoulder.

At the local precinct, she writes a report destined for obscurity. It's the sort of crime that is quickly forgotten—a hit-and-run without witnesses, a foreign victim with no name and no family, no keening relatives camped out at the police station, demanding justice.

Some days later, a detective studies the officer's report. The girl's handbag contained keys and lipstick, but no identification. She wore a dress and shoes, but no undergarments. A paramedic found, near her body, a pair of earbud headphones, but whatever they'd been plugged into could not be located. A phone, probably. No young person went anywhere without a phone.

On a hunch he calls DiDi, the car hailing company. Thirty-nine people requested predawn pickups in Lujiazui that Sunday morning, but only one had a foreign name. He writes it carefully on a notepad, unsure of the spelling: *Lindsey Litvak*. The syllables mean nothing to him. For instance: Is Litvak a man's name or a woman's? With foreign names he is never sure.

He studies the photograph taken at the hospital. The girl's eyes are closed, as though she is dead or sleeping. She looks young to him. Young enough to be a student? With Westerners it's impossible to tell.

The city has dozens of universities, students from every country on Earth. Like all foreigners living in China, they are required to register with the local police. The files are maintained by a centralized Records department, where the detective knows a guy.

Some days later, his friend in Records faxes over Lindsey Litvak's file. Attached is a copy of a US passport. The grainy photo shows a younger version of the girl lying in Xiehe Hospital, now twenty-two years old and breathing through a tube.

In a city of thirty million people, he has found her.

The rest of the file yields little information. On the Attestation of Temporary Residency, most sections had been left blank. Lindsey Litvak had supplied only her birthdate, passport number and a local address, the Modern Universe Service Apartments. The detective locates it on a map. The building is in the Jing'an section, west of the river. In his mind this raises a question: What brought an American girl to the financial district before dawn on a Sunday morning, dressed for a party but far from any nightclub?

The detective picks up the phone.

The comatose girl breathes deeply. A student nurse washes her arms and legs. The long limbs are slender and heavy. Her pale skin smells of milk. The student nurse studies the character inked on her shoulder. Except for a scraped elbow, her body shows no sign of trauma. All the damage happened above the neck.

The comatose girl dreams of rabbits. They are her little sister's favorite animal. Grace is eleven and enchanted by them. For months, now, she has lobbied their mother for a pet rabbit, so far without success.

Lindsey met her at the same instant their mother did. Grace was then seven months old, living in a state-run orphanage in Chongqing. There exists, in some family album, a photo taken that morning: Lindsey with a ponytail and a mouthful of braces, holding her new sister; Grace with pink eye and a persistent rash on her cheek. Invisible in the photo is Grace's scar, a white circle at the base of her neck, the size of a pencil eraser, where she'd been burned with a cigarette. She was not an abused child, they were told through an interpreter. Her birth mother had marked her so that she could be identified later, in this life or the next.

"Who was she?" Lindsey asked.

The interpreter relayed the question to an attendant, who responded at length. That she couldn't understand the answer is the great regret of Lindsey's life.

The interpreter's translation was four words long: "She was very poor."

Later, when Grace was older, their mother taught her the Chinese legend of the red thread, an invisible cord that connects each person to her future, to all those destined to love her in the course of her life. From the day Grace was born, the red thread connected her to the Litvaks. She was meant to be Claire and Aaron's daughter, and Lindsey's sister.

Of course, no one mentioned Grace's birth mother, the "very poor" woman so desperate to keep her that she'd burned her baby with a cigarette. This detail would have ruined the story. Would have proven, definitively, that the red thread could be cut.

New Hampshire is having a heat wave. For three days in a row, the temperature has reached ninety degrees. At Camp Friendship, the counselors pretend not to notice. Campers are sent on hikes with an extra bottle of water. No further concessions to the weather are made.

Camp Friendship is eighty years old—built for the youth of the last century, the sturdy children of New England Quakers. The cabins are spartan, cheerily uncomfortable. There are no curtains or window blinds; every morning, Grace wakes with the sun. The Quaker children, presumably, hadn't minded this. The Quaker children had never heard of air-conditioning and anyway, they weren't complainers. The dearth of power outlets didn't bother them, because they had nothing to plug in.

According to Grace's mother, Quakers see the Light of Goodness in every person. Also, they are pacifists. What this has to do with air-conditioning or power outlets isn't clear.

Her mother loves everything about Camp Friendship. She especially loves the Quakers, whose main principles—Peace, Simplicity, and some other ones Grace can't remember—are exactly what the world needs. Her mother thinks the Quakers are awesome. She's so crazy about the Quakers that, in Grace's opinion, she would have chosen the camp if it had no power outlets at all.

Grace's cabin, Monadnock, has six sets of bunk beds. She sleeps on the top bunk above a girl who never stops talking. Grace now knows everything there is to know about Austine, who lives in New

York City and is the only camper with actual breasts. Austine is a Pisces, which makes her intuitive and spiritual. Her favorite foods are pancakes and sushi. She is allergic to both tree nuts and peanuts, which are two entirely different things.

The counselors for Team Monadnock are Maya and Victoria. Like tree nuts and peanuts, they are two entirely different things. Maya has a boisterous laugh and can do imitations. Victoria's favorite word is "problematic." Her favorite activity is following rules.

Maya is the star of the Camp Friendship experience. Even if, like Grace, you came to camp with not the best attitude, Maya makes everything fun. Her first days at camp, Grace paddled a canoe and rode horseback. At Field Day with the neighboring YMCA camp, she ran the three-legged race with a boy named Jordan. She and Kira danced to a Rihanna song and won second place in the talent show.

Then disaster struck. Austine was caught sexting with a boy from the YMCA camp, which was extremely problematic. A cabin meeting was called. Team Monadnock sat in a circle around the firepit. One of the campers had made bad choices, in clear violation of the rules.

Their phones were collected into a pillowcase. "A tech break!" Victoria said brightly, as though this were some fun activity they'd all been looking forward to. Each night before Lights Out, they were given sheets of lined notebook paper and twenty minutes of Quiet Time, for writing letters. Letters!

Obviously, this was Victoria's idea.

If Grace were a different kind of person, she could have explained to Victoria that letters were useless. On a normal day, she exchanged a dozen texts with her sister in China—photos, videos, silly GIFs of dancing rabbits. She couldn't send a GIF in a letter and anyway, sending a letter to China was ridiculous! Sending a letter to China was like sending a letter to the moon.

When Grace talks about her sister in China, she knows what people are thinking. They picture a different type of sister, one who is Chinese-Chinese.

She sent a plaintive note to her mother (*Can I come home now?*), knowing it was hopeless. Her mother was anti-phone in general. Plus, the Quakers! In her mother's eyes, the Quakers could do no wrong.

*   *   *

Dear Linz,

Can you believe I'm writing you a letter??

You're probably sending me a million texts and wondering why I don't answer. The reasons is, I am in phone jail! Austine (bottom bunk) got caught sexting with a boy from the YMCA camp. (He is 15!) So Victoria (mean counselor) TOOK AWAY OUR PHONES!

Grace stops to stretch her fingers. Writing with a pen is hard work! Except for birthday cards to her grandmother in Florida, she never writes anything by hand.

Her handwriting looks babyish even to her. "That's not writing, that's printing," her grandmother says. Grandma Judy has beautiful old-lady handwriting, the letters all connected and slanting in the same direction. To Grace it is a marvel, a lovely but useless talent like churning butter or riding sidesaddle—life skills from another era, things people once knew how to do. Her grandfather could peel an orange in a single strip, the skin sliding off the fruit in a neat spiral. Grandpa Joe died when she was little and this is literally the only thing she can remember about him.

Grandma Judy has offered to pay a tutor to teach Grace how to write like an old person.

Grandma Judy's handwriting is literally impossible to read.

Grace studies what she's written. There's so much more to say! If she could talk to Lindsey, she'd explain how Camp Friendship is its own universe. Together day and night, Team Monadnock has become a dysfunctional family. A week ago they were strangers. Now Haley and Isabelle are mortal enemies, Sophia and Madison best friends for life. The alliances are volatile, constantly shifting. The girls agree on one thing only: Everyone hates Austine.

More, much more, to say. The extreme weirdness of showering with the other girls, the unspoken rules about seeing and being seen. Grace is the biggest in her cabin, taller and broader than the others. When they posed for a group photo on Field Day, she lurked in the back row until Victoria shooed her front and center. ("For balance!" she said.) Standing next to tiny Sophia, Grace felt hulking and awkward. A boy from the YMCA camp—there is always such a boy—teased her about it. "Chinese girls are supposed to be small."

Grace writes and writes. The thrill of dancing in the talent show, which for four magical minutes cured her of her shyness. Waking each morning to the smell of bacon, a food she used to hate and now eats every single day. The forest is dark at night—not the gray suburban twilight of Newton, Massachusetts, with its porch lights and streetlamps, but a deep, featureless blackness. The moon is larger and brighter than she ever imagined, the bunny ears clearly visible. It was Lindsey who told her about the rabbit moon. Now Grace can't see it any other way.

Writing all this down takes forever. She could've texted the same words in a matter of seconds, her thumbs flying over the screen.

When Quiet Time ends, Grace is still writing. Not until Victoria hands out stamps and envelopes does it occur to her: She doesn't know her sister's address.

*   *   *

The days pass slowly. Being disconnected from Lindsey is unsettling. For as long as Grace can remember—literally her whole life—they've been in near-constant touch. At night she lies awake in a gathering panic. What if a tornado hits, or a tsunami? What if the camp office catches fire, with all their phones inside? Her sister is on the other side of the world, unfindable. Lindsey will be lost to her completely and forever, if Victoria never gives back their phones.

*   *   *

Hundreds of years later, the punishment is lifted. The unhappy campers of Team Monadnock are reunited with their phones. For an entire afternoon they are invisible to one another, a dozen girls hypnotized by small glowing screens. Grace lies in her bunk, scrolling through text messages from her best friend, Iris, her former best friends Josie and Caroline. But from her sister—incredibly—there is only one.

Good luck in the talent show! Send pix!

The talent show is by now a distant memory. Lindsey's text was sent last Saturday, at four in the afternoon.
Grace replies immediately.

I just saw your text! They took away our phones!

She waits. When Lindsey doesn't respond, she fires off more texts, to catch her up on everything she missed.

It's boiling hot here! No AC

Austine got caught sexting and they punished all of us! Totally unfair!

Still Lindsey doesn't answer. Is her sister mad at her? Such a thing has never happened, as far as Grace can recall.

She rubs the scar at the nape of her neck, something she does when she's nervous. She studies Lindsey's last text, looking for clues.

Good luck in the talent show! Send pix!

The text is frustrating! How could Grace send or even take pix, if she didn't have a phone? She thinks of Grandma Judy, whose phone is bolted to the kitchen wall. When she was Grace's age, how did she send pix? Did pix even exist then?

Then, all at once, she remembers: In China, it's twelve hours later! Lindsey's text was sent at four in the morning!

This in itself is not so alarming. But Lindsey hasn't texted her in eight days!

Obviously, this is not normal.

Obviously, something is very wrong.

A phone rings in the Boston suburbs. The time is a minute before midnight. Claire Litvak is still awake, Not Writing. Against her better judgment she answers. Only telemarketers call the landline. Anyone who actually knows her would call her cell phone.

The caller, male, sounds young and nervous. "Ma'am, I apologize for the late hour. It's an urgent matter. I'm trying to reach Mr. Aaron Litvak." He explains that it's noon where he's calling from, the US Consulate in Shanghai.

Claire isn't alarmed, not yet. The reference to her ex-husband distracts her. It has the power to short-circuit her thinking, the very mention of his name.

"Aaron no longer lives here," she says. "Can you tell me what this is regarding?"

"It's about his daughter, Lindsey."

"She's my daughter too." It takes all her self-control not to shout it. "Did something happen? Is she all right?"

"There's been an accident," the consulate boy says.

Something is wrong with her hearing. His voice is suddenly very far away. On the notepad beside the phone she writes six words. *Xiehe Hospital hit and run Shanghai*. She doesn't immediately understand what she's writing. The word "Xiehe" means nothing to her. Twice she asks the boy to spell it. The looping script looks unfamiliar, a stranger's handwriting. She studies the words on the pad.

The consulate boy is still talking. Claire interrupts him in mid-sentence. "Wait a minute. Did you say *Shanghai*?"

For the last two years, her daughter has scratched out a living teaching English in Beijing. Not, Claire insists, Shanghai.

The consulate boy is stubborn. "I'm sorry, ma'am. According to the Chinese police, her local address is in Shanghai."

Claire closes her eyes. Relief washes over her. More than relief: a kind of mad exhilaration. It's a mistake, she tells him. That poor girl lying unconscious in a Chinese hospital is somebody else's daughter. Even as she says it, she understands that it makes no sense. And yet it buys Lindsey another minute. For one more minute, her daughter is safe.

"I'm afraid not, ma'am. The Chinese police have her passport on file. They've made a positive ID."

This is how it happens. Your life appears to be about one thing. Then the phone rings, and in a single moment, it is completely and irrevocably about something else.

* * *

That morning, on the last normal day of her life, Claire had coffee with a man her neighbor had met at a yoga retreat. "Gerry is special," Miranda said. "I've been saving him until you were ready." Claire didn't ask what, in Miranda's judgment, constituted "ready." She's been divorced for three years.

They met at a café in the town square of Newton—the comfortable suburb where she still lives, where she spent her entire married life. *It's only coffee,* she reminded herself as she circled the block, looking for a parking space. Dating at her age—she'd just turned fifty—felt slightly ridiculous. "Date" had fallen out of her vocabulary decades ago. There had to be a better word.

Gerry Duncan was sitting at a table near the window. She recognized him from a photo Miranda had taken at the yoga retreat. In the bright light he looked older than fifty-seven. She realized with a sinking feeling that he dyed his hair.

"You must be Claire," he said, getting to his feet. The top of his head was level with her eyebrows. Claire found this disconcerting. She isn't a tall woman, barely average height. Shorter men exist, but not in great numbers, and her high-heeled sandals gave her an unfair advantage. If they were both barefoot, she and Gerry Duncan might see nearly eye to eye.

"Do you live in the neighborhood?" he asked. He had a beautiful voice, deep and resonant.

"Sort of. I'm here all the time. My daughter goes to Country Day," she added, in the way of suburban parents.

"That's a high school?"

"K through twelve. Grace is in sixth grade. Seventh in September."

Gerry looked puzzled. "Miranda said she dropped out of college."

"That's my older daughter, Lindsey. She didn't *drop out*," Claire added, more sharply than she intended. "She's taking some time off."

"Ah. I've heard of this. A gap year, I think they call it?"

"Something like that. She's teaching English in China." Now that they were sitting down, the height difference was no longer apparent. Still, Gerry's delicate features — tiny nose, Cupid's-bow mouth — were a constant reminder of his size.

"China," he repeated encouragingly. It was a bit like talking to a therapist. "Are you estranged?"

"No!" Claire's cheeks burned, the beginnings of a hot flash. "Lindsey and I are very close."

Gerry chuckled.

"Is that funny?"

"Sort of." His eyes twinkled with merriment. "I mean, China is pretty far away. To get any farther, she'd have to leave the planet. How often do you see her?"

"It's been two years."

An awkward silence. Talking about Lindsey made her defensive; Claire knew this. She reached for a new subject.

"I hear you do yoga," she said.

Gerry grinned. "That's putting it kindly. I'm a rank beginner, but it kept me sane when my wife died."

"How long were you married?" Claire asked, relaxing a little. She was more comfortable asking questions than answering them. After Grace started preschool, she'd begun freelancing for the *Boston Globe*, writing obituaries. Day after day she interviewed widows and orphans, distilled entire lives into two hundred words.

"Eight years. It was a late marriage." Gerry emptied a packet of Splenda into his coffee. "We had a rough start. Barbara had a lot of baggage. Two ex-husbands, and the second one treated her badly. Her kids were already grown, but they'd watched the whole mess unfold and were pretty screwed up as a result."

"It happens," Claire said. His breezy summation offended her slightly. A casual observer might describe her own divorce in much the same way. "Well, what about you? You must have had baggage too." She felt oddly protective of the dead Barbara, who'd survived two shitty divorces only to spend her final years listening to Gerry Duncan's aperçus.

"Nope," he said cheerfully. "I had the opposite problem. I was a Catholic priest for twenty-four years."

A priest, Claire thought. It seemed that Miranda should have mentioned this.

"Of course, past a certain age, the lack of baggage is its own kind of baggage. It's no small thing to lose your virginity at forty-nine."

Claire studied him in wonderment. Unusually, she was at a loss for words.

"When I met Barb, what I knew about relationships would fit in a thimble, and most of it was wrong." For the second time, Gerry sweetened his coffee. "The Church's teachings on marriage are pure hogwash. It's not their fault; it's the way people who've never been married believe it should work. I loved Barb, but I thought we were too old to get married. That's what I said, but really, I thought *she* was too old. Because she was too old to have kids."

"You're joking," Claire said.

"I wish." He sipped his coffee and grimaced: *Sweet!* "In the Church's view, the whole point of the institution is to produce children. So a childless marriage isn't really a marriage. I figured if I was going to torch my whole life, give up a lifetime of consecrated celibacy, I wasn't going to settle for less. I actually said that to Barb. It was hurtful," he admitted. "I said a lot of things."

"What did Barb say?"

"She told me to go to hell." He laughed. "She used to say I was a fixer-upper. Most women would have run screaming in the other direction, but she didn't. It was the luckiest thing that's ever happened to me.

"We had a good marriage. Not perfect. We had eight happy years before Barb got cancer. Before that, I had a satisfying career for twenty-four years. I even helped some people along the way." Gerry sat back in his chair, seeming pleased with his summation. "All things considered, I've had a great life."

His serenity was enviable, if a little cloying. He seemed like a man who'd been successfully psychoanalyzed. Claire couldn't imagine dating him, but maybe she could write about him.

That was her intention when she sat down at her desk, before the telephone rang.

*   *   *

Claire stays awake all night. First she calls the hospital, an exercise in frustration since she doesn't speak a word of Chinese. Her ex-husband, predictably, doesn't answer his phone. That the consulate boy asked for him specifically bothers her more than it ought to. At some point, on some form or other, Lindsey must have listed Aaron as her emergency contact. *Why him?* Claire wonders. *Why not me?*

In the search window she types the word *Xiehe*. It means *concord*, according to Google Translate. A recorded voice pronounces it for her: *sheeya-hua*. Claire listens again and again.

Beijing, Shanghai. To her the names are nearly interchangeable. According to Google Maps, the cities are eight hundred miles apart.

At dawn she books a flight to Shanghai.

A Boeing 747 is cleared for landing at Pudong Airport. Aaron Litvak stares out the window as the wheels scrape the ground. The horizon is invisible, the sky and sea the same color, like watered-down root beer. The daylight is a little shocking. His assistant had booked him a direct flight, fifteen hours door to door. In the first-class cabin he stayed awake all night (was it actually night?), watching old westerns on his iPad: *Fort Apache, The Wild Bunch, High Noon.*

Deplaning takes forever. His fellow passengers carry a ludicrous amount of luggage — handbags, backpacks, shopping bags from the Duty Free. Aaron himself travels light. There's no telling how long he'll be in Shanghai, a city he's never had the slightest interest in visiting. Asian travel doesn't tempt him, long-haul flights across a dozen time zones. His company, NeoWonder, has made inroads into the Chinese market, but Aaron leaves the travel to his business partner, whose fascination with China is proportionate to his own indifference.

It's still possible that everything is fine.

He follows the throng through a quarantine area, where infrared cameras will measure his body temperature and, if he's running a fever, alert the appropriate authorities. His fellow passengers seem indifferent to the cameras, the uniformed agents stationed along the way. They move from checkpoint to checkpoint in a loose, disorderly swarm.

At Immigration Inspection a female agent studies his passport. "What is the purpose of your visit?"

It's precisely the question he's been asking himself. Claire's frantic phone call provided few clues. He gropes for an answer.

My daughter was in an accident. My daughter is in trouble again, or still in trouble. My daughter is troubled.

"Vacation," he says.

The agent holds his passport up to the light. His assistant had gone in person to the Chinese embassy and paid the hefty surcharge for a rush visa—single entry, valid for thirty days. *Thirty* days? Aaron thought but didn't say. He packed a week's worth of socks and underwear. It seemed like more than enough time to assess the situation and bring Lindsey home.

At International Arrivals he strides past a gauntlet of Chinese holding signs: Ramada Inn, Ritz-Carlton, Swissôtel. Finally he spots the name he's looking for, Cathay Royale.

"Welcome to Shanghai," says the driver, in careful English. "Did you have a pleasant flight?" As though fifteen hours on a plane, any plane, could be considered pleasant.

"It was fine," Aaron says. "A little long."

"Your wife hasn't arrived yet. Her flight is delayed." The driver raises his hands, palms up: *What can you do?* "We can wait for her in the lounge."

At one time Aaron would have corrected him: *ex*-wife. But he's been divorced for three years, long enough to relax about it.

Fatigue hits him all at once, like a physical blow. "Wow. Okay. I don't mean to complicate things, but can't you take me to the hotel now, and come back later for Claire?"

"Of course." If the driver is surprised, he doesn't show it. His wide, smooth face seems carved from stone.

Outside the terminal the heat is overpowering, the air humid. A dozen men stand smoking at the curb. Aaron inhales deeply. He quit years ago, but the urge has never left him. He eyes the pack in the driver's chest pocket.

The drive to the hotel is interminable. They crawl up an entrance ramp and onto an overpass. Below them are eight lanes of slow-moving traffic. Aaron expected dirt roads, bicycles, barefoot children, poverty. He picks out a Porsche, a Jaguar, several BMW sedans.

"Rush hour," says the driver.

"Not much rushing," Aaron says.

He reaches for his phone. He shelled out for the pricy international data plan—why exactly, he isn't sure, since any site he'd want to look at is apparently blocked.

He sees, then, the text message Claire sent yesterday from the airport: **Missed my connecting flight. I'm stuck in Seattle.** No point, now, in responding; they'll see each other soon enough.

Instead he sends a text to his younger daughter: **On the ground in China**. He nearly writes "your homeland" but catches himself. Grace doesn't think of herself as Chinese. Attempts to teach her about her heritage—the language tutor, the traditional dance classes—have gone nowhere. She even hates Chinese food. When Claire frets over this, Aaron reminds her: "She's a kid, for Christ's sake. She just wants to be like everyone else." His older daughter has the opposite impulse. Red-haired, six feet tall, Lindsey has chosen to live, of all places, in China, where she must be conspicuous as a flamingo. Her fascination with China began at age thirteen, when she traveled here with Claire to adopt Grace. At the time, Aaron was courting a major investor, an intricate dance that required his full attention. He was relieved when Lindsey clamored to go in his place.

In the past four days he's thought a great deal about that trip. If Claire hadn't brought her to China—he's sure of it—Lindsey would never have come to live here as an adult, to be struck by a hit-and-run driver and left for dead on the sidewalk. He knows it's simplistic and unfair, but he can't shake the feeling—profoundly familiar—that it's all Claire's fault.

She is an indulgent mother, a frustrated writer who's somehow never managed to write anything. Instead she pours all her formidable energy into raising their daughters, turning parenthood into more work than is actually necessary, just to have something to do. When Lindsey dropped out of Wesleyan, Claire coddled her. When she announced her plan to teach English in China, Claire—who'd spent her junior year abroad and never tired of talking about it—treated it like a reasonable idea. To Aaron, who'd already moved out of the house and thus had no say in the matter, it seemed a clear misstep, another wrong turn in a young life that had already gone disastrously off course. Still, it never occurred to him that the plan was dangerous. He took comfort from the fact that she wasn't going alone; her boyfriend, a big midwestern kid who seemed content to let Lindsey plan his life for him, would be tagging along. Zach was two years older, polite and respectful and maybe not the sharpest, but at least he'd managed to graduate. He and Lindsey filled out applications online and were quickly hired. The New Direction Language Academy arranged for visas and even paid their airfare. The entire process took less than a month.

Aaron and Claire drove them to the airport. It was the first time they'd been in a car together since the divorce. The parking garage was full, so he unloaded Lindsey's luggage and kissed her goodbye at the curb.

Since then they've kept in touch via email, though not regularly. It's been two years since he saw his daughter in the flesh. He's had to accept that Lindsey can take care of herself—or, if she can't, is unlikely to let her parents do it for her. All her major life decisions—applying to Wesleyan, dropping out of Wesleyan, coming to China—were made without consulting them. It's been years since she asked their advice about anything.

*　*　*

The hotel looks like the buildings on either side of it—a shimmering tower of mirror glass tinted salmon pink, the hue of a thousand vacation sunsets. The actual sunset is barely visible, a pink lozenge hanging just at the horizon, nearly obscured by smog.

The car stops beneath an awning. Beside it is an imposing fountain, decorated with marble nymphs and—bizarrely—a large inflatable Mickey Mouse. As Aaron gets out of the car, a sudden breeze kicks up. A spray of water hits his face, smelling strongly of chlorine.

The Cathay Royale came highly recommended. Peter Muir, his business partner, stays there often. To Aaron it's a hotel like any other—extravagantly air-conditioned, with patterned carpeting that makes his eyes cross. Next to the front desk stands another inflatable Mickey Mouse, man-sized. One white glove is raised in a jaunty wave.

At a shop in the lobby he buys a pack of Dunhills. Room 1511 is thoughtfully outfitted with matches and ashtrays. *How civilized,* he thinks, stretching out on the bed to smoke. After so many years, the nicotine hits him like a defibrillator. He's been awake for more than thirty hours. It's now 7 a.m. in New York, too early to call the office. Peter Muir is certainly awake, working out with his personal trainer, but doesn't answer his phone. And yet, after traveling to the other side of the world, it feels necessary to call *someone.* It's one of the small things Aaron misses about being married, the ritual of checking in from the road. For years he called Claire from hotel rooms and airports, just to let her know he was safe.

In the end he sends a text message to Erin Carpenter, a woman he

35

met on a dating site and has twice taken out to dinner. **Thinking of you. Hope all is well.**

To his surprise she responds immediately. **Where are you?**

The directness of the question startles him. Queasy from the cigarette, nearly blind with exhaustion, he responds without thinking: **Shanghai.**

Are you serious? she writes back—a full sentence, with appropriate capitalization and punctuation. It was the first thing he noticed about her: no cryptic abbreviations, no smiley faces. Her attention to grammar reassured him that he was dating an adult.

Yes, he writes back.

He nearly dozes off while waiting for a response. Mainly to keep himself awake, he calls her mobile phone. She answers on the first ring.

"Hi, Erin." Their homonymous names make for a certain awkwardness. Aaron feels, always, as though he's talking to himself.

"Hi yourself. What are you doing in *China?*" She's on her way to work; Aaron recognizes the ambient noises, the jovial recorded voice of the New York City subway system. *Stand clear of the closing doors!* The voice fills him with longing, an absurd nostalgia for the ordinary life he left just yesterday—the meetings and to-do lists, the daily commute. A week ago he delivered the welcome speech at the semiannual company retreat. Now he feels an odd tenderness for his former self, the Aaron of last week going about his business, innocently hailing cabs and returning phone calls and practicing his speech in front of the mirror, not understanding that everything was about to change.

"It was kind of sudden," he tells Erin. "There's a situation with my daughter."

"I thought she was at camp."

"My other daughter. Lindsey." Is it possible he's never mentioned her? More than possible: Erin had been reluctant to date him, leery about the age difference. Having a grown daughter—college-aged, though not actually in college—would have made him seem even older.

"She's been living in China the last couple years, teaching English. She's twenty-two," he adds, preempting the question.

There is a knock at the door.

"Hang on, Erin. Someone's at the door."

Through the peephole he sees a young Chinese woman standing on his doorstep. He opens the door a crack.

"Hello," she says in careful English. "Are you Tom?" She is dressed for a nightclub, high heels, a clinging black dress.

"Sorry, no. I think you've got the wrong room."

He closes the door and picks up the phone.

"Who was that?" says Erin.

"A Chinese girl, looking for someone named Tom. I think she was a call girl," he adds wonderingly.

To his consternation, Erin bursts into laughter.

"What?" he says.

She laughs harder.

"What's so funny?"

"I'm sorry," she says, recovering herself. "For some reason that is just hysterically funny. But continue. You were telling me about your daughter."

"Okay. Well, there's been an accident. Apparently she was hit by a car."

"Oh, God."

A silence.

"Aaron, I am so sorry. I feel like an idiot for laughing like that. Is she okay?"

"Unclear." He is aware of his heart working. "Her mother called the hospital, but the language is a problem."

"Her mother," Erin repeats. "She's there with you?"

Aaron has told her nothing about Claire, having learned from past mistakes. In the months after his divorce, newly single, he ruined more than one date by talking about his ex.

"No, just me." Technically, it isn't a lie: Claire's flight won't land for hours.

He says, "It's possible everything is fine."

The comatose girl dreams of mooncakes. Last year, at Mid-Autumn Festival, she ate two of them—one stuffed with red bean paste, the other with salted egg yolk.

Mid-Autumn Festival arrives each year, like a migratory bird returning—an annual gift to the people from their government, three days of paid vacation, a jolt to the national economy. Shopping malls do a brisk business. Mooncakes are exchanged and eaten. Families stroll through People's Park pushing prams and wheelchairs, the rolling conveyances of the very young and very old.

Yet because holidays must, it comes with a story. Long ago, on the night of the full moon, four animals encountered a starving man, never suspecting that he was the prince Śakra in disguise. When the man begged for something to eat, the monkey gave him fruit; the otter, fish. The jackal offered a lizard and a pot of milk curd. Having nothing else to give, the rabbit sacrificed its own body, leaping into a fire the man had built. Moved by the rabbit's great sacrifice, the prince drew its outline on the face of the moon.

In Shanghai the moon is invisible, the sky lit by a billion electric bulbs. Lindsey can't see the rabbit, but her little sister sees it for her. In a cabin in the New Hampshire woods, Grace creeps out of her bunk and peers out the window, looking for the rabbit moon.

The sun rises late in Shanghai. Claire wakes disoriented from a shallow sleep. Then comes the terrible moment when she remembers everything: her daughter lying in a Chinese hospital; a jumble of airports and taxicabs; her own frantic flight around the world. Somehow, in her brief, fitful sleep, she managed to forget these facts. Recalling them now, her terror and anguish are undiminished, as though she's hearing the news for the first time.

Her flight landed just after midnight. The hotel, luckily, had sent an English-speaking driver; but when Claire explained the situation, he refused to take her directly to the hospital. There was no point, he insisted. She would not be allowed to see her daughter.

She could have wept from frustration. By then she'd been traveling for almost two days straight—twelve thousand miles, half the circumference of planet Earth. The hospital was eight miles from the airport—technically, close enough to walk there. For a fleeting, insane moment, she considered setting out on foot, dragging her suitcase behind her.

The driver seemed to read her mind. She would not be allowed to see her daughter, he repeated. The best thing to do was get some sleep.

If only! After missing her connecting flight, she'd spent a night in the Seattle airport. By the time she boarded the plane to Shanghai, she'd been awake for twenty-four hours. Still, sleep was impossible. She'd never been more alert in her life.

The flight was interminable. In her ragged emotional state, sitting immobilized for thirteen hours was a brutal punishment. The safety briefing film on Hainan Airlines gave her a panic attack. To her American eye it was shockingly graphic, a convincing reenactment of a plane crash: overhead bins bursting open, suitcases spilling their contents into the aisle, a book, a red sweater, a stray flip-flop, the random possessions of these unknown travelers now plummeting to their doom.

"In case of an emergency bailout," the English subtitles cautioned, "remove high-heeled shoes." The practicality of this advice made sliding into the Pacific seem not so unlikely.

The things that can go wrong in a life.

Gingerly Claire gets to her feet. The bed is lower than she's used to. When she got up in the night to use the bathroom, the wooden frame attacked her shins.

The bed looks like a crime scene. The blood on the sheets makes no sense until she registers the familiar ache, low in her belly. When she turned fifty she declared herself menopausal, as though she could cease menstruating simply by deciding to.

In the bathroom she runs the water until it's cold—it takes a while—and soaks her underwear in the sink.

She dresses and ventures down to the lobby, a folded washcloth in her pants. There is no pharmacy in the neighborhood, but the concierge directs her to a nearby grocery store. Claire declines his offer to hail a taxi. The best way to get her bearings in a new city— she learned this years ago, as a college student backpacking across Europe—is to explore on foot.

Outside, rush-hour traffic is in full swing—three lanes in each direction, cars idling bumper to bumper. The volume of pedestrians is staggering, Chinese of all ages on their way somewhere—in professional dress, in jeans and T-shirts, in tank tops and spandex tights. A few wear surgical masks. An old woman carries an umbrella to shield her from the sun.

Claire joins the fray. At the busy intersection they stand shoulder to shoulder, close enough to smell one another—perfume and mouthwash, cigarettes and garlic. At nine o'clock in the morning, the heat is already sickening. She is uncomfortably aware of the terry cloth lump in her underwear, as though she has soiled herself.

The grocery store, when she finds it, is immense and bustling. The bright fluorescent lighting has a bluish cast. There is a smell of fish and spoiling produce, the lush stink of overripe fruit. She wanders, disoriented, past a vast selection of dried mushrooms, a hundred varieties of dehydrated noodle soup in bright paper bowls. Officious employees stand in every aisle, watching for shoplifters. In the refrigerated section, a plump woman offers samples of what might be yogurt. She is dressed entirely in red: a hat that looks vaguely military, a short jacket and bouffant skirt.

Claire takes an escalator to the basement, which stocks a massive inventory of housewares: plastic bowls and colanders, bamboo steamers and hundred-packs of wooden chopsticks, a huge assortment of cheap pots and pans. Boxes of sanitary napkins are stacked against the back wall. The packages are helpfully illustrated. Claire identifies several different varieties—panty liners, mini and maxi pads, with and without wings—but finds no tampons.

Her eyes fill.

While her daughter lies unconscious in a Chinese hospital, Claire Litvak is standing in a supermarket with a bloody washcloth in her pants, weeping over a tampon shortage. It is suddenly, blindingly clear that this is the lowest moment of her life.

*   *   *

Back at the hotel, she showers and dresses. The sanitary napkin is bulky as a diaper, but it solves the immediate problem: saving her from mortification, protecting the world from the sight of her blood. An hour later, fortified with coffee and decently diapered, she waits for Aaron in the lobby. Someone has left behind an English-language newspaper, *China Daily*. She scans the headlines—SHANGHAI CASTLE IS DISNEY'S LARGEST; OPENING OF SHANGHAI DISNEY TRIGGERS TRAVEL SURGE—and feels ashamed of her country, momentarily apologetic toward the Chinese people. In her view, the Disney franchise is yet another toxic American export, like carbon emissions or troop deployments or fast food or nuclear waste. Her own daughters had been Disney addicts, Lindsey especially. Without parental intervention, she'd have watched *Cinderella* twice a day. Claire found the cartoons insipid and weirdly moralistic, but grudgingly allowed them. She drew the line, however, at theme parks. Each time they visited Aaron's mother in Florida, Lindsey clamored to go to Disney World. Claire's answer, always, was a resounding "No."

On the facing page, another headline catches her eye. CHINA EXPERIENCES DRAMATIC DECLINE IN SUICIDES. The article is brief, heavy on statistics. There is a boastful tone to the writing: *Modern China has triumphed!!* It seems a strange thing to brag about.

"Claire!"

She looks up to see a man crossing the lobby toward her. Aaron was her husband for twenty years, and yet she doesn't, at first, recognize him. Context is the problem. He doesn't belong here any more than she does.

How did we get here? she marvels. *How is this us?*

They met at their five-year college reunion. *Reconnected,* Aaron would say, if he were the one telling the story; but this was inaccurate. They hadn't been connected in the first place. Stirling College was smaller than Claire's suburban high school—small enough that you knew everyone, or thought you did. But when Aaron Litvak approached her at the alumni reception, she was certain she'd never laid eyes on him in her life.

Apparently they'd taken a class together. Microeconomics fulfilled a requirement and had no prerequisites; Claire earned a solid B and hadn't thought of it since. But for Aaron, the course was life-changing. Professor Hubbard—"George," Aaron called him—became his mentor. On George's recommendation, he'd been accepted into Harvard Business School.

Claire nodded, barely listening. Across the room she'd spotted Troy Campbell, who was now writing for television. He'd flown in from LA for the reunion and was now charging in her direction. For this reason only, she let Aaron Litvak buy her a drink.

As they leaned in to clink glasses, Troy touched her shoulder.

"Claire McDonald! I was hoping you'd be here."

They did the reunion hug, the cheek kiss. "Troy, you remember Aaron Litvak," she said, briefly touching Aaron's arm. Helpfully, he was handsome—a full six inches taller than Troy, who'd put on weight and was losing his hair.

She'd met Troy senior year, in a writing workshop. Claire was the best writer in the class—a low bar to clear—and also the most demoralized. She was just good enough to know how good she wasn't, to recognize the chasm between the books she admired and what she herself could produce. Troy was a terrible writer, but through some blessed combination of luck and misplaced self-confidence, he managed not to know it. He swanned around campus in a floppy trench coat, talking about his "process." He sprawled on the library steps reading ragged paperbacks by Jack Kerouac and Hunter S. Thompson, whom he idolized. Not understanding that his work was bad, he kept writing and eventually got better.

Claire, paralyzed by self-criticism, didn't improve at all.

She left Aaron and Troy talking to each other, neatly extricating herself before Troy could ask the Question—there was only one— and feign surprise or sympathy at her response.

No, she was Not Writing.

It was a condition she shared with most of the human race, though other people seemed not to mind it. They simply didn't notice that they weren't writing, as they didn't notice they weren't juggling or throat singing or walking on their hands.

She forgot all about Aaron Litvak until, a few days after the reunion, he called her apartment, having wheedled the number out of the Alumni Office. Harvard Business School was hosting a welcome reception for the incoming class; would she be his date? His directness left no room for misunderstanding, no pretense of being Just Friends. She would learn later that this was typical of Aaron, who didn't deal in nuance and never did anything halfway.

Dating him was a well-organized experience. Aaron made reservations and bought tickets. He knew exactly where to park. They went to movies, to concerts, to restaurants—often with a group of his classmates from Harvard Business School. Suddenly Claire had a group of friends, something she hadn't realized she was missing. After graduation, she'd taken a job teaching French at a prep school in rural western Massachusetts. Her colleagues at the Burleigh School were her parents' age, and the village was short on nightlife. When she took the job, this had been part of the appeal. Her college friends had settled in New York, an easy train ride away, but Claire refused all invitations to visit. Solitude, she believed, would force her to write. To avoid doing so, she had a love affair with her only colleague under thirty, a history teacher named Jason Phelps. The relationship was brief and, thanks to a mystifying lack of sexual chemistry, technically unconsummated. (When she ran into him years later in Provincetown, hand in hand with a shirtless man, this finally made sense.) Their fellow teachers, starved for gossip in the somnolent village, took an unhealthy interest in the breakup, leading Claire to avoid them even more assiduously.

Having a boyfriend in Cambridge gave her a reason to disappear each weekend. And Claire liked Aaron Litvak. She especially liked sleeping with him. To her surprise, he was a skilled lover. He approached the task the way he approached everything: Faced with an unfamiliar mechanism, he was determined to understand how it worked. Her few prior lovers had been less ambitious. Before Jason Phelps there had been only Gilles, the French boyfriend who hadn't dazzled her. Later she understood that this was her own fault; she'd simply never taught him how to please her. At the time it hadn't seemed important. Her own orgasm was beside the point, which was to make him fall in love with her.

With Aaron she had no such agenda. Sex made them both happy, so they had it at every opportunity. When the term ended, they spent the summer together; a few of his classmates had pooled their resources to rent a house on Cape Cod. By August, he'd convinced her to quit her job at Burleigh. Taking a year off from teaching would leave her more time to write.

She did her best to oblige. Each morning she took her laptop to a crowded café near Harvard Square. Cambridge, it turned out, was a hotbed of Not Writers—students, professors, and sundry others, all engaged in the same doomed pursuit.

Life in Cambridge was highly social. Aaron's classmates planned brunches and dinners and movie nights, Sunday afternoons at Fenway Park. Their unofficial leader was Peter Muir, Aaron's closest friend at Harvard. To Claire he was like all of them, only more so: the most athletic, most privileged, best educated, most handsome. At the time he was engaged to an idealistic young doctor named Gabby, who'd aced a tough residency at Mass General only to take a job at a grubby clinic in Mattapan. When Peter bragged about her altruism—primary care was the least prestigious, least lucrative path a medical student could take—his smugness was grating. His outsize compassion for her Haitian and Cape Verdean patients seemed slightly suspect. Years later, Gabby's humanitarian work in Africa—she signed on early to Doctors Without Borders—would figure prominently in Peter's TED Talk. Having a saintly wife was good for his image. Peter had recognized this early on.

Outsize compassion, outsize everything. Peter Muir was just a little too much. Aaron's regard for him—admiration bordering on reverence—was, to Claire, exasperating. A blind man could see that Aaron was ten times smarter. Peter was a legacy kid, smooth and charming. He'd never had an original thought in his life.

On Thursday nights they convened at someone's apartment to watch television, a new sitcom the group was crazy about. The characters—six twentysomethings in New York City—were young and sexy and clever. Were, in fact, very much like them.

The show was pure fluff, but the biz school crowd loved it. Their tastes were mainstream. They seemed, always, to be doing market research. (*Why is this product successful?*) The MBA curriculum was rooted in the case method, the close study of successful companies. The wheel had already been invented, so they studied the best wheel makers. *What makes this organization a market leader? What can we learn here?*

One Thursday night, Claire spotted a familiar name in the closing credits: The episode had been written by her former classmate, Troy Campbell. In television he'd found his true medium. She recognized his snappy dialogue, his overdeveloped sense of irony, his palpable delight in his own cleverness—and was annoyed by him all over again.

"No way!" Aaron said, pointing at the screen. "That guy was in our class at Stirling. I met him at the reunion." Incredibly, *that guy* had been present the night he and Claire "reconnected." Aaron seemed not to grasp that Troy Campbell was the entire reason he and Claire were together, that she'd used him as a human shield.

At the next commercial she wandered into the kitchen, where Peter was mixing a pitcher of Bloody Marys.

"You could do that," he said, handing her a glass.

"What, be a bartender?"

"Write a TV show like that."

She said, "That's not the kind of thing I write."

Peter smiled as though she'd belched or farted, some awkward bodily emission he was too well-bred to acknowledge.

"Well, why not? People love it, and it's clever and funny. It does exactly what it sets out to do."

As always, his conclusions were unassailable. It was impossible to argue otherwise.

"Seriously, what would it take?" he persisted. "If you *did* want to write for TV, where would you begin?"

"I have no idea," Claire said.

Again the condescending smile. "Well, *somebody's* doing it. There are, what, thirty-five shows on prime time? Somebody's writing them." Peter filled his own glass. "What about your college friend? That's someone I'd get in touch with."

It was just *so Harvard*—the obsession with networking, the nearly Calvinistic belief in the power of social connections. The truth—that Claire didn't have the slightest interest in television, that she'd never in a million years get in touch with Troy Campbell—was none of Peter's goddamn business.

"Thanks, Peter," she said dryly. "I'll keep that in mind."

That night at home, she was violently ill. Peter's Bloody Marys rushed up her gullet like a sour geyser and turned the toilet bowl an upsetting color, as though she were bleeding internally. Her nausea lasted into the morning. She didn't know it yet, but she was four weeks pregnant. The next chapter of her life—and the first chapter of Lindsey's—had already begun.

They take a taxi to the hospital. Claire is in the back seat. Aaron sits up front, separated from the driver by a Plexiglas barrier. The car's air conditioner is broken. They sit in stopped traffic, idling in the heat.

The taxi driver glowers and mumbles. He seems to be having a one-sided conversation with the other motorists, the pedestrians crossing willy-nilly, the bicyclists and motorcyclists weaving through the gridlock.

"I *told* you," Claire says. "I told you something was wrong."

Aaron studies her face in the side mirror. *Of course* she told him. She's always telling him. Once a week he clears the hysterical messages from his voicemail: rants against Donald Trump, now improbably running for president; Lindsey's student loan debt, compounding monthly; her dim job prospects without a college degree. Aaron's position is always the same: He'll vote for anyone who will lower his taxes, and Lindsey's student loan is her own responsibility. Claire thinks he's being cheap, but this is unfair and inaccurate. If Lindsey had stayed in school, he'd have happily picked up the entire tab.

"Grace knew something was up," Claire says. "She hasn't heard from Lindsey in weeks. *Grace.*" It takes Lindsey a month to return a phone call from either parent, but she never loses touch with her sister.

"What did you tell her?"

"That Lindsey had an accident, but she's going to be fine." Claire riffles through her purse for a lipstick. Aaron has seen her apply it a thousand times—two quick strokes of color before pressing her lips together—but not recently. For just a moment, he feels married again.

"Thank God for the camp," she says. "I explained the situation to the director. They're letting her stay for the second session."

"Great," Aaron says. He doesn't ask what this favor will cost him. The Quaker camp, which Grace hates, looks like a penal colony and is priced like a five-star resort.

He stares out the window. Up ahead, a rickety bicycle is loaded down with construction materials: two-by-fours, a bundle of PVC pipes. Another carries—incredibly—a dishwasher, lashed to a plywood platform that sags precariously over its rear wheel.

"I can't believe we're in *China*," he says. "What the hell was she thinking?"

"It's called seeing the world. Being young." Claire's voice breaks and Aaron thinks, *Here we go.* He can feel her tears coming like a change in weather. When disaster strikes, Claire can always be counted on to lose her shit, her anguish eclipsing the original crisis in its demands for attention and care. If the house burst into flames, Claire's distress would demand the firefighters' full attention. It would be unforgivable, an act of monstrous insensitivity, to put out the fire first.

"All by herself?" says Aaron. "What happened to Zach?"

"They broke up. He went back to Indianapolis. She didn't tell you?"

"She doesn't tell me anything. I thought she was still in Beijing."

Claire leans back against the seat, her eyes closed, and fans herself. "The air quality is shocking. You read about this, but somehow I didn't believe it. I feel like I smoked a whole pack of cigarettes."

Reflexively Aaron feels for the pack of Dunhills in his pocket, to reassure himself that they're still there.

"When exactly did this happen?" he asks.

"Last weekend? What day is this?" Claire frowns, disoriented. "It took them a while to find us."

"A hit-and-run," says Aaron. "That's what they're calling it?"

"Apparently."

"How do we know that? Who told you that?"

"The US Consulate," Claire says. "That kid who called the house."

"He said that? Were those his exact words?"

"He's trying to get your attention," Claire says.

Aaron sees, then, that the driver is pointing toward a sign at the corner: XIEHE HOSPITAL. Claire pronounces it for him: *sheeya-hua*.

"It means *concord*," she says.

Aaron reaches for his wallet.

* * *

The room smells like an American hospital, the smell of inescapable realities. Lindsey lies on her back, her head elevated twenty degrees to reduce cranial pressure. Her arms are thinner than Claire remembers, her hair longer. Her skin is pale and smooth, unblemished except for a tiny hole in her left nostril. Her freshman year in college, to her parents' horror, she pierced her nose.

Now she wears a plastic bracelet printed with Chinese characters and a misspelled name, LINDY LITAK. A chair has been placed at her bedside. Claire sits there dumbly waiting for the doctor, holding Lindsey's hand.

Her firstborn, her onlyborn. Lindsey's hand is larger than hers, but otherwise a perfect replica, a photocopy enlarged by 10 percent. Except for her height—Lindsey is eight inches taller—their resemblance is striking. She inherited Claire's green eyes and high cheekbones and thick curly hair, though Claire's is blond now. Her natural color had grayed awkwardly, from red to a faded pink.

Where is this doctor?

She closes her eyes and listens to Lindsey's breathing. Somewhere down the hall, a television plays at high volume, a man speaking Chinese. His voice—deep and resonant, a newscaster's voice—washes over her like water: no words, no sentences, just an undifferentiated rush of sound. It is not, to her ear, a beautiful language. And yet, for some reason she'll never understand, her daughter has chosen to live in it.

Since earliest childhood, Lindsey has drawn up language like a cut flower in water. Her first words were Spanish, learned from a Dominican nanny. To Claire their chatter seemed encoded, an elaborate secret they were keeping from her. She was a different person then, her thinking distorted. Childbirth had wrecked her—not the labor itself but its aftermath. For a year she lived in a state of mental paralysis, a sadness so crippling that taking a shower felt like work. Lindsey was the child of that anguish, the innocent and unknowing catalyst of her despair.

Lindsey's first word was *"bueno"*; her second, "Mama." Her third word was "Flora," the Dominican nanny's name.

What was her fourth word, her fifth and sixth and seventh? Claire has no idea. The first years of her daughter's life are a blur. Later, properly medicated, she wished fervently for a do-over; but another pregnancy was out of the question. Then they found Grace.

She is a better mother to Grace than she was to Lindsey, a fact that shames her. With Grace she is accepting, uncritical, generous in a way that, with Lindsey, was simply impossible. The resemblance was the problem. Lindsey's pubescent awkwardness, her braces and teenage acne, flooded Claire with miserable memories of her own. She became the sort of mother teenagers hate, delivering a constant stream of unwanted advice. But because Grace looks nothing like her, *is* nothing like her, loving her is less complicated. Grace is her own remarkable person, completely and utterly herself.

Where in God's name is this doctor?

Claire touches Lindsey's hair, her cheek. The hospital gown has slipped from her shoulder, revealing a small tattoo—a single Chinese character, slightly larger than a quarter. Claire touches it wonderingly. Lindsey's skin is warm and dry.

Her daughter is beautiful—the best and worst thing that can happen to a girl, a trap Claire herself managed to avoid. Far better to be simply pretty, as Claire was and still is. Not being beautiful had protected her from the wrong kind of attention. Unencumbered by excess beauty, she was free to do other things, such as become a writer. (Except that she didn't become a writer.) Being pretty was good enough—ideal, really. Lindsey hadn't been so lucky. The eerie alchemy of genetics—pretty Claire plus tall, gangly Aaron—yielded an exquisite daughter. Lindsey is fatally, ruinously beautiful, the kind of beauty that makes a girl a target.

Once, in the Miami airport, a strange man handed Claire a business card. "Your daughter is stunning. Does she have headshots?"

On the card was the name of a modeling agency. Claire handed it back immediately.

"She's fourteen," she said.

Wherever they went, Lindsey attracted attention. In a single summer, puberty had transformed her. To Claire it was like science fiction, her daughter shape-shifting before their eyes. Her straight hair grew curly, her round cheeks slimmer. The braces came off her teeth. In a matter of months she grew four inches; the training bra she'd barely needed was suddenly inadequate. By the time she started ninth grade, she was five feet ten and wore a C cup.

That summer on the Cape, in her striped bikini, she drew lingering looks from boys and, disturbingly, grown men. Claire imagined taking them aside and explaining, gently, that her daughter still ate Count Chocula for breakfast; that among the clutter in her sloppy teenage bedroom was a complete collection of Harry Potter books and a plush Winnie the Pooh. On the drive out to Wellfleet, she'd woken with her hair in a tangle, having fallen asleep with gum in her mouth.

Lindsey seemed oblivious to the attention. A strong swimmer like her father, she bodysurfed in the freezing water until her lips turned blue. Claire loved watching her—her playfulness and effortless athleticism, her natural and uncomplicated joy. At that age, Claire had been crippled by insecurity. Trying on bathing suits in a department store dressing room was a traumatic experience, the cruel three-way mirrors offering her a rare glimpse of the scar on her back—eighteen inches long, a fleshy zipper running the entire length of her spine, the hideous souvenir of a childhood surgery to correct her scoliosis. The surgery was a success, as such things went, but to her young self the solution seemed worse than the original problem. For the rest of her life, she would wear that scar.

Lindsey's back was flawless, a long flat plane of unmarked flesh. Her straight spine was another gift from Aaron, whose superior genetic material had saved her from untold miseries. Lindsey would live in her body without shame. Lindsey was Claire perfected, the person she'd always wished to be.

Now she studies her daughter's face the way she studies her own, each night in the mirror. It's impossible to get this close to a conscious person. It feels somehow illicit, a violation of Lindsey's privacy. Privacy, that invention of adolescence: To Claire it had come as a shock that this body she'd carried inside her own, fed and bathed and held and soothed, should suddenly be withheld from her. "That's crazy," Aaron said when she tried to explain it. Claire didn't disagree—how could you? But he took entirely too much pleasure in pointing it out.

"Come back," she says softly, squeezing Lindsey's hand. Her voice sounds froggy, her throat aching with unshed tears.

They last spoke on Lindsey's birthday. What exactly they talked about, she literally can't remember. It was the last time she heard her daughter's voice.

Literally. Lindsey uses the word constantly, for emphasis—a verbal tic she's passed on to Grace. Claire used to find it annoying. Now she'd give a year of her life to hear Lindsey say it again.

Footsteps in the hallway, the click of high heels. Claire looks up to see a Chinese woman standing in the doorway, staring intently at Lindsey. She wears dark red lipstick. Eyeglasses dangle from a jeweled chain around her neck.

"Hello," Claire says, getting to her feet. "Are you the doctor? Do you speak English?"

The woman backs out of the room. Almost imperceptibly, she shakes her head.

*   *   *

Out in the hallway Aaron talks to Lindsey's doctor, a very young woman in operating scrubs. Head injuries are unpredictable, she tells him in halting English. A full recovery is still possible. They are watching Lindsey closely. The principal danger is swelling of the brain.

"Is this even a decent hospital?" Aaron asks. He doesn't mean to offend; it's an honest question. How the fuck can you tell?

The doctor tells him that it is very good, the best hospital in Shanghai. "All the Westerners come here," she adds, as if this should reassure him.

It does. "Well, that's something," he says.

She nods gravely. Yes, it is something. A stroke of luck, if such a thing could be called lucky, to be struck by a car just five kilometers from the best hospital in Shanghai.

They stand there a moment, not speaking. Aaron should be asking questions but can think of only one: *Is she going to die?* He is aware of his jaw clenching. If he opens his mouth, the question will fall out. He is relieved when a man approaches and speaks to the doctor in Chinese.

"This is Mr. Chen," she tells Aaron. "From the billing department. He would like to speak with you."

* * *

"What did he want?" Claire asks later, as they sit in yet another taxi with yet another broken air conditioner—headed, this time, for Lindsey's apartment. Mr. Chen from the billing department gave Aaron the address.

"What everyone wants," says Aaron. "To get paid."

Foreigners living in China, Mr. Chen explained, typically bought private health insurance. Did his daughter have such a policy?

"It's possible," Aaron said. He recalled, vaguely, that Lindsey's teaching job in Beijing included health coverage. In pitching the idea to her parents, she had stressed this point.

"Or perhaps through her work. Sometimes the foreign companies. What is the name of her employer?"

"I have no idea," Aaron said.

He studies the scrap of paper in his hand. Mr. Chen wrote the address in Chinese, to show to the taxi driver. All the characters look the same: bold pound signs, written with a flourish. It seems impossible that, to more than a billion people, these scratchings mean something.

"What did the doctor say?" Claire asks him for the third time.

"I told you."

"You told me nothing."

"Well, that's all she said."

"What's the prognosis, Aaron? What are they doing for her? Are they even *doing* anything?"

The driver brakes sharply, narrowly missing an old man on a bicycle.

"I can't believe you talked to her without me," she says, but of course she can believe it.

There is much, much more to be said about this.

The taxi changes lanes, provoking a clamor of car horns.

"She has a tattoo," Claire says. "Did you know that?"

"No." Aaron looks startled. "But, you know, a lot of kids have them. It's better than the nose ring."

The taxi turns onto a wide boulevard, lined on both sides with high-end boutiques. The street signs are in both Chinese and English: Yan'an Expressway. Nanjing Road.

"This can't be the right neighborhood. It looks expensive. What is *that*?" Claire points to a building up ahead, a massive structure with pagoda roofs leafed in gold. A throng of Chinese mill about on the sidewalk. Several tour buses idle at the curb.

For the first time the taxi driver speaks: "Jing'an Temple."

Claire cranes her neck out the open window. The temple takes up most of a city block. The ambient air smells of incense. Across the street is an Old Navy store.

Aaron has no interest in the temple.

"I still don't get what she was doing in Shanghai. Beijing is eight hundred miles away," he says. "It would be like you moving to Chicago for no reason."

"Obviously she had a reason."

"Like what?" Aaron says. "A boyfriend?"

Claire's face heats. It happens, now, with increasing frequency — when she drinks coffee or wine or eats hot soup, or when she's angry. That it's possible to have both hot flashes *and* menstrual cramps seems monstrously unfair.

"That's all you can come up with? A *boyfriend*?" She fans herself.

"Because, you know, no young woman ever does anything unless there's a man involved."

Of course Aaron would think that. What makes her even angrier is that she had the same thought.

"It's just a theory," he says placidly. "When did she break up with Zach?"

"Last spring." Claire doesn't add that she heard the news second-hand, from Grace. It's been years since Lindsey confided in her about anything.

"Also: What the hell was she living on? She must have been working *somewhere*."

At Aaron's insistence, they'd stopped paying Lindsey's bills when she dropped out of Wesleyan. Claire, who apart from alimony was broke anyway, reluctantly agreed.

Claire shrugs. "Teaching English, I guess. Like she did in Beijing."

The taxi races down a side street and lurches to a stop, in front of what looks like an office tower. A uniformed doorman, a large man with a shiny shaved head, waits at the door.

"*Here?* This is where she was living?" Claire is bewildered. She isn't sure what she expected. Somehow, not this.

She gets out of the car while Aaron pays the driver. The doorman speaks no English. He points to a sign on the wall: PROPERTY MANAGER 19TH FLOOR.

They take the elevator to the nineteenth floor, where another sign directs them to a corner office. The room is small and cluttered, loud with electric fans. An immense fish tank bubbles in a corner. At the desk a man shouts into a cell phone while eating his lunch, a slick pile of noodles in a Styrofoam tray.

When he hangs up, Claire approaches the desk. "Excuse me. Do you speak English?"

"Of course." The man blots his lips with a napkin and introduces himself: Sun, the property manager. His bottom teeth are missing. He seems slightly deaf, shouting to be heard over the fans.

Aaron introduces himself and Claire. "Our daughter is a tenant here. We need to get into her apartment. There's been an accident."

When he explains the situation, Sun nods gravely. "The city has become dangerous. Too many cars."

They take the elevator down to the sixteenth floor. Sun leads them to the end of a corridor.

"How long has she lived here?" Claire asks.

Sun says, "Fourteen months."

He takes an immense ring of keys from his pocket, unlocks the door, and flicks on a light. The apartment is small and tidy, a single room with a kitchenette and bath. A large window offers a view of the busy street, sixteen stories below. There is a low bed with a thin mattress, a glass-topped dinette table, a large TV set, and small leather couch. On the kitchen windowsill sits a jade plant in a blue-and-white china pot.

Sun closes the door behind him. Affixed to it is a photocopied notice, in both English and Chinese:

KINDLY REMINDING FROM THE POLICE STATION
FOREIGNERS, HONG KONG RESIDENTS, MACAO RESIDENTS,
TAIWAN RESIDENTS, AND CHINESE SETTLED ABROAD SHOULD
EACH TIME GO TO THE POLICE STATION TO COMPLETE THE
REGISTRATION OF TEMPORARY RESIDENCY WITHIN 24 HOURS

Claire thinks, *That's how they found us.* For a brief, unlikely moment, she is filled with gratitude toward the Chinese government. Somebody needs to keep track of people.

"Can we have a look around?" Aaron asks. "We need to find some paperwork. A health insurance card, that kind of thing."

"Of course. But first..." Sun inclines his head toward the door. "Mr. Litvak, may I speak with you for a moment?"

The two men step into the hallway.

"I am sorry to ask this," says Sun, "but the rent is due at the end of the week."

To Aaron the number is meaningless. He reaches into his jacket for his wad of Chinese banknotes and counts out hundred-yuan bills. According to the hotel concierge, no larger denomination exists, a fact Aaron finds incredible. A hundred yuan is fifteen bucks.

As he hands over the money, a mobile phone rings in Sun's pocket—a jubilant burst of electronic noise, like a slot machine making a payout. "*Wéi!*" he shouts into the phone, charging down the corridor.

Aaron follows him as far as the elevator, where a young Chinese of indeterminate gender stands smoking. Aaron reaches for his cigarettes.

"Excuse me." He pantomimes flicking a cigarette lighter. "Do you have a light?"

"Yes," he says in English. From his voice Aaron understands that he is a boy. He is very slender, dressed in narrow jeans and what looks like a silky black bathrobe. He appears to be wearing makeup. His ears are pierced with small gold hoops.

The boy takes a brass-plated Zippo from his pocket. He leans in to light Aaron's cigarette. His hands are perfectly hairless. On each wrist he wears two bracelets, made of red wooden beads. He smells of cigarettes and some floral perfume.

"You speak English," Aaron says, relieved. "Do you live in this building?"

"No. I work there." The boy points to an open door at the end of the hall.

They smoke in silence. Music streams from the open doorway, a woman's voice, American: *I fall to pieces.* It's a song Aaron remembers from childhood, a voice he ought to recognize.

"Are you Lindsey's father?" the boy asks.

"How did you know?" Aaron realizes at once the idiocy of this question. "Never mind, I guess it's obvious. You know her?"

"We are very good friends."

Hallelujah, Aaron thinks. For a fleeting moment, he is near tears.

"Then maybe you can help me," he says, recovering himself. "I need to know where she works."

The boy seems not to understand the question.

"Her job," Aaron says, more slowly. "Is she teaching English?"

The boy exhales cinematically. He smokes an unusual cigarette, rolled in dark paper. Around the filter are two thin bands of gold. "It's possible. Yes, I think so."

It is, altogether, a perplexing answer. Still, Aaron persists. "Do you know if she works for a company? Some kind of language school?"

The boy says, "I'm sorry. I don't know."

When Aaron tells him that Lindsey was struck by a car and gravely injured, that she is being treated at Xiehe Hospital, the boy's face doesn't change. It's like looking at a Siamese cat. He stares, very deliberately, at a sign above the elevator, a string of Chinese characters and the inexplicable words TIP TOP TOWN.

"Will she be okay?" he says finally.

Patsy Cline, Aaron thinks.

"Yes," he says, the only acceptable answer. Until that moment, no other possibility had entered his mind.

* * *

Alone, Claire paces the small apartment, so tidy it feels uninhabited. No personal mementos, no family photos. Aside from a laptop and a pair of stereo headphones, there's nothing here she's seen before. She has always been highly intuitive, sensitive to her surroundings; but about this place she feels nothing. A stranger lives here, an unknown Chinese person with orderly habits.

"Lindsey," she says out loud. "Where did you go?"

Fourteen months ago, her daughter moved eight hundred miles across China and never mentioned it to her parents, as if the fact simply slipped her mind.

At one time, such secrecy would have been unimaginable. For a long, magical stretch of Lindsey's childhood, she and Claire were closer than mother and daughter. They were best friends. Claire remembers that time like a book she read long ago: her marriage intact, her daughters thriving. It was true until, suddenly, it wasn't. Lindsey was a senior at Country Day when everything crumbled. The following year she went off to Wesleyan, pierced her nose and her navel (and, they could only hope, nothing else). She lasted four semesters. At the end of her sophomore year, she dropped out— why exactly, Claire still doesn't know. Lindsey refused to talk about it; parental questions only angered her. Now she lives on the other side of the world, and they communicate mainly through email. To Claire the silence is deafening. Weeks pass without hearing her daughter's voice.

The blank apartment offers no answers. Claire looks for Lindsey in drawers and cupboards. In the bedside table she finds lip balm and earplugs. The refrigerator is empty except for a carton of orange juice. An elaborate makeup kit, the size of a fisherman's tackle box, sits on the toilet tank. The medicine chest contains a blister pack of what looks like Benadryl, and several bottles of expensive perfume.

The narrow wardrobe closet is jammed with dresses in Easter-egg colors: pink, peach, lavender, yellow. With a shock, Claire notes the labels. Armani, Chanel, Ferragamo—names she recognizes from fashion magazines. There is a word for this type of dress—-trimmed, insistently feminine. A cocktail dress? Lined up on a shelf above them are several pairs of high-heeled satin pumps dyed the same improbable colors, as a bridesmaid might wear.

Claire studies them incredulously. Her daughter is six feet tall and lives in sneakers. Never in Claire's memory has she worn high heels.

The door opens. "Any luck?" says Aaron.

Claire says, "These aren't her clothes."

He looks at her as though she's speaking in tongues.

"I'm serious, Aaron. Are we sure this is the right apartment?"

"Maybe she went shopping," Aaron says.

Claire shakes her head vehemently, her eyes filling. Her daughter does not shop. Lindsey spent her entire adolescence in the same battered blue jeans, T-shirts fraying at the hem. Aaron, of course, doesn't know this. He has never done Lindsey's laundry, anybody's laundry. For twenty years Claire washed his dirty socks and underwear. Now he takes them to Family Cleaners at 64th and Lex.

"I mean it," she says, her voice quavering. "These aren't her things."

"Jesus Christ, Claire! *Focus.*" He takes a deep breath, loud and deliberate, to register his annoyance. "We need pay stubs. Paperwork. An insurance card. Did you even look?"

"Of course I looked. There isn't a scrap of paper in this apartment. She must do everything electronically."

"I was afraid of that." He sits at the table and opens the laptop.

"What are you doing?"

"What do you think?" He stabs at the keyboard. "Password protected, of course. Any guesses?"

Claire sits beside him. His shirt smells of cigarettes. They try Lindsey's birthdate, her childhood nickname (Mouse), the names of family pets long dead and buried (Sparky and Roosevelt, the golden retrievers; Stella, the Maine coon cat). To Claire it is a painful exercise. All these references are many years old. Of Lindsey's adult life, they know nothing at all.

"I give up," says Aaron. "My brain has stopped working. If I don't get some sleep, I'm going to lose my mind."

Sleep, she thinks dully. For a brief, deranged moment she is nearly sick with envy. Efficient sleeping is Aaron's superpower. He can fall asleep at will—anytime, anywhere—and wake on time without setting an alarm. His consciousness operates on a toggle switch: the two settings are wide-awake and dead asleep, with nothing in between.

"Try Dean Farrell," she says, her heart racing. They haven't spoken the name in years.

Aaron's face reddens. "I seriously doubt it," he says, but types the name anyway, in several permutations: DeanFarrell, DFarrell, FarrellD.

Claire holds her breath, but like all their other guesses, these are incorrect. It's a crushing disappointment and also, in a way, a relief.

*　*　*

In a past life, Dean Farrell had been a friend of the family. In their leafy suburb he was known and admired, his story often repeated: the promising rookie who, before blowing out his shoulder, played one magical season for the Sox. It was enough to make him a celebrity in Newton, Massachusetts, where the other husbands worked in law or finance and most of the wives did too, or did until the children came. The Farrells were reverse-typical: Trish, a vice president at Fidelity, worked long hours downtown, so it was Dean who took their daughter to the park and made small talk with the nannies and, one day, introduced himself to Claire. His Iris was in Grace's preschool class—in a town like Newton, an acceptable basis for adult friendship. Even Aaron, who preferred work to socializing and avoided their neighbors reflexively, took an immediate liking to Dean.

The two families barbecued together, hiked and picnicked and went to Sox games together. In baseball season, when coaching the Newton High School team took up most of Dean's evenings, Lindsey made extra money babysitting Iris, an ideal arrangement for all concerned. Claire believed this right up until the day when, putting away laundry in Lindsey's room, she discovered a plastic compact hidden in a dresser drawer, pills in four different colors. After the initial shock, she decided it was good news: Lindsey and the boy, whoever he was, were mature, responsible kids.

Confronted with the evidence, Lindsey told a different story. She was in love with Dean Farrell, and he was in love with her. How exactly this happened wasn't hard to picture. Every evening after babysitting, he drove her home in his car.

There began, between Aaron and Claire, a vicious, protracted argument: What should be done about Dean Farrell? To Claire, the answer was obvious. Their daughter had been molested. Dean Farrell was a child predator. Claire and Aaron would call the police, they would press charges.

"What charges?" Aaron countered. In Massachusetts, the age of consent was sixteen.

He said this with great finality—as if it mattered, as if such a preposterous law could be taken seriously. Under the law, it was perfectly acceptable for Dean Farrell to seduce a teenager. To Claire, it couldn't have been clearer: The law had been written by someone who'd never been a sixteen-year-old girl.

Of course, none of that mattered to Aaron. In the end, as always, he had his way. Without telling Claire, he had a talk with Dean Farrell. What exactly he said, she still doesn't know.

"I took care of it," he said simply. "They'll never see each other again."

He seemed to feel that this settled the matter, and in a way it did. In September Lindsey went off to Wesleyan. By the end of her freshman year, Aaron had moved his company, his entire life, from Boston to New York, and Claire had filed for divorce.

She couldn't forgive him. His insistence on confronting Dean personally—man-to-man—struck her as medieval. As if by taking their daughter's virginity, Dean had insulted Aaron's honor; as if Aaron, not Lindsey, had been wronged.

Their whole married life, he'd paid lip service to equality. Major decisions—a new car, a significant investment—were always discussed beforehand, but to Aaron this was no more than a formality. In the end he called the broker or bargained with the dealer, and whatever he and Claire had agreed upon usually went out the window. His decision to confront Dean Farrell was perfectly in character. Consciously or not, he believed that important matters were to be settled man-to-man.

The crowning irony was that Lindsey forgave him. Their relationship was damaged, but not totaled; somehow or other, Aaron managed to escape the full force of her wrath. In the court of teenage resentment, he was tried as an accomplice. In Lindsey's eyes, it was Claire who'd ruined her life, and Aaron did nothing to correct this perception. He'd been perfectly happy to throw her under the bus.

In the end Lindsey blamed her completely. Claire was outraged, but not entirely surprised. Her own mother had been the family disciplinarian, enforcer of curfews and assigner of chores. Claire and her sisters railed against these strictures—evidence, they felt, of their mother's dreary nature, her essential joylessness and pettiness. Their father was easier to love—jokester and prankster, amateur magician and virtuoso whistler, a man whose bear hugs had the power to right the world. His professional success—he sold real estate—was a direct result of his personal charisma, his warmth and joviality and easy laugh. His daughters idolized him and still do; it wasn't until Claire became a mother herself that she saw the injustice of it. Her father had reaped all the benefits of parenthood while her mother had done all the work.

Lindsey gave her father a pass. Aaron, too, seemed to forgive himself everything. For most of her adolescence he'd been absent, flying to and from Silicon Valley to cultivate partnerships, court investors, develop new IP. At home he was preoccupied, distracted. If Lindsey had burst into flame at the dinner table, he might not have noticed; he spent the entire meal staring at his phone. It apparently never occurred to him to wonder why she was so vulnerable to Dean Farrell in the first place—fatally hungry for male attention, the affection and approval of an older man.

In the weeks and months after Aaron left, Claire argued with him in her head.

Back at the hotel, Claire makes a phone call.

"Grace Litvak. She's in Monadnock," she adds, the name of Grace's cabin.

"Hang on," says the bored teenager at the other end of the line. "This could take a while."

In fact, it takes an eternity. Birdsong in the background, children's voices, a distant radio. The landline in the dining hall is the only way to reach Grace by phone. When the counselor confiscated the kids' cell phones, Claire was privately delighted. Grace spent entirely too much time staring at hers. A break from screens seemed like a fine idea, in the Before time.

(Before Lindsey lay in a coma in a Chinese hospital. Before a hit-and-run driver left her for dead on the side of the road.)

Claire stretches out on the low, hard bed and idly flicks on the television. The hotel information channel is available in Chinese, English, Korean, and Japanese. From the menu she chooses "Safety Procedures." She watches a vivid reenactment of a hotel fire, smoke billowing through the corridors, entire Chinese families wrapping their faces in wet towels.

Finally Grace comes to the phone.

"There you are!" For a moment Claire feels overwhelmed with relief, though she understands it's ridiculous. The camp is well-run, reputable. Grace is being looked after. This daughter, at least, is perfectly safe.

"I can't believe you're in *China*," Grace says.

Shanghai is a remarkable city, Claire would have said in the Before time. *Someday you'll have to see it.* For years now she's been a walking tourist brochure for the People's Republic of China—its history, its traditions, its natural wonders. According to the adoption counselor, this would empower Grace to explore her Chinese identity.

In the After time, she lets the moment pass.

"We saw Lindsey," she says, a tremor in her voice.

"Is she okay? Are you coming home?"

Claire ignores the first question. "Not yet, sweetie. She needs to stay in the hospital for a while."

"Can I call her?"

"She's resting," Claire says, because what's more restful than a coma? "She needs time to heal. We just need to be patient."

Silence on the line.

"It's *so weird,*" says Grace. "I keep texting her, but she doesn't answer."

"Wait a minute. I thought they took away your phones."

"That was just temporary. It was Victoria's idea," Grace says. "Maya would never have done that. She's, like, a reasonable person."

"Well, they both seem very nice." On drop-off day, Claire met both counselors. Victoria is Japanese American, the only Asian counselor at the camp. Claire had specifically requested that Grace be assigned to Victoria's cabin, hoping the two would hit it off; but instead it's Maya whom Grace talks about incessantly.

"Is Daddy there?" Grace asks.

"He's taking a nap."

Voices in the background, a bell ringing.

"Mom, I have to go. It's breakfast."

"Okay, sweetie. Go eat something," Claire says, but stays on the line. She is physically unable to let go of the phone. It's magical thinking, but she believes it absolutely: No further calamities can befall them, as long as she can hear Grace's voice.

Grace is her happy child: energetic, affectionate, uncomplicated. Adopting her transformed Claire's life. For the first time in many years, she was neither writing nor Not Writing. She was simply Grace's mother—and that, miraculously, was enough.

In those years she lived in the moment, as Grace did. It was a capacity she'd never known she possessed. Her earlier failure as a mother still haunted her, but Lindsey had survived her inept parenting. By all appearances, she was thriving: a standout student at Pilgrims Country Day, so far ahead of the curve that she'd skipped the eighth grade. Claire had resisted the idea, but Aaron, who'd skipped a grade himself, was adamant. Lindsey's standardized test scores were exceptional; for a gifted child, boredom in school was the greatest danger. In the end, he was right. In her new grade, Lindsey made friends quickly; she was outgoing and popular. Recognizing her unusual talent for languages, the upper school bent the rules, allowing her to study both Mandarin and French. At home she was sweet-tempered and helpful—devoted to Grace, an exemplary big sister. If Claire had accomplished nothing else as a mother, she'd given her daughters each other. By any measure, it was a remarkable gift.

Claire and her girls were a tight unit, a happily self-sufficient family of three. At the time, Aaron was often absent. Growing the company consumed him completely. He and Peter traveled constantly, courting investors. He lived entirely for his work, as young Claire McDonald had expected to live for hers. But the solitary writing life she'd imagined never materialized. Motherhood brought her far greater satisfaction than writing ever had. This continued for a few years and might have gone on forever, if she hadn't brought Dean Farrell into their lives.

They met at the town park. On weekday mornings it was abuzz with small children, supervised by mothers or nannies. Grace—then three years old—required minimal attention. A self-sufficient child, she was happiest playing alone in a corner of the sandbox, blissfully absorbed.

One morning Claire looked up from her *New Yorker* to see that Grace had made a friend, a towheaded girl exactly her size. They were playing together with great energy, building what Grace later explained was a sand bakery: cakes and pies and cupcakes and cookies, all made of moistened sand.

When Grace's new friend tripped and stumbled and let out a wail, Claire heard a male voice behind her.

"Iris! What's the matter, sweetheart?"

Iris's dad was young and handsome, with the body of a college athlete. He headed for the sandbox at an easy jog.

Iris wailed louder. Then Grace, in apparent solidarity, began crying too.

"Yikes—sorry," the man called to Claire. "I guess it's contagious."

She saw that he was her own age: gray at the temples, his blue eyes crinkling at the corners.

"I was sleeping on the job. Please don't tell my wife."

Claire would remember this later, how he'd mentioned his wife immediately. It made her trust him. He bragged shamelessly about Trish's accomplishments, her meteoric rise at Fidelity. "She's the brains of the operation," he liked to say. "I'm Mr. Mom."

She saw him at the playground every morning. If she and Grace happened to arrive first, her daughter was inconsolable until Iris arrived. Claire marveled at the intensity of it, Grace's instant, all-consuming attachment. In a teenager you'd call it puppy love, but in a very small child it raised a compelling question: What did it mean, exactly, to fall in love?

While the girls played together, their parents shared a park bench. Claire, being Claire, asked a million questions. Dean answered at length, charmingly and in great detail. Twenty years ago he'd been a top draft pick for the Red Sox, pitched in six games before blowing out his shoulder. The injury was irreparable. Many surgeries later, he could paint the house and shovel the driveway and carry Iris to bed each night. But never again would he throw ninety-eight miles an hour.

This is the worst part of the story, the part that shames her: When she first met Dean Farrell, and for some months after, Claire had flashed on him. That was how she thought of it, a flash—the kind of instant attraction a younger, less experienced person might mistake for love. She believed at the time that the feeling was mutual, that as mature, married adults, they'd tacitly agreed not to act on it.

The mad hunger for love—Claire knew this—served an evolutionary purpose. But at the time she was forty-four; there was no longer any question of her propagating the species. The impulse had outlived its biological usefulness and yet she still felt it, that visceral, atavistic need.

Mature, married adults. How mortifying to discover, later, that it was her teenage daughter Dean wanted, Lindsey, who looked so much like her. That he preferred the larval version—unformed, pliable, inexperienced, undemanding—was a crushing existential disappointment, a bleak confirmation of a truth she'd always known. In the end, Dean was no different from the callow French boys who'd pursued Claire during her junior year abroad: tickled to meet an American who was actually *named* McDonald, undeterred by her halting, barely intelligible French. Speechless for the first time in her life, "Claire McDo" was a mute listener, seemingly incapable of wit or insight or complex thought. It was shattering to learn that men actually preferred her that way—a timid, simplified, wholly inarticulate version of herself. To Dean Farrell, Lindsey's emotional and intellectual immaturity were no impediment. They were part of her appeal.

Dean Farrell was a predator. Blinded by her attraction to him, Claire simply hadn't seen it. She had failed to protect her daughter. Everything that happened later was entirely her fault.

Back in his hotel room, Aaron cranks up the air-conditioning and slips between the sheets. After the smog and torpor of the city, the frigid room is an oasis of freshness. Exhaustion grips his arms and legs, his back and shoulders. Every part of him aches with the need for sleep. When he closes his eyes he sees hordes of Chinese people carried toward him on a great tide: old and young, on foot and on bicycles. A veritable sea of people talking on mobile phones, speaking a language he will never understand.

When he wakes, he feels that he's been asleep a long time. The crack of light between the curtains tells him it's still daytime, or daytime again; at first glance, it's impossible to tell. The digital clock reads 6:00, his usual waking time—though it takes him a moment to understand that it's 6:00 *p.m.* If not for the twelve-hour time difference, he'd have awakened perfectly on time.

He takes a very long, very hot shower—his one vice, something Claire used to give him shit for. "You're a one-man environmental disaster," she often said, as if Aaron's showers were responsible for all the planet's misfortunes. The hotel's water pressure is excellent. The towels, a little too short and a little too thin, are bleached a blinding white.

The room is so cold that steam rises off his body. He puts on a clean shirt, clean everything, and checks his phone. Two missed calls from Peter.

They'd started NeoWonder a lifetime ago, their second year at Harvard. Peter still has the storied bar napkin where they'd hashed out a rudimentary business plan, a prop he used to great effect in his recent TED Talk. Their partnership has outlasted every relationship in Aaron's life, including his marriage. Four years ago they sold Neo to Neutrino, the West Coast tech giant, on the condition that they continue to run it themselves.

It's now 6:15 in New York—a little early for a phone call, but Peter, famously, rises at dawn.

"Pete, what's up?" Aaron asks, his usual greeting. "Everything okay there? I can't access my Gmail."

"Dude, no VPN? Are you crazy? Hang on, I need to see you."

There is a moment of silence as Peter switches over to video. He is known for his insistence on face-to-face conversation, a principle he expounds on at length in interviews and in his TED Talk. Aaron finds this mystifying. Even a normal phone call is more personal contact than he needs with most people. Everything he needs to communicate can usually be conveyed in a text.

"Aaron, my man." Peter looks tanned and fit, sweaty from his morning workout. "You should have downloaded a VPN before you left. It's the only way around the Great Firewall." He drinks some bright green liquid from a tall glass. "How are things in Beijing?"

"Shanghai," Aaron says.

"Wait, *what*? I thought she was in Beijing."

"She was. Apparently she moved to Shanghai."

Peter looks flabbergasted. "Unbelievable. I was just there for the conference."

Aaron has no interest in the conference. Peter, being Peter, intuits this. "How're you holding up, buddy? How's Lindsey?"

Aaron tries to remember how much he told Peter before he left. His last day in New York is like something he dreamed. He has no memory of packing or getting himself to the airport, though clearly he did these things.

"Still unconscious. We were at the hospital all morning. I don't think she had any clue we were there."

"We?"

"Me and Claire."

"Oh, wow." Peter runs a hand through his sweaty hair. "Jesus, poor Claire. How's she handling it?"

"How do you think? She's a fucking wreck."

There is a silence.

"How's the hospital?" Peter asks. "Is she getting good care, anyway?"

"Hard to tell. Are the hospitals any good here?"

He hears the whir of a blender, Peter making himself a second smoothie.

"Depends," Peter says. "On the high end, they're as good as anywhere. On the low end, it's Appalachia."

How exactly he knows this, Aaron doesn't ask. Peter travels to China several times a year—to meet with government officials, with manufacturing partners. Jack Ma is a personal friend.

"Can you bring her back to New York?" Peter asks.

"Oh, man. She's in no shape." Burning in his throat, a feeling he recalls from childhood. Aaron hasn't cried in decades, as far as he can recall.

"How are you managing with Claire?"

"Fine. She looks good," Aaron adds, surprising himself. Why tell Peter this? Why should it even matter?

Peter says, "Give her my regards."

A bell rings in Peter's apartment, a sound like wind chimes. He is surrounded, always, by electronic noises, peals and chirps and customized ringtones.

"That's Gabby, calling from Darfur. I should go." Peter drains his glass. "Before I do: Is there anything I can do for you?"

He is famous for asking this question — evidence of his generosity and also (according to Claire) his outsize ego. Her resentment of Peter has always baffled Aaron, her reflexive impulsive to think the worst.

"Anything, buddy. Just say the word."

Aaron feels suddenly parched, his chest flooded with heat.

"Pete, I have questions. My daughter was *hit by a car,*" he says, very distinctly. "Some animal plowed her down and left her for dead by the side of the road and I'm supposed to be satisfied with that explanation."

At the bathroom sink, he fills a glass with water. He takes one mouthful — it tastes like a spent match — and spits it into the sink.

"A *hit-and-run,*" he continues. "I mean, whose conclusion was that? Was there even an investigation?"

"Well, there must have been," Peter says, quite reasonably. "They found you, didn't they?"

"Someone is *responsible.* Someone *did this* to her."

"Have you talked to the police?"

Aaron says, "Not yet."

*　　*　　*

Downstairs, the hotel restaurant is crowded. Aaron half expects to find Claire exactly where he left her — on a sofa in the lobby, staring blearily out the window — but there is no sign of her.

He heads for the concierge desk. "I need to find a police station," he says.

The concierge — a small, neat man with a trimmed mustache — looks alarmed. "Sir, is everything all right?"

Well, no, Aaron thinks. *Nothing is all right.*

"It's not an emergency," he says quickly. "Nothing like that. I just need some information."

The concierge signals a bellman and tells him something in

Chinese. Aaron follows him outside, waits next to the fountain as the man hails him a cab. Water clatters loudly into the marble basin, and Aaron feels a sudden urge to urinate. The Mickey Mouse balloon is now partially deflated, shrunk to half its original size.

A taxi stops at the curb and unloads its sole passenger, a Chinese girl in a slinky evening dress. She is shorter and curvier, but no less beautiful, than the one who came to his hotel room looking for Tom.

That morning at breakfast he told the story to Claire, exactly as he'd told it to Erin on the phone. "I think she was a call girl."

Erin had found this inexplicably hilarious, but Claire was not amused. "That's offensive," she snapped.

Her reaction was confounding. Had she always been this humorless, this hypersensitive, this judgmental? Or was Aaron simply more offensive than he used to be?

When he gets into the cab, it still smells of the girl's perfume.

*   *   *

The police station sits on a busy boulevard. Aaron pays the taxi driver with the Chinese cash he tucked into his wallet. The money looks fake to him. The crisp paper hundred-yuan notes lack the grubby authority of US dollars—the dusty green color of bread mold, soft as an old T-shirt run many times through the wash.

Unlike any place he's yet encountered in China, the police station is uncrowded. On each side of the lobby, a pair of baby-faced soldiers stands guard. To Aaron they look impossibly young, like kids playing dress-up; but the rifles strapped across their chests are undeniably real.

He approaches an information desk, manned by a uniformed officer. "Do you speak English?" he asks.

The man frowns. Through a combination of nodding and pointing, Aaron is directed to a chair and instructed to wait.

Moments later, another officer appears and speaks to him in Chinese.

"English?" says Aaron. "Does anybody here speak English?"

Once again he is left to wait. His chair sits directly beneath a skylight. He watches the progress of a shadow reaching across the lobby. A ray of sunlight pierces the low gray sky.

Finally a woman approaches him—middle-aged, dressed in slacks and a yellow sweater, and carrying a notepad. She's the only person in the place not wearing a uniform. In slow, clearly enunciated English, she introduces herself as Mrs. Li.

"How may I help you?" she asks, pen poised over her pad like a waitress taking his order. Her exact function is not clear. Is she a translator? Some sort of public information officer?

"My daughter was in an accident," he says. "She was hit by a car."

Mrs. Li seems unfazed by this revelation, as though this sort of thing happens all the time. Possibly it does. Possibly they keep her around for just this purpose, to deal with the victims—unlucky foreigners mowed down by Shanghai's crazy drivers, left for dead without a backward glance.

Aaron says, "I need to speak to the officer who investigated the accident."

Mrs. Li takes down Aaron's name and phone number, the approximate date of the accident. Twice he spells his daughter's name: L-i-n-d-s-e-y. Mrs. Li makes a series of unintelligible marks on her pad.

"I will give the message to the officer."

"What's his name?" Aaron asks.

Mrs. Li says, "He will call you."

*   *   *

From the police station, he sets out walking, unsure exactly how to hail a taxi. The air is stifling. When he turns a corner, he recognizes the Buddhist temple across from the Old Navy store. He is blocks away from the high-rise he and Claire visited this morning—the Wang Building, his daughter's last known address.

He finds it easily. The door of the lobby is propped open. The bald doorman is smoking a cigarette. He drops the butt to the sidewalk and grinds it out with his heel. Like Aaron, he is sweating through his shirt. There is a smell of bus exhaust and raw sewage and a surprising top note, unexpectedly enticing, something like fried basil. Aaron's stomach rumbles. He hasn't eaten since breakfast and is suddenly ravenous.

The source of the smell is a bright storefront across the street. In its window is a pink-and-blue neon sign shaped like a bowl of noodles, a sign that transcends language. A few solitary patrons sit at a counter looking out at the street.

The place is small and brightly lit, with all the charm of a bus station, but the delectable aroma is overpowering. Aaron waits in line to order, studying the menu on the wall, helpfully punctuated with color photographs. Pointing at the menu, he orders a steaming bowl of something. The old man behind the counter runs his cash through a counterfeit detector. Then he nods toward the front counter, where Aaron takes a seat.

Within minutes, a bowl and a mug of hot water are set in front of him. He ordered—apparently—several large, fishy dumplings in a salty, saliva-colored broth. Curled around the dumplings are (he is fairly certain) two generous coils of tripe.

He eats with great focus. Claire used to complain that dinner conversation was impossible when Aaron was absorbed in his food.

The saliva-colored broth is surprisingly delicious. When the tripe and dumplings are gone, he slurps it straight from the bowl. Claire, if she were here, would be mortified. He feels vindicated when the Chinese men on either side of him do the same.

He slurps and studies the building across the street, which resembles a Midtown office tower. Its upper windows are illuminated with fluorescent lights. It's hard to believe Lindsey actually lives there. Lives, lived? What exactly will happen when she wakes up is a question he hasn't considered in any conscious way. He realizes, now, that he simply assumed they'd take her home to Boston, the old house in Newton—a house where, in point of fact, Aaron no longer lives.

Home. Paternal instinct, if such a thing exists, boils down to this one imperative: to keep his family safe and close. By this standard—by every standard—Aaron has failed abjectly.

Of course, this is an oversimplification. The reality is more complicated, because it involves Claire.

She is a disappointed woman. He hadn't realized this when he married her, though he should have. He spent twenty years of his life trying to make her happy, but in the end it couldn't be done. Aaron understands this on a cellular level, having been raised by such a woman. His mother, Judy, is underwhelmed by life. Her disappointment seems congenital, a condition of her being. It's impossible to imagine her any other way.

His parents met as teenagers at a campground on Cape Cod. Joe Litvak was nineteen, a mechanic's apprentice at Otis Elevator. Judy had just graduated high school. They fell in love instantly and married quickly, and a year later, Aaron was born. Was his birth the beginning of Judy's disappointment? Or had she always been that way?

Her disappointment seems intimately connected to her younger sister, who married rich. In the lifelong competition of the Zeichner sisters, Nadine has swept all categories. Her winning streak began with her marriage to Joel Landau, a law student who went on to become an ambulance-chasing attorney, specializing in medical malpractice.

Apart from marrying sisters, Joe and Joel had nothing in common. Aaron's dad dropped out of high school to join the Navy, where he trained as an electrician. He could build anything, fix anything. As a boy he dismantled a television just to see how it worked. For thirty-five years he repaired elevators for Otis. In retirement he grew an extravagant vegetable garden that took up every square foot of their suburban backyard. Joe could coax tomatoes from the poorest soil. He could grow pole beans out of rock.

Aaron's uncle Joel was a different phenotype, nearly a different species—a man who swept through life with good-natured impatience, winning settlements and making investments, as though his extra consonant entitled him to a greater share of life's bounty. In their impeccable Tudor house in Scarsdale, New York, Nadine raised two overachieving sons and, in her spare time, ran a high-end catering business. Despite being a gourmet cook, she could still squeeze into her wedding dress, having preserved her girlish figure with Jazzercise.

Aaron's mother, a terrible cook, is thirty pounds overweight. She's been on a diet his entire life.

In any interaction with his Scarsdale cousins, her disappointment was palpable. Aaron was acutely aware of being part of the booby-prize package, along with a vinyl-wrapped tract house in New Britain, Connecticut, a part-time gig selling Avon cosmetics, and marriage to Joe Litvak.

As a kid he'd been the only Jew in his class—his parents' fault. They'd sent him to parochial school for a better education. Joe and Judy had a working-class respect for price tags: St. Boniface *had* to be better than what the public school handed out for free. Aaron was an excellent student; in any subject involving numbers, he dominated his class. At his mother's insistence—and because his cousin Phil had done so—he skipped the eighth grade.

That same year, he attended Phil's bar mitzvah in Scarsdale, a tense experience. Aaron can't recall the ceremony or even who was present. He only remembers his pants. His mother had taken advantage of the post-Christmas sales to buy, on layaway, Aaron's first suit. What made it a stupendous bargain, she said, was the label sewn into the lining—the name of a designer Aaron had never heard of, a label no one would even see. That spring he experienced a wild growth spurt. By the time the bar mitzvah rolled around, the trouser cuffs barely cleared his ankles. His mother pretended not to notice.

Aaron himself had no bar mitzvah. He didn't want one, and his father agreed. Joe scorned any display of religiosity. His objections weren't philosophical but economic. The vertiginous cost of three tickets to High Holiday services offended him existentially. "At that price we could see the Rolling Stones," he annually said.

After attending his cousin's bar mitzvah in flood pants, Aaron didn't set foot in a synagogue for fifteen years, until his shiksa bride dragged him to services on Yom Kippur. He was so in love, then, that he was easy to drag.

How bizarre to meet her in a hotel on the other side of the world, this woman he's spent his entire adult life shackled to. Blond now, dressed in clothes he doesn't recognize, but still unmistakably Claire. What he said to Peter is true: She still looks good to him. She always did; that was never the problem. The problem was everything else. Has she always been this prickly, this critical? Is "prickly" even the word for it?

There is no word for it.

The problem is that with Claire, he is always wrong.

In twenty years of marriage, he got used to it. A person could get used to anything. At a certain point he stopped resisting; he simply accepted her judgment. It was easier that way.

He doesn't miss that, his constant wrongness. He misses other things. Sex. Dinner together. Her ferocious smartness about nearly everything, her way of reading the world and seeing what he can't. He understands, now, how much he relied on it—Claire's insight into human nature, her almost supernatural ability to grasp other people's motives, which were invisible to him and still are. Without her he feels incapacitated, as though some essential sense has been lost to him forever, though over time he's made peace with it. The world is full of blind and deaf people who manage, somehow, to navigate. In the same way people learn to live without sight or hearing, he has learned to live without Claire.

"It gets easier," said Aaron's lawyer, Jack Monaghan—among local graduates of Harvard Business School, the divorce attorney of choice. Jack was old-school, Boston Irish, a thirty-year veteran of the Massachusetts courts. The main service he offered was commiseration: The Commonwealth's ball-busting divorce laws were notoriously hostile to husbands and fathers—Jack could tell you some stories. Aaron learned this the hard way, at considerable cost. He liked Jack Monaghan, enjoyed their expensive conversations. Despite paying him a small fortune to do almost nothing, he liked Jack very much. He'd have liked to have a beer with Jack, watch a game with Jack, but not at six hundred bucks an hour.

Claire was represented in the divorce by Marcia Schulman, a sixtyish lesbian who seemed to find Aaron both reprehensible and ridiculous. In their brief interactions, Attorney Schulman found ingenious ways to communicate this. She spoke to him Jew to Jew, her favorite way to shame him, her speech peppered with Yiddish words he didn't understand.

The divorce agreement wasn't complicated. Aaron would pay a modest alimony for five years, until Claire got on her feet. The sum was based on his income at the time they separated, which was meager. Obsessed with growing the company, he'd paid himself a paltry salary. Still he felt sheepish. With a trust fund to live on and no kids to support, Peter drew no salary at all, a grand gesture Aaron couldn't possibly match.

Then, a year after the divorce was final, they sold the company to Neutrino. Almost overnight, Aaron became a wealthy man. Claire could easily have dragged him back into court—because he'd built Neo over the course of their marriage, she could reasonably argue that she deserved a share of the proceeds, according to Jack Monaghan. A different type of woman would have sicced Marcia Schulman on him immediately, but Claire had never cared about money. She made only one request: that he pay off Lindsey's student loan.

"You can afford it," she told his voicemail; but to Aaron it wasn't that simple. His daughter—once a brilliant student—had abandoned her education, dropped out of college with no plan to return. Paying off her loan would mean that he supported her decision—and Aaron, adamantly, did not. Quitting high school had been his dad's greatest regret; Joe Litvak, if he'd lived, would have been appalled to see Lindsey squander her opportunities. His belief in personal responsibility was firm and unequivocal, his own private religion. The Navy had taught him that decisions had consequences, a lesson he'd drilled into his son.

This is what Aaron is thinking when the boy comes out of the building—the Chinese boy with the brass-plated cigarette lighter, the boy who knows Lindsey.

Aaron grabs his jacket—it's ninety degrees in the shade; why the fuck did he bring a jacket? In the five seconds it takes him to rush outside, the boy has disappeared into the throng on the sidewalk.

Aaron pushes his way through the crowd—an ocean of Chinese people, as in his dream. Is he even going in the right direction? The boy could be two feet in front of him and he'd never know it. He is surrounded on all sides by pedestrians with glossy black hair.

He's ready to give up when he spots the boy twenty yards ahead, crossing a busy intersection marked CHANGSHU ROAD.

Aaron breaks into a run.

He reaches the corner just as the light is turning. A woman in a fluorescent-yellow vest blows a whistle, two long, piercing blasts. Emblazoned across her back is the word TRAFFICASSISTANT. On Changshu Road the traffic charges forward, but Aaron keeps running. There is a clamor of car horns.

He is two feet from safety when a blue scooter nearly creams him. The rider is an elderly man who appears to be wearing oven mitts. The back of his T-shirt is printed with English words: REFRESHING WIND PEACEFUL SURFRIDER.

Again the TRAFFICASSISTANT blows her whistle. Aaron looks around frantically, but there is no sign of the boy.

He's ready to give up when he spots the boy just ahead, hurrying down a staircase into a subway stop.

"Wait!" Aaron cries. "It's me. Lindsey's dad."

The boy turns his head furtively. For just a moment their eyes meet.

"I need to talk to you," Aaron shouts.

The boy scurries down the stairs.

Aaron tries to follow, but it's like pushing his way through a mosh pit. By the time the human wave carries him down the stairs, the boy is gone.

* * *

Well, now what?

Aaron pauses, out of breath. His side aches from running with a belly full of dumplings. His shirt is plastered wetly to his back. The boy saw him; he's sure of it. So why did he run away?

He climbs the staircase to street level. The sun has set, but the headlights and neon signs make their own daylight. *My daughter lives here,* he thinks. He tries to picture Lindsey sitting in one of the cafés or boarding a bus or browsing shop windows but finds it impossible. When he thinks of her, it's a little red-headed girl he pictures:

the Lindsey he made snowmen with, rode bikes with. Adult Lindsey is a stranger to him.

He picks a direction and sets out walking. Idling at the next light is the blue scooter that nearly killed him. Aaron sees, now, that the driver's oven mitts are actually attached to the handlebars, secured with layers of grimy duct tape. Another TRAFFICASSISTANT stands by smoking as traffic swarms in all directions. The WALK signal promises nothing; it is no more than a suggestion. It seems to be saying, *Now is your best bet.*

Aaron crosses carefully. The Chinese pedestrians seem unfazed by the taxicabs squealing through the intersection, the bicycles and motorcycles darting in all directions. When a cyclist runs the red light and jumps a curb onto the sidewalk, colliding with a pedestrian, no one seems to notice. Naturally Aaron thinks of Lindsey—an innocent bystander, her young life hijacked by a hit-and-run driver. How many times a day did she cross these treacherous streets?

He passes a rotund woman with a soup-bowl haircut. Her purple T-shirt is printed with white letters:

THE STYLE
LET'S MAKE A CONCERTED EFFORT!

On the next block is a brick building several stories high, draped with a red banner lettered in gold. Aaron reaches for his phone to take a photo. At Peter Muir's suggestion, he downloaded an app that reads Chinese characters.

According to the app, the banner says: GATE OLD MOUTH CHINA.

He continues walking.

Halfway down the block, he spots a woman squatting in an alley behind a restaurant. His first thought is that she's taking a dump. A moment later he understands that she is eating, the two bodily functions so closely related that from a distance, in a poorly lit alley-way, one looks much like the other, a distasteful thought. She is his own age—a kitchen worker in a hairnet, on her dinner break, crouched in a position Aaron would find physically impossible. Just looking at her makes his knees ache. She wields her chopsticks at superhuman speed, shoveling in noodles from a bowl held close to her mouth.

Aaron passes a girl on Rollerblades, her T-shirt emblazoned with the word COLLEGE. No college in particular, just COLLEGE, as if attesting to the value of higher education.

He waits for another light to change. Across the street, at the opposite corner, a young couple clutches each other in a clinch that could be either angry or amorous. Their voices pierce through the roar of traffic, arguing or maybe not. With the language barrier, it's impossible to tell.

When the light changes, he crosses toward them. It's clear, now, that they are fighting, the boy declaiming loudly, the girl yowling back at him, clinging to his arm.

Aaron feels a surge of adrenaline.

"Is everything all right here?" he calls.

The boy and girl eye him blearily. He sees that they are very drunk.

He tries again, speaking this time to the girl. "Is he hurting you?"

She stares blankly. It's clear she has no idea what he's asking. Behind her a small crowd has gathered. When an old man yells something in Chinese, the boy answers deferentially, ducking his head.

Aaron backs away, his cheeks flaming. Hurriedly he crosses the street. At the next corner he glances over his shoulder. The boy and girl are now walking side by side, his arm tight around her shoulders.

Aaron passes a man in a blue ballcap, also printed with English words: ONLY BRAVE FOR SUCCESSFUL LIVING.

The next time he turns to look, the young couple is gone.

"I am a fucking idiot," he says aloud, to no one in particular. No one seems to disagree.

He imagines Lindsey walking down this very street, waiting at the corner for the light to change. If a man put his hands on her in anger, would any of these people have stepped forward to intervene?

No one had helped his daughter. Aaron himself had not helped his daughter.

He tries to remember the last time they spoke. The twelve-hour time difference is a complicating factor. Lindsey is a late riser; most mornings she sleeps until eleven. By the time she's conscious, Aaron is already asleep for the night.

This is the story he tells himself.

*   *   *

Dean Farrell took his daughter. Aaron has heard the expression before, an archaic euphemism for sexual intercourse. Now he understands the literal truth of it. After Dean Farrell, Aaron's daughter was lost to him forever. There was no getting her back.

The distancing had begun years earlier. Lindsey's puberty came between them. At the time it seemed natural, the fate of fathers everywhere. Claire acted as an intermediary, keeping him apprised of key developments: the first period, the mysteriously named training bra (training for what?). They agreed it was the best way to handle things, the most comfortable for Aaron and Lindsey both.

When Claire found Lindsey's birth control pills, she called Aaron in a panic. At the time he was in Palo Alto, courting an angel investor. In those days he was often traveling, but Claire seemed unbothered by his absence. She was happy then, by Claire standards. The girls were doing well in school. Claire kept busy with freelance work from the *Globe,* writing detailed obituaries for the most renowned of the local dead.

When she found the pills, her reaction was reasonable. She wasn't a prude, and neither was Aaron. His own family had been up-front about sexual matters, if short on wisdom. ("Keep your pecker covered" was his father's only advice.) Apart from the wish that he not impregnate anyone, Joe and Judy had no objection to him having sex. As parents, Aaron and Claire were of the same mind. Lindsey was seventeen, an excellent student. She'd applied Early Decision to Wesleyan and been accepted; her high school graduation was three months away. To be deflowered by some awkward, lovestruck teenage boyfriend seemed an appropriate rite of passage. In getting herself to Planned Parenthood, she had exhibited sound judgment. By any reasonable standard, she was doing just fine.

But Claire's conversation with her hadn't gone as expected. When confronted with the evidence, Lindsey confessed everything. There was no awkward, lovestruck teenage boyfriend. She was in love with Dean Farrell, and he was in love with her.

To Aaron it was like a meteor strike. He'd liked Dean Farrell, respected him even. The guy had a way of meeting your eyes, a frank and forthright manliness that made you trust him. Even Claire, with her uncanny sixth sense about human nature, had been fooled.

He and Farrell had talked about getting a beer together, but never did. Between his own travel and Farrell's practice schedule, they never found the time. Would Farrell have had the brass to sit there drinking a beer with him, knowing he was fucking Aaron's teenage daughter? Yes, he probably would.

Dean Farrell was probably a sociopath. Aaron and Claire agreed on this point. It was the last time they ever agreed about anything.

Aaron flew back from Palo Alto that weekend. From the airport he drove straight to Dean Farrell's. It was a Sunday afternoon in late spring, unseasonably warm, the dogwoods blooming. Farrell was mowing his lawn in shorts and a T-shirt, printed with the Nike slogan: JUST DO IT. When Aaron pulled into the driveway, Farrell turned off the mower and came toward him, wiping his sweaty forehead with the hem of his shirt.

Aaron stepped out of the car. He had come without a plan. He had no idea what he was going to say until he saw Farrell's bare abdomen — the firm, slightly thickened midsection of an aging athlete, covered in brown hair. The stomach plus the Nike motto, with its vaguely lewd connotations, made Aaron see it all with hideous clarity, the hairy middle-aged man who'd Just Done his daughter.

"You piece of shit," he said.

It wasn't a strategic approach, but it got the conversation started.

"My daughter," he said.

"Aaron." Farrell looked furtively in both directions — making sure, probably, that the neighbors' windows were closed. "Can we go somewhere? Some place where we can talk."

Without waiting for an answer, he went around to the passenger side and got into Aaron's car.

They drove in silence. Farrell directed him to the high school parking lot, empty on a Sunday. The only sign of life was a landscaper mowing the athletic field.

Aaron cut the engine. They sat for a long time without speaking. Later it occurred to him what they must have looked like: two closeted suburban husbands looking to get into each other's pants.

Say something, motherfucker, he thought but didn't say. It was a rule he'd learned from Peter, who dominated every negotiation they'd ever undertaken: Make the other guy talk first.

Finally Farrell spoke. "Who told you?"

Aaron said, "Claire found her pills."

"But..." Farrell was flushed, visibly shaken. His pulse was visible in his throat.

He's looking for his angle, Aaron thought. *Plausible deniability.*

He could almost see the guy's mind working, trying to figure out how much Aaron knew.

"Lindsey told her everything." Aaron stared straight ahead, at the big commercial machine buzzing across the soccer field, mowing in wide strips. "She's in love with you. She says you're in love with her." *Discuss,* he thought—that word beloved by English teachers. Last fall, when Lindsey was writing college application essays, it had become a running joke between them. "Linz, your room is a mess. Discuss." The memory nearly unglued him. Humiliatingly, his eyes filled.

Farrell didn't notice.

"Of course I love her. She's an amazing kid. An amazing young woman," he amended hastily, as though he felt the ice cracking beneath him. "But I have a family. Trish and Iris are my whole life. They can't ever know about this."

The words were enraging.

"*Your* family? I'm supposed to give a fuck about *your* family?"

"Aaron, I'm sorry. It never should have happened. I have no excuse."

The mower was getting louder. Aaron watched its progress across the field. It occurred to him that Farrell had known the parking lot would be empty. He'd known exactly where to go.

"Is this where you brought her? For privacy. Is this where you came to fuck my daughter?"

Wisely, Farrell didn't answer.

"I'll do whatever you want," he said, blinking rapidly. "Anything. Tell me what to do, and I'll do it. Just please don't tell Trish."

You spineless weasel, Aaron thought. He wished Lindsey could see Farrell at this moment, begging to save his marriage. Lindsey was young and foolish, but she had character. When confronted, she'd defended the man, and told the truth as she knew it. "I love him and he loves me." Dean Farrell had no such instinct. He rolled over like a little bitch. It was enraging to think that Lindsey had wasted her love on such a person, a man who cared nothing for her. It made Aaron hate him even more.

"You're never seeing her again," he said.

"Done," Farrell said quickly. "Of course. But first I'll have to explain it to her. At least let me do that."

"Are you out of your mind?"

The lawnmower stopped abruptly. The silence was brutal, unexpected, like some meteorological event.

"*Never. Again,*" Aaron said. "You don't talk to her. You don't text her. You see her even once, and I'll tell Trish. I'll tell the school board. I'll write it in the fucking sky."

* * *

"You did *what?*" Claire said.

They were standing in the foyer of the house in Newton, Aaron's wheeled suitcase on the floor behind him. With different dialogue, it might have been the final scene in a dying marriage, the disgraced husband being kicked to the curb. For Aaron and Claire, that scene wouldn't happen for another ten months.

"I saw him." Aaron was out of breath, as though he'd run home from Palo Alto. "I wanted him to look me in the eye and admit what he did." As he said it, he realized it hadn't happened. Farrell hadn't admitted anything.

"*Why?*" Claire looked stricken. "Why on earth would you do that?"

"I took care of it," he said. "He's never going to see her again."

"How does that take care of anything?"

There was a terrible silence.

"Look," Aaron said. "We can't undo what happened. I wish to God we could, but we can't."

Claire's eyes were wild. "We can hold him accountable! We can press charges! He is a *child predator*."

"Not legally he isn't. The age of consent in Mass is sixteen."

"That's impossible," Claire said.

"I talked to a lawyer," he lied. (He had Googled it.)

"You're telling me all this is perfectly legal?"

"That's what I'm telling you. If she were fifteen it would be statutory rape, but she isn't. Legally, there isn't a goddamn thing we can do."

Claire grabbed her hair with both hands, a terrifying gesture he hadn't seen since the dark time, postpartum, when she lay in bed weeping while Flora buckled Lindsey into her stroller and pushed her around the block. Normally a calm baby, Lindsey would shriek like a howler monkey if she saw her mother cry.

"I can't believe you," Claire said in a low voice. "I can't believe you did this without telling me."

"It's better this way. Trust me, he'll never see her again."

"*Trust* you?"

"Look, I know you think—"

"*Trust* you?"

"Claire, this is the best we can hope for."

It wasn't enough; it never would be. She wanted to see the man punished. Claire Litvak wanted blood. It was a side of her Aaron had never seen. It made him glad he'd never crossed her. In all their years together, he'd never betrayed her.

Claire said, "I will never forgive you."

As always, she'd kept her word.

The comatose girl is agitated. Her hand opens and closes like a crab's claw. She is reaching for her iPhone, a thread of a different color—the cord that connects her to the world, the dear and treacherous business of life on this Earth.

The thread connects her to Grace, who at that moment is running a relay race. Grace hates running, her teammates, the camp entire. She wants only to be left alone in the woods, to read and draw and look for rabbits. In New Hampshire rabbits are everywhere. All you have to do is be still and wait.

The thread connects her to Mei, who once seemed like a friend but has become something else entirely, and to Johnny Du, who is closer than a lover. He is the great friend of her life.

Somewhere out in the ether, her invisible mailboxes are overflowing with voicemails and emails and text messages. The messages are everywhere, they are nowhere. They don't live on Lindsey's iPhone, now outfitted with a new SIM card and stored in a street cleaner's pocket. They live in the air, between charged particles, the nowhere space the Apple corporation has named, cleverly, the Cloud.

Dashu cruzin me on the boat.

Graduation was amazing! We missed you Sending pix now.

Girlfriend I knocked on your door this morning where are u?

Xiaoying, I need you Tuesday night. Maybe Wednesday too. I will text the details.

I just saw your text! They took away our phones!

Austine got caught sexting and they punished all of us! Totally unfair!

Girlfriend are you ok?

Linz where are you?????? Mom said you had an accident!!!

Peace Hotel, 19:30. I will send a car.

Year of the Monkey

Statistically speaking, every meeting is improbable. Doubters can test this theory at home. Track your movements for seventy or eighty years and express them mathematically, a series of points plotted on a graph. Repeat one hundred seven billion times, for each person who has ever drawn breath on Earth. The odds of any two paths intersecting are vanishingly slim.

And some intersections are unlikelier than others. Two baby girls born twenty years apart, on different continents, under different heavens: one in a starving village in Anhui province, at the boiling point of the Cultural Revolution; the other in the moneyed Boston suburbs, on the very day her father graduated Harvard Business School. Statistically speaking, Mei and Lindsey shouldn't have met anywhere, and yet here they were on a Saturday afternoon in springtime—the rainy season in Shanghai—sitting one table apart in a tourist bar near the Bund.

The bar was Zach's choice—crass, overpriced, a fake Irish pub catering to Westerners, the sort of place Lindsey despised. They'd come to Shanghai for a long weekend, on the cheap: a last-minute flight on a bargain airline, bunk beds in a youth hostel. The trip had been Lindsey's idea. After ten months in Beijing, her Chinese had improved dramatically. This had created a distance between her and Zach, who knew ten words of Mandarin before they arrived and now knew eleven or twelve. Exploring a new city would, she hoped, make him fall in love with China—another unlikelihood, but it seemed worth a try.

In Shanghai the weather was miserable—*méiyǔ*, plum rains.

Lindsey was determined to see the city anyway. For two hours they walked the parks, the boulevards. They toured the former residence of Chiang Kai-shek, Zach complaining all the while because the audio guide didn't work and the exhibits were labeled only in Chinese. At the bar, soaked to the skin, they ordered expensive beers and immediately began fighting, the same fight as always. Zach hated Beijing, hated teaching English. Without telling Lindsey, he had applied to law school. When the term ended at New Direction Language Academy, he would pack his bags and fly back to Indianapolis, with or without her. After only ten months in China, he was ready to go home.

* * *

If Zach had chosen the bar next door, certain things would still have happened. Their breakup, for instance: By the time he and Lindsey boarded the flight to Shanghai, their paths had already begun to diverge. His own bent inexorably westward—to Indiana University, marriage and children, contract law and recreational golf. Zach's life would have turned out no differently, if he had chosen the bar next door.

But for Lindsey, his choice was determinative. If he'd chosen the bar next door, she might have stayed on in Beijing without him; she might have decamped to Hong Kong or Taipei or even—it's possible—gone home to Boston. This much is certain: On June 26, 2016, at four o'clock on a Sunday morning, she would have been somewhere other than a deserted street corner in the financial district, in the path of an oncoming car.

The white Mercedes would have encountered no obstacle; it would have roared forth unimpeded, tearing up the deserted streets of Lujiazui, if Zach had chosen the bar next door.

* * *

After he stormed out of the bar Lindsey sat alone, shivering in wet blue jeans. She drank two beers she didn't want, because they were already paid for and it was still raining and she had nowhere else to go.

"*Bù, xièxiè,*" she said when the waitress offered to bring another. "*Wǒ hē gòule píjiǔ.*"

No, thank you. I've had enough beer.

At the next table a woman turned to study her. She wore dark red lipstick. In perfect English she asked, "You speak Chinese?"

She was in her forties or fifties, that long, undifferentiated middle stage of life Lindsey thought of, vaguely, as Adulthood. Expensively dressed, in a leather skirt and red blouse that might have been silk. Eyeglasses dangled from a delicate chain around her neck. Except for the bartender and waitresses, she was the only Chinese in the place.

The woman was friendly and talkative. She introduced herself as Mei, a name that would always remind Lindsey of the plum rains. Because Mei seemed interested, and because Lindsey was wet and dejected and profoundly lonely, she explained that she'd studied Mandarin in high school. On Saturday mornings she'd worked with a private tutor, an MIT grad student born and raised in Guangzhou.

Mei seemed to find this fascinating. Was Lindsey still a student? Did she live here in Shanghai?

Lindsey explained that she was visiting for the weekend, that she taught English in Beijing.

Mei studied her, a probing gaze that took in everything: her grimy jean jacket and sodden hoodie and scraggly wet hair, transformed by the rain into a cloud of frizz.

"Beijing is expensive," she said. "Shanghai too. It must be hard to manage on a teacher's salary."

"It is," Lindsey said. Split two ways, their rent in Beijing was barely affordable. How she'd manage when Zach went back to the US wasn't clear.

"Your Chinese is good. That isn't common." Mei took a slim gold case from her bag and handed her a business card. Lindsey caught a whiff of jasmine perfume.

"This is my company. We're always looking for young people."

(*To do what?* Lindsey did not ask. At the time she didn't even wonder.)

"Chinese-speaking is a big plus," Mei added. "The next time you're in Shanghai, please call."

*　　*　　*

Zach's final weeks in Beijing passed with agonizing slowness. Their impending separation made them tender, rueful. In bed they clung to each other as they hadn't in months. They revisited their favorite places: the teahouse, the karaoke bar. They were careful with each other, gentle and considerate. They wandered hand in hand through Purple Bamboo Park, not speaking of what was to come. A casual observer would have guessed that they were deeply in love, but Lindsey knew it was an illusion. They would revert to their old pattern—the petty resentments, the constant bickering—if Zach changed his mind and decided to stay.

On his last morning they rose early. Though she wanted to, he wouldn't let her go with him to the airport. It was better this way.

She crawled back into bed and slept for twelve hours. When she woke, she made tea and took stock of her life. She posted an ad on the language school's intranet—**ROOMMATE WANTED**—and quickly deleted it. The apartment, a cramped studio with a tiny separate bedroom, was barely big enough for a couple. Two people could live there only if they shared a bed.

To afford it alone, she'd have to earn more money. The obvious solution was to pick up an extra class. But news traveled fast at New Direction Language Academy. After Zach gave his notice, it was understood that Lindsey would soon be single, and her (older, married, decidedly unattractive) British supervisor asked her out to dinner. She declined his invitation. A week later, her request for an additional class was denied.

The situation was untenable. To stay in China she'd need a new job or a new apartment, or possibly both. The alternative — running home to Newton, Massachusetts — was too awful to contemplate. The worst moments of her life had happened there: the Dean Farrell debacle, her family imploding. In Newton she'd be surrounded by her own mistakes, incontrovertible evidence of the destruction she'd caused.

She remembered, then, the woman she'd met at the bar in Shanghai. *We're always looking for young people.* In the pocket of her jean jacket she found Mei's business card.

"I don't know if you remember me," she said when Mei answered. Mei remembered.

Their conversation was confusing. Lindsey switched to English halfway through, to make certain she hadn't misunderstood. Mei's clients were successful men with business interests in Shanghai. They came from faraway parts of China, from all over the world. In their free time, they wanted to enjoy all that the city had to offer — restaurants, nightclubs, cultural activities. Mei's girls were educated and sophisticated, perfect companions for discerning gentlemen.

Mei said, "They are just like you."

At the time Lindsey was flattered. Later the words would haunt her. *They are just like you.* What had led Mei to this conclusion? At the bar they'd spoken for just a few minutes. And yet, without knowing a thing about Lindsey's fucked-up history, Mei had seen her clearly. Mei knew exactly what she was.

(What Mei said and what she didn't, what Lindsey filled in for herself.)

She avoided thinking about what she was doing, because what was she doing? She hadn't done anything yet. On the train to Shanghai, she had the sensation of observing herself from a great distance, buying her ticket, finding her seat, pretending to herself that she hadn't yet decided. That at any moment she might change her mind.

* * *

Late spring, Fuxing Park in full flower. Lindsey arrived with a single suitcase and a battered canvas rucksack. Mei took her to a furnished apartment on the sixteenth floor of the Wang Building, guessing—correctly—that she had no furniture, that she owned nothing at all.

On her second morning in Shanghai, they went shopping. In the elegant boutiques on Nanjing Road, they were often the only customers. A half-dozen salesgirls hovered, waiting to help. Lindsey stood behind a curtain in her underwear and tried on dresses. She modeled each one for Mei, who studied her from all angles. Lindsey was instructed to sit, to stand, to walk the length of the store.

Mei was a discriminating shopper. She knew exactly what she liked. In this way she was the opposite of Lindsey, who liked either nothing or everything. Every dress she tried on seemed wrong for her. When she imagined them on someone else, every one seemed right.

When she tried on a sleeveless dress of dark green silk, Mei touched the tattoo on her shoulder. "What is this?"

"I got it in Beijing," Lindsey said.

Mei put on her glasses to study it, her nose wrinkling as though she smelled some unpleasant odor. Her eyeglasses chain was studded with rubies, tiny stones the color of blood.

"I know someone who can remove it," she said.

"I don't want to remove it." The tattoo was a promise to herself, a reminder to do better. It had cost her four thousand yuan, but she would have paid twice that. She'd gotten it on a cold February night, in a grand-mal fit of loneliness, to feel closer to her sister.

Mei had the salesgirl take away two dresses, both sleeveless. For a fleeting moment Lindsey thought of her mother, the imperious way she'd send back an overcooked steak.

The dresses had no price tags. When Lindsey asked what they cost, Mei waved away the question. She had the longest fingernails Lindsey had ever seen, painted pearl pink.

They ate lunch in the upper room of a teahouse, eight delicate courses: a thimbleful of soup; a single bite of meat in sweet sauce; one perfect, lacquered shrimp.

In the afternoon they went to see to a doctor, an old man who wore trifocals. Lindsey sat on a table in a paper gown, her feet in plastic stirrups. The doctor did not speak. She studied the movement of his eyes, focusing and refocusing. The bottom third of the lenses was for close range, the top for distance. The middle window was for Lindsey, her labia spread open before him like some exotic specimen, a rare butterfly pinned in place.

"That was weird," she told Mei afterward. "He didn't say anything."

"He must have assumed you didn't speak Chinese. Also, I am sure he has never examined a redhead before." Mei took Lindsey's hands in hers. "You have long fingers, like eagle's claws. But you bite your fingernails. It's a problem."

They took a taxi across town. In a refrigerated salon they put on thin robes. The manicurist looked like a child, slender and sweet-faced and no taller than Grace. Mei's long fingernails went from pink to red. Lindsey had no nails to speak of, but the girl did her best.

Afterward, she was led into a back room. At another table with plastic stirrups, the child manicurist sat between Lindsey's thighs.

She stirred a pot of goop that smelled like crayons, pronouncing, carefully, the one English sentence she had mastered: "It is very hot."

On the sixteenth floor of the Wang Building, Lindsey hung three dresses in her empty closet. Matching shoes would be delivered later. The shoes had to be specially ordered. No Chinese woman had size 11 feet.

* * *

The clients called her Lily, a name Mei had suggested. Remembering the new name was sometimes a problem. It was best to choose one that sounded like her own.

Three or four nights a week, men took Lily to dinners and receptions. In June, for the Dragon Boat Festival, a private jet flew her to a party in Hong Kong. She was introduced to the best restaurants and most of the consulates, the theatres and good hotels and exclusive private clubs near the Bund.

The work was not even work. When Lindsey thought of it at all, she considered herself a consultant. For most of her childhood, her dad had been chief technological officer at NeoWonder, the company he'd started. "Aaron's baby," her mother called it. As a little girl Lindsey had taken this literally, and felt a despairing sibling rivalry: Neo was her father's number one son, the favorite child who demanded his full attention. And so it came as a distinct shock when, halfway through her freshman year at Wesleyan, her father sold his baby at a kingly profit. That he stayed on as a consultant made the whole business seem even colder, as though he simply didn't care that the company was no longer his. Working for Mei seemed benign by comparison. Lindsey wasn't selling anybody's baby. She was selling nothing she pretended to love.

Men, all sorts, rich or lonely or lazy enough to spend untold sums of money to take an American girl to the opera, a formal dinner, a cocktail reception at the British Consulate. Lily made small talk in English and Chinese, dusted off her rusty Spanish. She said nothing very profound, but the men were easily impressed.

She gave little thought to what she was doing, because what was she doing? She was meeting men. According to Johnny Du, it was the very definition of success: to be paid for something you wanted to do anyway.

This is why she loves him.

The best part of the date was getting ready beforehand. The mood was festive. Lindsey and Johnny played music and danced. Hair-styling was involved, makeup, wardrobe. She was like an actress preparing to go onstage. Here, Johnny's skills were invaluable. In normal life, Lindsey wore mascara and ChapStick. It was Johnny who taught her to curl her eyelashes, to draw her eyebrows, to outline and fill in a pillowy frosted mouth.

It was more fun than she could possibly have imagined. As a tall, gawky teenager, she'd felt foolish in high heels and dresses—an unconvincing female impersonator, an awkward drag queen with no fashion sense. Johnny taught her the pleasures of primping. As a little girl she'd dressed Barbie in elaborate outfits, sparkly dresses with tiny matching shoes. Now she herself was the doll.

The second-best part of the date was telling Johnny about it the next morning. His knock was her alarm clock. Lindsey came to the door in her nightshirt, still groggy. They lay together in her bed as chastely as sisters, and she told him everything.

She felt as though she'd always known him, was born knowing him. As though they'd grown up side by side, watching the same Disney cartoons. Lindsey's favorite was *Cinderella*; Johnny's, *Sleeping Beauty*. He told her how, as a small child, he'd imagined himself into the story. He cast himself, always, as Princess Aurora, kissed awake by a prince.

Each morning after his father left for work, Johnny's mother took the DVD from its hiding place in her closet. *Sleeping Beauty* was their secret. Without ever being told so, he understood that they couldn't watch it when his father was at home.

* * *

Lindsey's apartment had a place for everything. In the bathroom, a hidden clothesline could be pulled across the shower to dry laundry. In the base of the bed were two capacious drawers, big enough to hold her suitcase and rucksack and grungy Nikes, the remains of her American self.

In Shanghai she felt unburdened. In Beijing the past was inescapable; the ancient capital contained multitudes, dynasties layered one atop another, the psychic weight of eight centuries. Shanghai, aggressively modern, seemed to have been built yesterday. The city was young and vibrant, refreshingly indifferent to its own history—a bracing antidote to her educational New England childhood, where every other building was the birthplace of some Whig or Federalist she'd never heard of, marked with an engraved plaque. Shanghai had no time for looking backward. Wandering its streets was like traveling into the future. It was a city for getting on with her life.

She explored the neighborhood—the souvenir shops and tourist cafés near Jing'an Temple; the side streets with their fruit stands and corner groceries and noodle bars. Each morning she bought a milk tea from an automated stall. She poked at a touch screen to choose her desired temperature (iced, cold, warm, hot) and sweetness level (0, 25%, 50%, 75%, 100%). She chose warm, 50%, the middle road all around. In less than a minute her beverage was dispensed, in a foil-sealed cup.

She drank the tea at her kitchen window, overlooking Shanxi

Preparatory School. Each morning the students lined up for calisthenics in the school courtyard, neat rows of girls in white shirts and dark pants, a red kerchief at the throat. After calisthenics they set off running, moving like a single organism—a many-legged parade dragon, streaming down the wide sidewalk of Yuyuan Road.

At the kitchen table she plugged in her laptop. Not every day, but most days, she wrote in her journal—a practice she'd adopted reluctantly, on the advice of the therapist she'd seen at Wesleyan.

"Do I have to?" she'd protested. A lifetime of absorbing her mother's anxieties—the unending drama of writing or not writing—made her leery of the whole business.

"Yes," Wendy said. "Yes, you do."

Wendy had been recommended by Student Health, for reasons that weren't clear. Her specialty was eating disorders, the one type of disorder Lindsey didn't actually have.

At first the journal felt like homework. What exactly was she supposed to write?

"Memories," said Wendy. "Dilemmas. Strategies. Whatever you dreamed last night."

"I don't dream," said Lindsey.

"Everyone dreams," Wendy said.

In the beginning she pretended she was writing to Wendy, chatty letters that proved she was getting better, that she was making an effort. Later—after she dropped out of college, after Wendy moved across the country to start an eating disorder clinic in Seattle—she simply kept writing. Keeping a journal made her less lonely. It was like confiding in an imaginary person she could trust completely, a best friend she'd never met.

Naturally she wrote about Dean Farrell. For a long time she wrote about nothing else. She wrote to exorcise him, to purge him from her system. She wrote so that she could keep him forever. Every fragment of memory, literally every word they'd said to each other. Once written, these things could never be lost.

The knotted muscles of his back and shoulders, the blond arms and chest. Being her first, he had an unfair advantage. Every lover after him would suffer from the comparison.

With Zach the effect was devastating, but Lindsey slept with him anyway. In bed with her devoted, unmarried, age-appropriate boyfriend, she sometimes wished Wendy could see her. Having sex with Zach felt salubrious, evidence of her emotional recovery—a positive step toward wellness, like taking vitamins or joining a gym. That she didn't actually desire him felt like a detail. She feigned enthusiasm when necessary, but it was seldom necessary. Zach was so pleased to have her in his bed that he assumed she felt the same.

She didn't miss him at all.

But: Dean Farrell. He'd studied her body as though he were memorizing her. "Let me look at you." In those moments Lindsey was the whole world to him, the center of the known universe. The feeling was intoxicating. She would chase it for the rest of her life.

The first time they made love, his hands trembled as he unbuttoned her shirt.

His body was a revelation. She'd seen naked men before, a thousand times on the internet, but this had in no way prepared her for the reality of him. Sandpaper beard scraping her breasts, the startling heat of his skin. His velvet chest smelled of the soap he washed with. The smell underneath was something like potting soil, dirt that was somehow clean.

Let me look at you.

Afterward he drove her home, dropped her at the foot of her driveway. The warm September day smelled of charcoal, the neighbors having a barbecue. A plane buzzed overhead, its contrail slicing the sky.

The normality of everything was astonishing. Crossing her front yard, Lindsey looked up at the plane and imagined the passengers could see her—a girl illuminated from the inside, as though she'd swallowed a light bulb. Her light, surely, would be visible from the sky.

Let me look at you.

He was a grown man, a husband and father. To have his full attention was so startling, so altogether improbable, that she didn't at first believe it. It was as though she'd discovered she could fly.

When he talked about leaving his wife, a cavern opened up inside her. There was a world inside the world, a shadowy adult reality whose existence she had never guessed. Who knew that grown-up lives were so fragile? That they could be shattered in an instant by a girl who knew nothing, who'd simply returned a particular look in a particular way.

"I could leave her," Dean said.

The more he talked about it, the sicker she felt. Leaving his wife would mean that Dean loved her. She was supposed to want this.

She couldn't say, *Don't do that.* She couldn't say, *I am seventeen years old.*

She woke each morning in a cold sweat, a bath of suffocating dread. A chain of events had been set into motion, moving inexorably toward disaster. There was no way to pause the action, no way to rewind it.

She believed this right up until the moment her mother found her pills.

In the beginning she'd been careful, hiding the compact between her box spring and mattress. Later she got lazy. She stashed the pills in her underwear drawer, where Claire made regular deposits of clean laundry.

"It's almost as if you wanted her to find them," said Wendy. "Did you want her to know you were sexually active?"

At the time Lindsey had resisted this suggestion. Later she wondered if Wendy had been right. Loving Dean Farrell was the most exciting thing that had ever happened to her. An insistent, irrepressible part of her wanted the whole world to know.

When she found the pills, Claire's reaction was insulting. She assumed Lindsey was having sex with some lame teenage boyfriend, one of the clueless dorks in her class at Pilgrims Country Day. Lindsey had worried for months that she and Dean were being too obvious—needlessly, it turned out, because her mother hadn't been paying attention. The most important development in Lindsey's life was literally invisible to her.

Was it really so unthinkable that Dean loved her, wanted her, had chosen her?

"He's a predator," her mother said, as if Lindsey were a child. As if Dean's love for her were inherently wrong.

Then, without warning, Dean disappeared completely. He stopped texting, stopped calling. When she showed up at his baseball practice, he refused to talk to her.

He didn't even bother to dump her. To Lindsey this was the worst part, a blow from which she would never recover.

What exactly her mother said to him remained a mystery. Dean refused to tell her, and in the end it didn't matter. Lindsey never saw him again.

* * *

Her pills from Planned Parenthood had come in a plastic compact, arranged by color: white pills first, then pink, peach, and green. The Chinese pills were plain white. They came in a blister pack, twenty-one days' worth. Every three weeks Lindsey started a new pack, to avoid having a period. Mei had assured her that this was perfectly safe.

Mei paid her in cash. Every Friday an envelope of hundred-yuan notes was hand-delivered to her door. The amount varied from week to week, for reasons that weren't explained. Mei handled each negotiation personally: hourly or flat fee, her own commission. She didn't disclose this information to Lindsey.

"It's better that you don't know, Xiaoying." This was all she had to say on the matter, and in a way she was right. Lindsey was happier and more relaxed, and thus better at her job, if she forgot about money entirely.

Xiaoying, Mei called her. Little Eagle.

Of course, the not knowing had consequences. She was never completely sure what the client expected. If she knew the price he'd paid, she could make an educated guess.

On this point Mei offered no guidance. "It's a date, like any date. What you do is up to you."

Lindsey saw, later, that her uncertainty was part of the service. Any talk of money would shatter the illusion. "It's psychologic," Mei explained. "They want a girlfriend, not— "

She finished the sentence with a languid wave, as though clearing the air of smoke.

What Lindsey did with the client was up to her. A surprising number wanted only to lie next to her, to drink themselves into a stupor and fall asleep in her arms. An exotic few wanted no physical contact whatsoever. An engineer from Johannesburg sent her home with a jaunty salute.

There were rules, but only a few. Transportation was provided by a car service. The driver, who called himself Bill, met Lindsey at the Hotel République, a block away from her apartment. Mei was insistent on this point: Under no circumstances was she to give the client her phone number or address. Lindsey believed, at first, that Mei was concerned for her safety. Later she understood that the reason was practical. If a client wanted to see her again, he'd have no choice but to pay for another date.

Each morning she swallowed a pill from the packet.

The sudden blunt intimacy of seeing a stranger unclothed.

The first time it happened was surreal, dreamlike. The client, an investment manager from Toronto, was seventy-four years old—the oldest person she'd ever seen naked, literally old enough to be her grandfather.

His ugliness was startling. The ductile flesh, the skin tags, the crusty elbows. His meaty back was studded with cancerous-looking moles. The client seemed to know this. He undressed with apology in his eyes. Seeing this, she felt a rush of tenderness. His shame made her generous, his ugliness, his frailty. Lily caressed him with loving pity, like an aged family pet.

Her skills were solid; she knew this. She took real pleasure in her competence. The feeling was wholly unfamiliar. Her life was a disaster of her own making—her family shattered, her education abandoned, her student loan debt compounding at a dizzying rate. But in this one area, her proficiency was inarguable. The men suffered from a common ailment Lily could cure in minutes, with—literally—one hand tied behind her back.

Occasionally a client made a special request. Lily granted it with perfect equanimity. Her sweet smile affirmed that such desires were perfectly normal. The men seemed reassured by this, the confirmation of their own banality. They trusted Lily's judgment in these matters, bowed to her professional expertise.

There was a Russian who wanted only to smell her. For a solid hour he nuzzled at her groin, his head heavy in her lap. Lily stroked his hair and stared at the ceiling, bored but strangely moved. Of all the clients' idiosyncrasies, this one seemed the purest and most innocent—the blind animal need to soak up another's smell.

She was a first responder, cool in a crisis. If the client was impotent, she didn't panic. At such moments Lily was like a nurse in wartime, dispensing lifesaving medicine, emergency doses of solace and hope.

Her ministrations were effective. The patients submitted gratefully to her touch. In the end they came victoriously, which made her love them. No matter how fitful their arousal, how slow and tedious, it always ended in triumph. It was so easy to make them happy. Their pride was joyful to behold.

Their gratitude afterward was fervent and genuine. They fell asleep curled against her, trusting as infants. At such moments she felt the purest sort of pleasure—the simple human happiness of being kind.

To do such work in the States would have been unimaginable, but she was in China—living her daily life in Mandarin, meeting men from all over the world. That she could fuck in four languages made the whole business seem educational—an edifying cultural exchange, a self-guided junior year abroad.

An Englishman named Jack removed his wedding ring in her presence. "I guess I don't need this."

He took off his ring and unzipped her dress.

He was younger than most of them. They went to a party at a grand hotel on the Bund and Lindsey drank a great deal, a sweet lemonade that smelled strongly of gin. To her surprise, she wanted him to touch her. It had something to do with the shape of his shoulders, his hand at the small of her back guiding her through the room. She wanted him to touch her and was afraid that he wouldn't.

" 'Jack.' " He said it with audible quotation marks, as though he wanted her to know it wasn't really his name.

In the taxi his hand went up her dress.

He did not, objectively, resemble Dean Farrell. And yet, in his arms, she felt a hard jolt of recognition. The weight and feel of him, the relative temperature of their skin. What the body remembers. It made her wonder what else was locked away in her limbic brain, what other secrets she was keeping from herself.

He fit inside her like a cork in a bottle.

Unlike any client before or after, he talked to her while they fucked.

It was the talking that confused her. For days afterward, she imagined seeing him again. When he didn't call, she was crushed in a way that dismayed her. She thought of her grandma Alice, who before the massive cerebral hemorrhage that killed her had suffered a series of mini-strokes. Lindsey's anguish over "Jack" was a mini-heartbreak, a pale shadow of what she'd suffered when Dean Farrell dumped her. A mini-stroke did invisible damage, but it didn't kill you.

She made a rule for herself: no more talking.

Each morning she swallowed a pill from the packet.

The clients called her Lily, which was helpful. The things she did with and for and to them didn't stick to her. A hot shower washed them away.

Lily stepped into the shower and came out Lindsey, clean as the day she was born.

In the beginning they were all Westerners: British, Scandinavians, boatloads of Australians. Later there were no Westerners. They were, Mei said, a waste of her special talents. In Shanghai, English-speaking girls were as common as dumplings. For Lindsey, she had other things in mind.

*   *   *

Her first Chinese date called himself Tony. He was a small round man with a soul patch and long sideburns. One Saturday night, they flew in his private plane to the island of Macau.

In Macau, gambling was legal. The flight took three hours. Tony drank orange juice and chain-smoked Chunghwa cigarettes. He talked about Stanley Ho, who'd built the original Casino Lisboa. Stanley Ho, he said, was the Godfather of Macau.

They landed late in the evening. At the airstrip, a car was waiting. Tony took a fresh pack of Chunghwas from his pocket. They drove in the direction of the waterfront. Tony pointed out the Canidrome, where tourists bet on the dogs.

When they arrived at the casino it was after midnight. The floor was crowded with men, a mixed crowd of Westerners and Chinese. A few girls circulated among the tables—all Lindsey's age, all Chinese. They were dressed as she was, in high heels and clinging dresses. "They work for the house," Tony said.

Tony played blackjack and baccarat; he played Sic Bo and Pai Gow. Tersely he explained the rules. In Pai Gow the best hand was Supreme Pair, followed by Matched Pairs, Unmatched Pairs, Wongs and Gongs.

They stayed in Macau for fourteen hours. In that time, Tony never left the casino. In the morning, Lindsey wandered the waterfront alone, hungry and thirsty, until the rain started. From her phone she learned that *sic bo* meant *precious dice*. She could make no sense of Wongs or Gongs.

When she returned to the casino, Tony was playing Fan Tan—the most difficult game of all, a game of pure chance. As directed, Lindsey stood behind him at the table. The banker placed two handfuls of buttons on the tabletop and covered them with a silver bowl.

Tony placed his bet and gave Lindsey a long kiss, tasting of orange juice and cigarettes. The other players—a half-dozen Chinese men, in varying stages of dishevelment—seemed not to notice. Their eyes never left the table. They seemed hypnotized by the silver bowl.

Bets were placed, the bowl removed. Four at a time, the croupier swept away the buttons with a bamboo stick.

Tony bet Fan, he bet Hong, he bet Kwok, he bet Nim. After each bet, another long kiss.

When he'd lost his final bet, he turned away from the table. Lindsey followed him out the door. At the curb, the same car and driver were waiting. They rode in silence to the airstrip.

She never saw Tony again. It wasn't her fault, Mei explained later. The client hoped, always, that a new girl would bring him luck. In fact this had never happened, but he continued to believe.

* * *

Lindsey went on dates four nights a week. The other nights she went dancing with Johnny Du, who wasn't her boyfriend or roommate or sister but some magical combination of the three. She never thought of Zach and only rarely of Dean Farrell, whom she'd loved in a way she would never love anyone else, a thought that had once depressed her and now filled her with relief.

From the window of the all-night noodle shop, she and Johnny watched the sun rise.

On summer afternoons, they lay on a blanket in Fuxing Park and watched the boys go by. Their taste in men was strikingly similar. For Johnny it was thrilling to speak so boldly. At school he'd been surrounded by girlfriends who knew what he was but never spoke of it, understanding that it was a conversation he didn't wish to have.

They lay shoulder to shoulder, speaking in low voices. There was an Italian he'd met several times in a club. Johnny understood, without ever having been told so, that the man had a wife at home. This was evident in his intimate habits, the long stretches of time spent kissing and touching, which Johnny found pleasant but unnecessary and which women were said to like.

To Johnny she surrendered her secrets. Unlike Wendy—who'd literally been paid to listen to her, to care about her or pretend to—Johnny owed her nothing. He knew all about her and Dean Farrell, shameful truths she'd never confessed to another living soul.

At Mid-Autumn Festival, they exchanged mooncakes. That night, under the full moon, Johnny took her to see a construction site, cordoned off with yellow tape. During the Japanese occupation it had been a dance hall, the Gate of a Hundred Pleasures. Foreign jazz musicians came to play there. Men bought tickets to dance with the girls. One girl was especially popular. Her name, Rose Orchid, was known all over Shanghai. One summer night, a Japanese soldier came looking for her. He bought a ticket and held out his arms for a dance.

When Rose Orchid refused him, the Japanese soldier shot her in the throat.

After the war, jazz was outlawed, the dance halls shuttered. The empty building fell into disrepair. Since then it had been renovated many times, but the disguises were unsuccessful. In each iteration, the cursed building was visited by tragedy. Its roof was struck by lightning and caught fire. During typhoon season the facade crumbled, crushing and killing a passerby.

"It is said that Rose Orchid still dances here," Johnny said on the night of the full moon.

Lindsey eyed him skeptically. "Do you believe that?"

Johnny repeated, "It is said."

Every Saturday morning, Lindsey called her sister.

In Newton it was still Friday night, just after Grace's bedtime. Lindsey imagined her in her Hello Kitty pajamas, her clean hair smelling of strawberry shampoo. The calls were top secret. Under no circumstances was Grace to tell their mother.

Lindsey's mother made her crazy.

Lindsey's mother had literally ruined her life.

This was the story she'd told Wendy: Claire, once her best friend, had revealed herself to be an agent of destruction. Single-handedly, she'd dismantled Lindsey's happiness. Wendy's reaction wasn't what she'd expected.

"You don't believe me," Lindsey said.

"I believe you believe it," Wendy said.

In the terrible weeks after Dean Farrell dumped her, Lindsey saw her mother with new eyes. Their long-ago trip to Chongqing had seemed, at the time, a great adventure — "the rescue mission," they'd called it. Remembering this later, Lindsey felt ashamed. She'd been too young, then, to understand the wrongness of it. Her mother wanted a baby without the hassle of being pregnant, so she took someone else's. What made it worse — what made it truly unbearable — was her self-righteousness, the smug certainty that she'd saved Grace from some terrible fate. Claire was a good liberal — constantly signing petitions, canvassing for candidates, donating to progressive causes. Hilariously, she'd even marched in demonstrations against human trafficking — "to raise awareness," she said, though she had yet to raise her own. When the *New York Times* ran a story about a baby-selling ring at a Sichuan orphanage, she refused to hear about it. The story had nothing to do with them, she insisted, because Chongqing wasn't part of Sichuan province. When Lindsey pointed out—someone had to—that the city was only forty miles from the provincial border, Claire seemed not to hear her. She had a superhuman ability to ignore inconvenient facts.

The rescue mission. Claire Litvak, the white hero, had saved her Chinese daughter from untold horrors, whisked her away to an idyllic suburban childhood, music lessons and expensive orthodontia, private school and Santa Claus. She'd given zero thought to all that Grace was losing: birth mother, motherland, mother tongue. Trying to explain any of this was hopeless, because Claire was always right.

Her mother loved her out of all proportion; Lindsey knew this. Her mother's love was a boulder on her back. Her dad needed less from her; he was, essentially, a selfish creature. Lindsey was grateful for his selfishness. It made him easier to bear.

She spoke to each of them once a month, give or take, though lately the interval had gotten longer. She offered lame excuses: the time difference, her busy teaching schedule, poor connectivity in the Beijing apartment where she supposedly still lived. Telling them otherwise would lead to questions she couldn't answer.

Grace asked her no questions, ever. They talked about TV shows, Grace's ballet recital, upcoming auditions for the school orchestra. (She was learning to play the viola.) Though she wanted to, Lindsey never asked about Iris Farrell (*Have you seen her dad? Does he ask about me?*). Then one day, apropos of nothing, Grace informed her that she and Iris were no longer friends.

"Why not?" Lindsey asked, feeling her heart.

Grace's explanation was unsatisfying. Iris had gotten weird and boring. She spent all her time with Kylie, a girl from gymnastics who was also weird and boring. Anyway, it didn't matter. Grace's new best friend was Josie.

In that moment Lindsey would have done anything to be eleven years old.

*　*　*

Dean Farrell had been the end of her childhood, though at the time she hadn't thought so. The very suggestion would have offended her. When they fell in love she was sixteen going on seventeen, like that asinine song from *The Sound of Music*. She considered herself an adult.

The astonishment of being chosen. The first time Dean saw her, in his basement rec room in Newton, he knew that his entire life had been leading up to that moment. When he first told her this, Lindsey didn't believe him. Later she believed him absolutely. His adoration was a drug to her, a high like no other. When he said her name, it literally gave her chills.

The evenings she spent babysitting were interminable, but also thrilling. Sitting still was impossible. After Iris was asleep, Lindsey put on her headphones and danced. She danced in the kitchen, the basement, the vaulted great room. She danced all over the suburban McMansion Dean shared with his wife. Her joy and anticipation could not be contained.

He taught her how to touch him, the correct speed and pressure, the sensitive spot near the head. She felt, at such moments, that they were both inside his body. That she knew precisely how it felt to have a penis, lovingly licked and caressed.

He was every man to her. The urgent dance of their bodies seemed entirely his creation, an elaborate ritual he'd invented himself.

He bought her small gifts, white cotton tank tops to be worn bra-less, thong panties of sheer white lace. When instructed, she took selfies. When they video chatted, she lay on the floor of her bedroom closet in the underwear he'd bought her, legs wide-open so he could see her through the lace.

She was bald there now, smooth as fruit. This felt correct to her. The monthly salon appointment was painful but oddly satisfying—a small, belated way of saying no to him, all these years later. Of erasing the part of her he'd loved the most.

*   *   *

She went away to college. A new start, her parents said, and it was true: At Wesleyan no one had heard of Dean Farrell. Once, at a party, she met Adam Somebody, a senior who followed the Sox with religious devotion. "Farrell," he repeated. "Ninety-one, right? He was a first-round draft pick." Lindsey was so grateful she could have kissed him. She did kiss him. She went back to his room and let him show her his records, a vast collection of vintage vinyl. Then, because he seemed to expect it, she let him undress her.

She felt nothing at all.

Her parents' divorce unmoored her completely. This wasn't hard to do, since she was barely moored. She'd been seeing Wendy for four months. After a shaky start, she'd begun to find her footing academically. She had just met Zach. The antidepressant made her tired, but each day she managed to drag herself to class. When her parents divorced, she understood that her efforts were futile. There was no way to repair the damage, no end to the destruction she'd caused.

At the beginning of spring semester she started cutting. Why exactly she did this was hard to explain, even to herself. The relief it gave her, the bright comfort of seeing her own blood. The pain proved beyond all doubt that she was a person, demonstrably alive no matter how dead she felt inside.

She cut conservatively, judiciously—a small incision on her left shoulder, barely an inch long. Later she made a second cut and eventually a third one, three parallel lines a centimeter apart. The cuts were clean and precise, made with a brand-new razor. Once healed, they resembled the lines on notebook paper, college-ruled—a grim souvenir of her time in exile, her brief, pointless flirtation with higher ed.

When she came home on spring break, she kept the scars covered. In March—still sweater season in New England—this wasn't hard to do. Once, while she was brushing her teeth in their shared bathroom, wearing boxers and a tank top, she saw Grace staring at her shoulder.

"Linz, what happened?"

"I cut myself," she said.

"On what?"

Lindsey's heart pounded. For a brief, insane moment she imagined unburdening herself to her sister, confiding the fucked-up secrets no little kid should have to hear.

"A barbed-wire fence," she said—the first and last time she ever lied to Grace.

She never cut herself again. A year later, in Beijing, a tattoo artist covered the scars with a Chinese character.

雅

Yōuyǎ

Grace

* * *

In September, the rains came.

Typhoon season had begun in July—gradually, inexorably. By September, natural disaster was a daily occurrence. Mornings were stagnant and humid, the air rich with particulates. The invisible sun bleached the sky a grainy white. Pale clouds sank by increments. Then, in late afternoon, the ceiling dropped.

The heavens exploded without thunder, without lightning. The only sound was the rush of wind.

A shattering rain pelted the sidewalks. Rain swept the boulevards in purposeful sheets. Shanghai smelled of its streets and alleys, wet concrete and asphalt. Cars raced through puddled intersections, sending up sprays of grime.

One morning in typhoon season, Lindsey woke coughing. In her dreams she'd been drowning, her lungs and sinuses filling with rain. Mei took her to see an herbalist. The old woman examined Lindsey's tongue and the whites of her eyes, felt the pulse in her wrists, throat and feet. She was sent home with medicines mixed for her specially—a foul-smelling tincture in an unlabeled glass bottle, a packet of fishy tea.

Johnny appeared at her door with a huge bag of Little Yang dumplings—the best in the city, he insisted. (In Shanghai, this was an inflammatory claim.) He'd brought more than seemed reasonable, because Westerners had huge appetites and Lindsey (he said) would surely eat twice what he did. This offended her slightly, but it turned out to be true.

They lay in her bed watching DVDs from his personal collection: *Snow White, The Little Mermaid,* American versions with Chinese subtitles. Johnny had watched them all a hundred times. This, he explained, was how he'd learned English.

"That's demented," Lindsey said. How was it even possible? His English was as good as her Chinese, and no one had taught him. Lindsey, meanwhile, had been taught constantly. At her fancy private school, the Mandarin teacher was a native speaker with a PhD from

Harvard. A private tutor came to her house once a week. Her parents had subsidized this ongoing instruction. What exactly it cost had never occurred to her to wonder. Naturally she'd never thanked them. Lying next to Johnny, she felt spoiled and a little ashamed.

*　*　*

In October, Lily went back to work.

At a lavish dinner at the Lotus Club, she excused herself to the powder room. As she touched up her makeup at the mirror, a blond girl approached her. She wore a lace dress that matched her hair.

"Let me guess," she said. "You're one of Mei's girls."

Gails. Her accent was distinctive, familiar from movies.

"How did you know?" Lindsey said.

"I saw you get out of the car. Bill used to be my driver. Now I ride with Bob."

The Australian girl—she introduced herself as Heather—was warm and chatty. "You're the one who speaks Chinese," she said. "Mei talks about you. Not by name, of course. We're not supposed to know each other."

"Why not?" Lindsey asked.

Heather shrugged elaborately, like a dancer stretching.

They exchanged phone numbers and met the next day for lunch, at a Cantonese restaurant Heather had suggested. Lindsey arrived first and waited at a table. At each place sat a shrink-wrapped package holding a small plate, a soup bowl, a teacup, and a china spoon.

Heather made a grand entrance. "First things first," she said, unwrapping the scarf from her hair. "That's not actually my name."

Her real name was Hester—*Hister*—a name she'd always hated. "What were my parents thinking?" she demanded, laughing but not really. In this way, working for Mei had been liberating. If nothing else, she'd unloaded that hideous name.

They ordered soup, pork and noodles. Hester ate ravenously. In between bites, she gossiped about Mei.

"Her husband is stinking rich, apparently. They live in some swank penthouse in Pudong. Do you want this?" she asked, pointing her chopsticks at the last spring roll.

"I'm stuffed," Lindsey said.

In addition to the stinking-rich husband, Mei had an elderly mother and a young son. Lindsey found these details astonishing. It was impossible to imagine Mei as an actual person, somebody's wife or daughter or mother. To Lindsey she revealed nothing; she was a master at dodging personal questions. When Lindsey asked how she'd spent Golden Week, Mei had pretended to misunderstand the question.

"It was very nice," she'd said.

And yet she could be maternal. That day at the herbalist's, Mei had gone into the examining room with her. While the woman felt for her pulse, Mei had held Lindsey's hand.

Hester had worked for Mei for two years. She, too, had flown to Macau with Tony and watched him lose at Fan Tan.

"He speaks English?" said Lindsey.

"Sort of," Hester said. "It's fun, isn't it? You know, as long as you're careful."

Something in her tone invited a question.

"What do you mean?" Lindsey said.

"There was one of Mei's girls. I met her at a party last summer. She was from New Zealand, completely adorable. Stop me if you've heard this."

"I haven't heard anything," Lindsey said.

Hester leaned in confidentially. "Her date tied her up and left her in his hotel room. Then he checked out of the hotel and didn't tell anyone. She was stuck there for hours."

"No!" Lindsey said. It was entirely too easy to imagine. At least once a week, she met a date in a hotel lobby—or, if he requested it, went directly to his room.

"The chambermaid found her the next morning, naked, tied to the bed." Hester lowered her voice. "She had to wee, so she went on the sheets."

"Oh, God." Lindsey put down her chopsticks. "Did they catch the guy?"

"*Catch?* He was staying in the hotel. They knew exactly who he was." Hester popped the spring roll into her mouth and held up a finger—*Wait!*—until she finished chewing. "A Westerner." *Wisterner.* "He was Swiss, I think. Or Swedish. One of those."

"Well, *Mei* knew who he was," Lindsey pointed out. "She must have. She arranged the date."

"What could she do? It wasn't as if she could call the police." Hester refilled their teacups. "And anyway, Mei is a businesswoman. You can bet it cost him serious money to keep it quiet."

"That's demented," Lindsey said.

"I don't mean to scare you. Some of the clients are brilliant. I've met some amazing people this way." Hester smiled as though she were thinking of someone in particular. "Of course, most of them are deadly boring. They're just regular men, but with money."

Lindsey couldn't disagree. Her best date, so far, had been an evening at an acrobatics show. She'd lost herself in the performance, the stupefying strength and agility of the performers' bodies. The man who'd taken her there had made no impression whatsoever. She literally couldn't remember his face.

"What happened to her?" she asked. "The girl from New Zealand."

"She was humiliated, of course. I heard she went back to Auckland. I never saw her again." Hester stacked their dirty dishes with cheerful competence, like an expert waitress. "At the end of the day, you have to trust your instinct. If you get a bad feeling about the client, get the hell out of there. Excuse yourself to the loo and skip out the back door."

"You can do that?" said Lindsey. "Just—leave?"

"I have," said Hester. "Twice, actually. Mei was livid, of course. But I can't worry about that, can I? It's my arse on the line, not hers."

Pudong was the newest part of the city—born, like Lindsey, in the 1990s. This struck her as magically significant. The streets and sidewalks were as young as she was.

She met the client at a private club east of the river. When Bill dropped her in front of the club, her date was waiting on the sidewalk, poking irritably at a mobile phone. According to Mei's instructions, his name was Sean, an alias Lindsey found comical. She'd graduated high school with a half-dozen Seans, the Irish Catholic sons of Greater Boston. This Sean was Chinese, with longish hair. His square spectacles gave him a scholarly look. He appeared to be in his thirties, tall and well-built. Lindsey would have called him handsome until he spoke.

The date wasn't his idea; his colleague had arranged it. The party would be full of potential investors, Chinese, English, American. A girl who spoke both languages would be ideal. Sean explained this brusquely, in rapid Mandarin. He kept his eyes on the ground.

At the cocktail reception he ignored her completely. To the other guests—bigwigs in the telecommunications sector—he was witty and charming. To Lindsey he was businesslike and cold. Only once, at dinner, did he speak to her directly.

"Why did you want to learn Chinese?" His tone was accusatory, as though he suspected her of some crime.

"I came here when I was thirteen," she said. "I didn't understand anything. I hated that feeling. What about you?" she asked, thinking they might at last have a conversation. "Why did you want to learn English?"

"I didn't. I speak English when I am forced to. When I travel, I can't escape it. Wherever I go, it is pushed down my throat." For the first time that evening, he met her eyes. "You can't possibly feel that way about Chinese."

Lindsey admitted that she didn't. She resisted the urge to apologize for the English language, invading foreign countries like some aggressive cancer.

When the dinner ended, Sean walked her to the curb, where her driver was waiting. "Good night," he said curtly, eyes on the sidewalk.

No client had ever treated her so rudely. And yet, riding back to the Hotel République, she felt vaguely ashamed, as though she'd performed poorly on a test. Not once had he touched her, not even a handshake. She was both disappointed and relieved.

* * *

"He literally wouldn't look at me," she told Johnny. "He couldn't wait to get rid of me."

She was sitting in his chair, wearing a cape of red plastic. They had their best conversations this way, while watching each other in the big mirror. His scissors took tiny bites at her wet hair.

"Seriously, he hated me. He probably called Mei and asked for his money back."

"He didn't hate you." Johnny fluffed the hair at the nape of her neck and made a judicious snip. "I think maybe he was testing you."

"I don't get it," said Lindsey. "Testing me for what?"

Johnny said, "Some men are this way."

He was prone to such statements, vague but insistent pronouncements on the basic nature of men. A different sort of person would feel compelled to back up his assertions, but Johnny didn't see the need.

He removed the plastic cape and shook the wet trimmings to the floor. Lindsey paid for her haircut and stuffed the change into her pocket. At that moment her phone vibrated, a text from Mei. **The client from Shenzhen would like to see you again.**

* * *

The reception was held in a hotel ballroom, two blocks away from the last one. Lindsey recognized a few faces from last time: a Japanese man who got rambunctiously drunk; a silent German who studied her body coolly, like a painting he might decide to purchase. Sean noticed it too. For just a moment—so briefly she might have imagined it—he pressed his hand to the small of her back.

At the end of the evening they walked outside. Lindsey hugged her coat around her. She steeled herself for another cold farewell at the curb.

"Would you like a coffee?" Sean asked.

"I would love one," she said.

They walked to a café around the corner, still serving at midnight. The smell of the place was achingly familiar, the aroma of a thousand Starbucks. To Lindsey Litvak, to an entire American generation, it was the smell of home.

They sat at a counter facing the window, staring out at the empty street like two strangers. An overhead speaker played a Muzak version of "A Hard Day's Night."

Freed from the obligation to meet her eyes, Sean was more talkative. He lived with his wife and six-year-old son in Shenzhen, 1,500 kilometers to the south.

"Nothing," he said when she asked what was most interesting about the city. Twenty years ago, Shenzhen had been a backwater.

Now it was flush with foreign money. Factories had popped up like cases of croup.

"Nine years," he said, when she asked how long he'd been married. He and his wife had grown up side by side, in the same housing development. He'd known her since they were four years old.

"Why didn't you bring her to the party?" Lindsey asked, genuinely curious.

Sean laughed as though she'd said something uncommonly witty. "She hates this kind of thing." Late nights were impossible for her; she woke at dawn and occasionally fell asleep at the dinner table. Moreover, she had no interest in speaking English.

"You ask a lot of questions," he said.

"Sorry." Lindsey's cheeks heated. "Maybe you could ask *me* something."

Sean seemed confounded by this suggestion.

"Anything," she said. "Ask me whatever you want."

He stared out at the street. "You told me, last time, that you visited China when you were thirteen. Why did you come here?"

She was astonished that he remembered, that he'd even been listening.

"My parents adopted a baby. My sister, Grace. We went to Chongqing to get her." She described the crowded orphanage, the young childcare worker who'd placed Grace in her arms.

"And this is why you studied Chinese?"

"Yes," she said. "In high school, and later at college. University."

Sean turned to her. He looked positively dumbstruck. "You went to university?"

"For two years," she said. "Then I quit."

There was a silence.

"Quit," he repeated.

"It wasn't for me." Lindsey hesitated, unsure how to explain it. "I liked the classes. Well, some of them. But really, there was nothing I was dying to study. I guess I never found my passion."

Another silence.

"What did your parents say?" Sean asked finally. "When you left university. Were they angry?"

"They weren't thrilled," she admitted. "But you know, they sort of got it. My mom spent her junior year abroad, and I've been hearing my whole life how it was the best thing that ever happened to her. So when I decided to come to China, she couldn't really argue."

Sean stared at her in mute incomprehension—a look familiar to foreigners everywhere, travelers speaking gibberish in languages not their own. What was she even saying? Was there even a Chinese word for "junior year abroad"?

She tried again.

"I mean, there are other ways to learn besides sitting in a classroom. I felt like I was missing my life. How about you?" she asked, feeling foolish. "Did you like being a student?"

Sean stared out at the street. She sensed that she had offended him. Once again, she blamed her Chinese.

"I'm sorry," he said. "I think I don't understand the question."

"I mean, did you enjoy it? Was it fun?"

"*Fun?*" he repeated loudly. "No, it wasn't fun! It was miserable. The teachers were cruel. For four years I hardly saw my family. I barely slept. I did nothing but study."

"So why did you continue?" Lindsey asked, genuinely curious. "If it was so bad, why didn't you leave?"

The song ended and another began, a guitar riff the whole world recognized. A Chinese girl with a baby voice sang, *I can't get no satisfaction.*

"To go to university in China there is an entrance exam," Sean said. "You know this from the time you are born. It's the purpose of your whole life, to prepare for this test." He sipped at his coffee. "The day of the exam is like a holiday. When I rode the bus to the test center, there were crowds on the sidewalk waving. The whole city came out to tell us *jiāyóu*."

I can't get no, the baby voice sang.

"My parents didn't go to university," he continued. "My father had a tea stall near the train station. Every morning he was there at five in the morning, making the tea. It was too much for him, but he would never let me help him. My job was to be a student, he said. Going to university was the only thing that mattered. My parents were poor, but they paid for me to have a private tutor. They wanted me to have a better life."

I can't get no, the baby voice sang.

"Wow," Lindsey said. "That's amazing."

"No! It is not amazing. It's *normal*. It's what all parents do." Sean turned to look at her, his eyes blazing with some emotion she couldn't identify. "When I was accepted to university it was the best day of my father's life. You know what he told me? 'I can die now.' That's what he said."

I try. And I try. And I try. The singer's voice was breathless, plaintive. To Lindsey it was painfully clear what the song was suggesting.

"So, no. University was not fun. It was very, very hard. But I never had the thought to quit. It would be like cutting off my leg."

The music was impossible to ignore. The baby-voiced girl was now whimpering pornographically, trying desperately to get off.

To her surprise, Sean spoke to her in English: "This song is terrible."

"Terrible," she agreed.

"Let's get out of here," he said.

* * *

Outside, the temperature had dropped. A stiff wind was blowing, carrying a whiff of ocean.

Sean and Lindsey set out walking. To her surprise, he took her hand.

They made a wide loop around the financial district, not speaking. The streets were deserted at this hour, the empty office towers brightly lit. Lindsey didn't ask where they were going, because it didn't matter. Nothing mattered, as long as he held her hand.

Finally they reached their destination, a pale concrete tower that looked like all the others. A bright red awning marked the entrance. Sean tapped out four digits on a keypad to open the door.

In the mirrored elevator they stood shoulder to shoulder, their eyes finally meeting.

At the fifth floor they stepped off the elevator. Lindsey followed him down a long hallway, lit with fluorescent lights. Sean stopped at a door and typed four more digits into a keypad.

"This is a company apartment," said Sean. "I stay here one week a month."

She followed him inside. The rooms were small but immaculate. In the bedroom the blinds were open, the room filled with a watery gray light, the billion distant electrical bulbs of Shanghai at night. He undressed her in the cold light, studying her. His skin was smooth and heavy as suede.

His real name, he told her, was Shen.

* * *

Days passed. Lindsey made a concerted effort not to think about Shen. To distract herself, she took long walks around the city. She wandered the hip art galleries of Xintiandi. She explored the old French Concession, with its colonial mansions and tree-lined streets.

In the evenings she went on dates. On free nights she went dancing with Johnny and his friends. On the dance floor she was completely happy, a mindless antenna for the techno music coursing through her body, the whomping bass line vibrating her bones. The rest of the time she was waiting. Then, three weeks later, Mei sent her a text: **The client from Shenzhen would like to see you again.**

* * *

The address was a hotel in Xujiahui, the trendy neighborhood where Lindsey and Johnny sometimes went clubbing. Never before had she been sent there on a date. She agonized over what to wear. In the end she settled on her favorite of the dresses Mei had bought her, deep red lace that matched her hair.

Per Mei's instructions, she waited in the hotel lobby, watching the elevator. Why hadn't he asked her to come up to his room?

"Sorry I'm late," said a voice behind her.

Lindsey turned. He'd come in from the street, through the same revolving door she'd used. He was dressed—puzzlingly—in jeans and a sweater.

"I'm not actually staying here," he said. "It just seemed like a convenient meeting place."

"I'm confused. I thought the reception was in Pudong."

"That was a lie. There is no reception." Shen grinned mischievously. "I just wanted to see you. To do something normal."

The day was clear and bright, smelling of ocean. They strolled hand in hand along the crowded sidewalks, ignoring the impatient pedestrians scurrying past on both sides.

The movie theater was on the fifth floor of a shopping mall. They waited in line at the box office, surrounded mostly by teenage boys. In her high heels and cocktail dress Lindsey felt like someone's overdressed mother.

The film was a new release, the latest sequel in a long series.

Watching it required 3D glasses. Shen helped Lindsey put them on, fitting the temple pieces around her ears. They sat shoulder to shoulder, grinning like idiots.

"We look ridiculous," she said happily, whipping out her phone to take a selfie.

The lights dimmed.

The film was ludicrous. A team of tomb raiders faced a long series of mortal challenges: armies of roaches, corpses that came suddenly to life. There was an evil empress who led a platoon of CGI snakes. The corpses sang a deadly song that lulled the tomb raiders into madness. The two heroes were distinguished by their superpowers. One had slick martial arts moves. The other charmed snakes by playing a flute. Shen had chosen a showing with English subtitles, to make it easy for Lindsey to follow, but this was unnecessary. There was almost no dialogue.

Lindsey's mind wandered, though not as much as she'd have liked. The booming soundtrack made thought impossible. Shen was thirty-four, a grown man. He seemed both older and younger. A husband and father, a rising star at his company. And yet he was enraptured by this terrible film, a mindless collage of CGI animation. He had the tastes of a teenage boy.

When the film let out, the weather had shifted. Storm clouds gathered in the west. They sat drinking hot chocolate in a coffee shop called the Lost Heaven Café.

"I'll be in Shanghai for one more night," Shen said. "Can I see you tomorrow?"

"I'd love that," she said. "But I have to work."

There was a silence.

"*Work.*" His mouth twisted sardonically. "That's what you call it?"

Lindsey flinched as though he'd hit her.

She said, "It's my job."

Another silence.

"I don't understand you," he said finally. "Some girls, maybe they have to do this. But you went to university. You could have a better life."

Lindsey's cheeks flamed. Her face felt flooded with blood. "Better than what?"

Shen stared past her, blinking rapidly behind his glasses. "Better than going with men for money."

"It isn't like that," she said, but how was it? Even in English, it would have been hard to explain.

She got to her feet. Her body, at least, remembered Hester's advice: *You have to trust your instinct. If you get a bad feeling, get the hell out.*

Her legs were a little shaky. "I should go," she whispered, reaching for her coat.

Outside, a light rain was falling. She picked a direction and set out blindly. Normally her driver lingered in the neighborhood, a phone call away. But Lindsey was in the wrong part of town, far from Pudong and the reception Mei believed she was attending. Tonight she was on her own.

When she saw a Metro stop in the distance, she quickened her pace, ducking to avoid strangers' umbrellas. The satin pumps were tight as tourniquets, cutting into her heels. In that moment she saw the logic in the ancient tradition of foot-binding. It was how you kept a woman from running away.

Quick footsteps behind her, a man running.

"I'm sorry," Shen called. "Please come back."

Lindsey stopped short, so abruptly that he nearly ran into her, and turned to face him. He was out of breath, his forehead glistening.

"I shouldn't have said that," he said.

"Is that what you really think of me?" A car roared past at top speed, spraying her legs with wet.

"I think you're beautiful. You're like no person I have ever met."

They took a cab to the company apartment. In the bedroom they undressed in the half-light. When Lindsey moved to close the blinds, he stopped her.

"I want to see you," he said.

The heat of his skin shocked her. He didn't talk the way some men liked to. Without his glasses he looked younger and gentler, curiously undefended. It was more intimate, in a way, than seeing him naked.

They kept their eyes open, an unspoken agreement between them. Closing her eyes would have felt like evasion or capitulation.

They never closed their eyes.

*   *   *

"Shen from Shenzhen," Hester said. "That is just too perfect."

"Right?" said Lindsey. "Maybe that's why he didn't tell me. In the beginning he called himself Sean."

They were sitting at a Mongolian restaurant in the French Concession, eating skewered lamb and steamed bread.

"Oh my God, bread! I miss it so much." Hester stuffed a wad into her mouth and pushed the basket toward Lindsey. "Take this away from me. You have to save me from myself."

Lindsey tore into a piece of bread. "Why do they do that? The fake names. It seems sort of . . . unnecessary."

"I can't speak for the Chinese. Honestly, I don't know why they do anything. But for the Westerners," — *Wisterners* — "it's just what you think." Hester changed her mind, reaching for the basket of bread. "They're all married, obviously. They're just garden-variety cheaters. From their perspective, the less we know about them, the better." *Betta.*

"Shen isn't like that," Lindsey said. "He isn't like anyone I've ever met." And then, because she had to tell someone: "He asked for my phone number."

Hester's eyes flickered. "But you didn't give it to him."

"Of course not," Lindsey lied.

They split the bill down the middle. Lindsey stuffed the leftover bread into her handbag. As she crossed the street to her apartment, her phone vibrated in her pocket.

我想你

I miss you.

Shen came to Shanghai the first week of each month, worked long days at his company's office in Lujiazui. In the evenings they met for late, inexpensive dinners. They went back to the company apartment, played video games, and eventually went to bed. At a certain point Lindsey rose and dressed in the dark, careful not to wake him. She tiptoed silently out the door.

For the first week of each month, Lily was unreachable. Her phone went directly to voicemail.

When Shen asked her to spend the night, she knew it was a mistake. But by then it was too late. She was already in love with him.

That he was married didn't trouble her. In some way she couldn't have explained, it made him more attractive. It was one of the terrible discoveries of her time with Dean Farrell, how sleeping with a married man could feel like winning. It was better to be cheated with than cheated on.

Sharing his bed felt luxurious, an intimacy she'd never shared with Dean Farrell. She lay awake most of the night, listening to the humming refrigerator, the forced-air heat that came on periodically with a roar. Lying naked in Shen's arms was the greatest pleasure imaginable. Sleeping would have been a waste of time.

The company apartment was snug but comfortable. Sometimes she pretended they lived there together. She imagined them doing ordinary things, drinking coffee, shopping for groceries. She pictured the bedroom closet filled with their clothes. Of course, this could never happen. At the end of the week, Shen would return to Shenzhen. The company apartment would be used by other ambitious young men, exhausted from long days at the office, eager to make their mark on the world.

One morning as she was leaving, he stopped her at the door.

"You forgot something." From his pocket he took a ponytail elastic. Threaded through it was a long auburn hair.

"I'm sorry," she said quickly.

"I ask you to be careful. It's the only thing I ask of you."

Technically this was true. His other expectations were unspoken: her time and attention, her body in his bed one week each month. That this was a week in which she earned no money didn't occur to him. Her work was a subject they avoided strictly. Shen paid close attention to his own budget, but Lindsey's, apparently, never crossed his mind.

At the end of the month, Mei called her with a booking. "For next week. It's a very important client."

"I can't," Lindsey stammered. And then, because an explanation seemed to be required: "I'm not feeling well."

Silence on the line.

"I have noticed that the same thing happened last month," Mei said. "Are you taking the pills correctly?"

Lindsey saw her escape. "I started the pack late," she lied. "I didn't want to tell you."

"Xiaoying, we discussed this. It is very important to stay on schedule, to regulate the cycle."

"I'm sorry," said Lindsey.

"We don't want any surprises," Mei said.

Chinese New Year fell on a Monday. Like every year, it was preceded by a mass migration: hundreds of millions of Chinese piling into trains and planes and buses, the vast megacities drained of their multitudes. Trains roared out of Hongqiao Station packed to capacity, heavy with human cargo. In the aisles, whole families slumped over piles of luggage, the floor shuddering beneath them for ten or twenty hours, the thousands of kilometers between city and home.

The run-up to the holiday was hectic. Grocery stores were packed, bakeries, florists, gift shops. Hair salons did a brisk business. For the entire first week of February, Johnny Du worked twelve-hour shifts.

Johnny viewed the coming year with caution. In the Year of the Monkey, he explained, gross misfortune was almost inevitable. Lindsey found this slightly comical.

"The whole year?" she teased. "For all of humanity?" For a brief, unsettling moment, she was aware of being Aaron Litvak's daughter. Her dad was so stubbornly rational that it was a little obnoxious. Illogical statements offended him personally; an unsubstantiated assertion was a provocation to argument. He had no tolerance for superstition, religion, magical thinking of any kind.

"Yes," Johnny said, very seriously. "Normally this is true."

"Well, it has to be lucky for *someone*," she said, having absorbed the inescapable lesson of a capitalist childhood: If someone in the world was suffering, someone else was getting rich.

Johnny considered this. "Babies," he said finally. "Everyone wants a Monkey baby. They are very cute."

It wasn't reassuring, it was definitely a bad sign, that Lindsey thought immediately of Shen. At that moment he was blasting across China in a bullet train, to his parents' home in Hunan province. The whole family would greet the New Year together: Shen, his parents, his wife and young son.

It was now possible, with permission, for couples to have a second child. Once, in a weak moment, Lindsey asked if he'd considered it. The answer was bound to cause her pain, and yet she couldn't help herself.

"My wife would like to," he said. "But I think we are too old."

The words affected her powerfully. Jealousy washed over her like a sickness. She felt suddenly overheated, distinctly unwell.

He seemed puzzled by her distress. "Why do you ask me these questions?"

"I can't help it," she said—the truest answer she could possibly give.

His son was the center of his world. Lindsey accepted this. The little boy was a preexisting condition; Shen had made him with another woman without knowing there was a Lindsey in the world. But for him to have a second child with his wife would be an unspeakable betrayal, an anguish too terrible to bear.

*   *   *

On New Year's Eve, the Wang Building was tomblike. The tenants of the World Peace Guest House had gone back to wherever they'd come from. The nail salon and driving school were closed. Even the sky was quiet: For the first time in local memory, New Year's fireworks displays were forbidden. The city's dire air quality was blamed. Lindsey holed up in her apartment and watched CCTV—China Central Television, the annual broadcast of the Spring Festival Gala. She thought of her grandmother in Florida, who spent every New Year's Eve in front of the television. The way Grandma Judy waited for the ball to drop in Times Square, a billion Chinese watched Chunwan.

The production was lavish. The curtain rose on a jubilant chorus, a multitude of voices welcoming the new year. At the front of the stage, children in golden monkey costumes mugged and frolicked. Behind them were a hundred girls in pink lotus-shaped ball gowns. Each held a massive fabric flower suspended from a pole. The lotus girls twirled in unison. The golden flowers spun hypnotically, in time with the swelling music:

Spring fills the universe, arriving early
Spring returns to the earth, bringing good spring sight

Lindsey tried to imagine where Shen was at that moment—Shen the family man, celebrating the holiday with his wife and son. Once, while he was in the shower, she'd snuck a peek at his beeping cell phone. His wife had texted him a photo of their son, who'd just lost a front tooth. Lindsey studied the photo hungrily—the boy with his wide gap-toothed smile, his mother at his side. The woman looked older than Shen, doughy and round-faced. She held the boy's baby tooth between two fingers. On her right hand was a gold wedding band.

Picturing Shen with this woman, making love to this woman, was like cutting into her own flesh, but Lindsey did it anyway.

Mountains and rivers joyfully dance with the spring breeze
The divine land resounds with joyful songs, echoing the spring tide

The monkey children scampered offstage. Next came a horde of dancers in red costumes. The girls wore red go-go boots. Their hair was identically styled, in two high rolls that resembled Minnie Mouse ears.

He didn't wear a wedding ring, a fact Lindsey found striking. In all the time she'd known Dean Farrell, he'd never taken off his ring. He and Trish had been married for twelve years. At family barbecues, at Red Sox games, Lindsey watched them closely: laughing often, finishing each other's sentences. Occasionally they held hands. That she'd never sensed anything amiss between them made her distrust Dean, and men generally. How could you know if they really loved you? If they were lying, how would you ever know?

She fingered the tattoo on her shoulder. The scars beneath it were invisible, but they were still there.

Loving Dean had taught her that jealousy was addictive: the perverse thrill when her worst fears were confirmed, the terrible vindication of learning she'd been right all along. In some demented way, it was deeply satisfying. Jealousy was like outsmarting love. Explaining this to Shen was impossible. When he married his wife, both were virgins. There was nothing in her past, or his, to be jealous of.

One night when they were drinking wine together, Lindsey told him about Dean Farrell. She hadn't planned on it. The words had simply spoken themselves. She needed him to know that another man had loved her. That she could be loved.

The knowledge affected him powerfully. That night he made love to her almost angrily, with a new intensity.

It was not a manipulation on Lindsey's part. She had needed — truly needed — for him to know.

*   *   *

The lunar year dawned soundlessly. Lindsey woke too early and watched the sun rise. The silence was disconcerting. The roar of traffic—the city's grinding soundtrack, constant as the ocean—was simply absent, as though some higher power had pressed MUTE.

Last year, she and Zach had watched in wonderment as Beijing contracted. On New Year's Day, they strolled the empty sidewalks arm in arm. The lunar New Year meant nothing to them; the holiday—celebrated by one-sixth of humanity—was to them a quaint ritual. To be far from their families was not painful. To feel alone in a Chinese city—ever, for any reason—was a kind of miracle.

On the first day of the Year of the Monkey, Lindsey wandered Shanghai alone. The dormant streets seemed sterile and ugly, stripped of life like defoliated trees. The neighborhood stores were shuttered—the noodle shop, the fruit market. Even the automated tea stall was out of service. Its screen flashed New Year's greetings in English and Chinese.

In a store window she caught a glimpse of her reflection: UGG boots, stocking cap, a down coat over her flannel pajamas. She looked like a crazy person, an unhoused schizophrenic arguing with the voices in her head.

Back at her apartment, the refrigerator was empty. She had neglected to stock up on lucky New Year's foods, whole fish and long noodles. Congee was the unluckiest food, but she ate it anyway, for comfort. It slid down as easily as strained peaches, baby food for adults.

The day wore on.

The afternoon was impossibly long, as though the laws of physics had been suspended. To distract herself she found, in a kitchen cupboard, a bottle of whiskey Johnny had brought to celebrate Golden Week, untouched these many months. Mixed half-and-half with orange juice, the liquor went down easily.

She sent a text to Shen.

*　　*　　*

When she woke her phone was beeping, her head pounding. She'd fallen asleep on the couch. The lights were on, the whiskey bottle nearly empty. It was now seven in the morning, dark and rainy. The air felt heavy and still.

The evening came back to her in a rush. The sweet drinks, the sudden, exhilarated certainty that she and Shen were meant to be together. The chance to be loved was rare and fleeting. Her time with Dean Farrell had taught her this. When he talked about leaving his wife, Lindsey had choked. If she hadn't, her entire life would be different.

Rare and fleeting, and there were no do-overs. With Dean she had been too cautious. She wouldn't make that mistake again.

Now she scrolled through her phone. Her first texts to Shen had been effusive. **You make me so happy!** Later they became pathetic. **I miss you. I need you.**

In the end they turned angry. **How could you marry her? I know you don't love her.**

I can't live this way. I'm tired of living.

In the space of four hours, she'd sent him fifty-seven text messages. His eventual reply, early this morning, was written in English.

I am blocking this number, he wrote. **Please don't contact me again.**

*　　*　　*

Days passed. How many days exactly was impossible to say. Lindsey could think of no reason to leave the apartment. From CCTV she learned that the holiday was over, the mass migration of Chinese happening in reverse.

When she ventured outside she found the city repopulated, hordes of people packed into subway cars as though they'd never left. From her kitchen window she watched the girls at Shanxi Preparatory School doing their morning calisthenics, running down Yuyuan Road. Lindsey stood at the window, her breath fogging the glass, until they disappeared from view.

Each morning she swallowed a pill from the packet. In this way, she marked the weeks.

At a certain point she lost her cell phone. How this was possible in a small apartment was hard to explain. The phone turned up some days later, in the pocket of a jacket that had slipped from its hanger. The battery was dead and she didn't recharge it. There was no one she wanted to call.

In dreams she wandered the streets of Lujiazui, looking for the company apartment. The city blocks were endless. Her dream self hobbled on bound feet, wishing she'd worn different shoes.

The door code to the company apartment was 2331. She'd watched Shen enter it many times. All four digits were in the top row of the keypad. Her dream self got it right on the first try.

In the bedroom blinds were drawn. Shen was sleeping on his side. Lindsey unzipped her dress and unhooked her bra, slid in naked behind him. To her surprise, he was wearing pajamas. He'd always slept naked when they were together.

When she slid her hand under his pajama top, he woke with a start.

"*Nǐ shì shéi?*" he shouted. *Who are you?*

Her dream self sprang out of bed. When the lights came on, she saw that the man in the bed was not Shen but Dean Farrell. He was wearing red pajamas. He stared at her naked body in open-mouthed horror, and she saw that his bottom teeth were missing.

When Dean called her a whore, his Chinese was better than she'd have expected.

"*Duìbùqǐ,*" she said. *I'm sorry.*

The word repeated and repeated in her head.

*   *   *

She woke to the sound of knocking. The apartment, to her surprise, was filled with gray daylight. Groggily she made her way to the door.

She opened it a crack.

"Miss Litvak." Sun, the building manager, studied her from top to bottom. She wore panties and an old T-shirt that ended at her upper thighs.

"I was sleeping," she said, crossing her arms over her chest.

Again his eyes went up and down. "I am sorry to bother you. This will only take a moment."

Lindsey blinked, disoriented. Like Dean Farrell in her dream, he was missing his bottom teeth. She marveled at this detail. It was as if her subconscious had known that Sun was waiting on her doorstep. As if, on some level, she'd been expecting him.

She wished she could tell Wendy.

Sun said, "Your rent was due on Saturday."

Lindsey squinted into the bright hallway. A fluorescent bulb flickered overhead. "What day is today?"

"Tuesday," he said.

No answer would have surprised her. It might as easily have been a Monday or a Thursday or a Sunday.

"I'm sorry," she whispered. "I've been sick. I'll go to the bank tomorrow."

Sun looked confused. Was she speaking in Chinese or English? Sometimes she wasn't sure.

"I'm sorry," she said again, and gently closed the door.

*   *   *

The bank was a lie. There was no bank. Everything she earned went into an envelope, kept in the hidden drawer beneath her bed. After

Sun's visit she checked the envelope. Inside were six hundred-yuan notes.

She hadn't been on a date in weeks. Since New Year's Day, she'd avoided looking at her phone.

She plugged in the phone and waited. It took some minutes for the screen to illuminate. When it did, she began scrolling. Missed appointments, voicemails from her parents, dozens of unread texts from Johnny and Hester and Grace. Each was a pinprick, largely insignificant; but the combined effect was deflating.

Lindsey was losing air.

She located the last text Mei had sent her, the day after New Year's. **A very important client wants to meet you tonight. Let me know if you are free.**

Lindsey had never replied.

For the first time in weeks, she studied herself in the mirror. Her hair was fuzzy and shapeless as an old wool sweater. Her nails were uneven, the cuticles ragged, her legs bristly, her groin itchy. Her biweekly salon appointment—charged to Mei's account—had come and gone. The leg and bikini wax, the mani-pedi, were luxuries she couldn't afford.

*   *   *

"Girlfriend, your hair is so long!"

Lindsey sat at her kitchen table, a towel around her shoulders. Johnny combed her wet hair into neat sections, securing each with a plastic clip.

"Thank you for doing this," Lindsey said. "I'll pay you next week, I promise. As soon as I talk to Mei."

After the shock of powering up her phone, she'd fired off a barrage of text messages, variations on a theme: **Sorry to be out of touch! I've been under the weather. Let's catch up soon.** Then, gathering her courage, she telephoned Mei. The call went immediately to voicemail. A recorded greeting informed her that no message could be left.

She sent Mei a text much like the others, but with more exclamation points. **Sorry to be out of touch! I was extremely ill, but now I am completely recovered! Please call me!!! I can't wait to get back to work!**

Johnny said, "I don't think she will call."

His face was impassive, revealing nothing.

"She has to! I mean, I'm still working for her. Technically," she said. "She didn't actually fire me."

"I think maybe she did," said Johnny. "Chinese way."

Spring came, the return of the plum rains.

Lindsey's birthday fell on a Sunday. For the first time in weeks, she treated herself to a milk tea. At the corner market she bought a dragon fruit and a bag of dried jujubes.

She drank her tea and watered the plant Johnny had brought her. A jade plant in a west-facing window would attract money luck. Lindsey was skeptical, but she watered the plant faithfully. Her dad, if he were here, would laugh at her. He was so, so proud of not believing in anything.

She straightened the apartment and waited for the phone to ring, though who might reasonably be expected to call wasn't clear. It was literally the middle of the night in America. Johnny was at that moment sitting down to Sunday lunch with his parents. Hester was on a plane to Taiwan, where an annual meeting of international semiconductor manufacturers was being held.

She flicked on the television. CCTV was showing aerial footage of the new Shanghai Disney. The grand opening was days away. Johnny had spent hours online getting them tickets; when the park opened they would go together, a belated birthday present. That she'd never been to Disneyland astonished him. It defeated the entire purpose of being American.

Her phone rang.

For a brief, demented second, she was sure that it was Shen calling. That she'd never told him her birthday seemed an unimportant detail. Some small, insistent part of her was certain he'd know.

She picked up the phone.

"Lizzer, happy birthday! I miss you!"

The voice was female, American. Hope Childress had been her roommate at Wesleyan, a lifetime ago.

Lindsey said, "I miss you too." Though she hadn't thought of Hope in months, it was suddenly true: There was no one in the world she'd rather talk to.

Hope updated her on Wesleyan gossip, recent developments in the lives of people she used to know: a nosy RA they both had found ridiculous; a boy Hope had met at a party and dated for just a minute; a girl on their freshman floor who'd fucked her way through an entire frat. Meghan's overnight guests had been spotted regularly in the floor's one bathroom—male feet visible beneath the door of the stall, large and hairy and pointing in the wrong direction.

Ashley Burdick, Connor Whalley, Meghan Ford. To Lindsey the names were vaguely familiar, like characters in a book she'd read long ago. When she dropped out of Wesleyan, she stopped updating her Facebook profile. For the entire year she'd lived in Beijing, her Facebook self was still in college, pulling all-nighters and shuffling to the dining hall for a late breakfast. The outdated posts—long-ago birthday wishes, goofy photos and inside jokes—were a psychic bookmark, keeping her place in the old life in case she ever wanted to go back. When she came to Shanghai, she deleted everything. The sensation was chilling and weirdly satisfying, as though she were erasing herself.

Hope talked and talked. For Lindsey, it was hard to believe that Wesleyan still existed. Now she remembered late-night dorm conversations, drunk-dancing at loud parties, plastic cups of watery beer. The leafy campus in springtime, the first warm day after the long Connecticut winter, music playing, Frisbees flying. To her surprise, she missed it. For a single, aching moment, she missed being young.

They said their goodbyes. In three weeks, Hope's parents would throw her a graduation party at their house in Montclair, New Jersey. "It's going to be *epic*," Hope said. "You have to come!"

Graduation. The word was like a relic from some extinct language, its meaning irretrievably lost.

"Maybe I will," said Lindsey. "It would be great to see everyone. To come home."

* * *

Home.

Having said the word aloud, she couldn't stop thinking it.

Home was the house in Newton, the basement wall scored with pencil marks where, on each birthday, her dad had marked her height. She could go back there whenever she wanted; her parents would be happy to buy her a ticket. She imagined landing at Logan, walking through the glass doors of Terminal E, International Arrivals, Grace waiting to meet her.

Home.

* * *

At 8 p.m., her mother called.

"Happy birthday, sweetheart! Any plans for your special day?"

"My students are taking me out to dinner," Lindsey said, which was nearly true. Two birthdays ago, in Beijing, Zach had organized a small birthday party at a restaurant, a handful of students and fellow teachers sharing hot pots. She wasn't telling a lie, merely an outdated truth.

I'm coming home, she nearly said.

"Can I talk to Grace?" she said instead.

Grace was the only person she wanted to tell. *Home, home. I'm coming home.*

"She isn't here," said Claire. "There was a sleepover at Iris's house."

"I thought they weren't hanging out anymore."

"They weren't. I'm not sure what happened, but apparently they kissed and made up." There was the sound of a door opening, her mother getting into the car. "Grace can fill you in when she gets home. I'm supposed to pick her up in Belmont at nine."

"Belmont? What are they doing in Belmont?"

"Trish moved." Claire's voice vibrated with some unexpressed emotion. "I guess I didn't tell you. She and Dean are getting divorced."

"Now?" Lindsey felt the wind go out of her, like she'd caught a football hard in the solar plexus. "They're getting divorced *now?*"

Claire said, "Apparently there's a girl."

A girl, Lindsey repeated in her head. English words had begun to seem strange to her, arbitrary syllables with no inherent meaning.

"She's eighteen, so at least she's legal," Claire said neutrally. Lindsey appreciated the effort this must have cost her. By some heroic feat of self-control, she'd managed to keep the satisfaction out of her voice.

"He's a predator, Lindsey. This is what he *does.*"

It was the old Claire, her voice strident. The mother who'd ruined her life.

"Mom, why are you telling me this?" Lindsey's heart raced. "Seriously, am I supposed to be happy about this? Is this some kind of twisted birthday present?"

"Don't be so dramatic," her mother said.

"You want me to know that he never loved me. That I was just some young girl he wanted to fuck." The crass syllable landed satisfyingly, the blunt, ugly word Lindsey had never said in her mother's presence.

"How can you say that?" Claire inhaled noisily, a moist, snotty sound. "How can you even think that?"

Before hanging up Lindsey said, "Happy birthday to me."

Xiaoying, it's been a long time. I was surprised to hear from you."

This time there was no fancy tearoom. They met outside a noisy cafeteria near the Wang Building. Lindsey felt inexplicably nervous, as though she'd been granted an audience with the queen. After leaving a half-dozen voice messages, she'd been stunned when Mei finally answered. To Lindsey's delight, she suggested meeting for lunch.

Mei went through the line first, choosing fish and bean curd. At the cash register she opened her wallet and paid for her own lunch.

Lindsey waited at the cash register, her heart racing. She had chosen two steamed buns and a small bowl of curry soup, with the fine vermicelli Johnny called "rain." The bill came to sixty yuan, ten more than she had in her pocket.

If she'd known she'd be paying for her own lunch, she wouldn't have gotten the soup.

"*Duìbùqǐ*," she told the cashier. *I'm sorry.*

She backtracked through the line and set the soup under the heat lamp where she'd found it. When the cashier barked something unintelligible in Shanghai dialect, Lindsey understood that she was being scolded.

"It isn't permitted," Mei explained. "It is against the health regulation." She opened her wallet and handed the cashier ten yuan.

Her cheeks flaming, Lindsey retrieved her bowl of soup.

They found two spots at a noisy table and ate mostly in silence.

Mei inquired after her family, the health of her parents. To Lindsey, who'd never mentioned having any, the questions seemed bizarre.

When they had finished eating, Mei got to the point.

"I left you several messages," she said. "After the holiday is a busy time, always. I had to hire two more girls."

"I'm sorry to be out of touch. I wasn't well," Lindsey said, the apology she'd rehearsed.

"I had several requests for you specifically."

A flutter in her throat, as though she'd swallowed a bird or butterfly, some living creature desperate to escape. "Was it the client from Shenzhen?"

"No." Mei eyed her intently. "He stopped calling some time ago."

The room seemed suddenly loud.

"It is very strange," Mei said. "He used to call us often. He was a regular customer."

It was a lie; it had to be. Shen had never wanted a date in the first place; his colleague had forced him into it. At least, that's what he'd told Lindsey.

"I didn't know that," she said carefully.

"Oh, yes. Many times a year. Each time he came to Shanghai, he would call us for a date."

There was a long silence.

"There is one other thing, Xiaoying. Your residence permit will soon expire." Mei studied the Formica tabletop, patterned with tiny fish. "The permit is for foreign workers only. Since you are no longer working, it will be impossible to renew."

"But I can work!" Lindsey said, too eagerly. "I'm available right now. Tonight."

"I'm sorry, but I have nothing for you at the moment."

"Nothing?" Lindsey felt a wash of panic. "I don't understand.

Hester—Heather—says it's been very busy. She has a date almost every night."

The moment she said it, she knew it was a misstep. For a fleeting moment, Mei looked startled: *You know Heather?*

Mei recovered quickly.

"Heather has many repeat customers. They call on a regular basis, asking for her. She is very reliable." She reached for her purse and coat. "Xiaoying, I am sorry to see you go. It was good to have a girl with your special talents. I am only sorry that we couldn't work together longer."

"Wait!" Lindsey said. "I owe you an apology. I'm very sorry I let you down. I should have let you know that I was sick. I was irresponsible."

A silence.

"I'm ready to work now," she said. "The client doesn't have to be Chinese. English, American, anything."

Mei seemed to consider this.

"I have one client who comes to Shanghai regularly. He likes to have a date for the symphony. But I think you are not the right girl for him."

"Why not?" Lindsey said, her heart hammering.

"The language is a problem. He wants a girl who is French-speaking."

"That's no problem! I can do it." In fact her French was mediocre—her grammar shaky, her vocabulary pathetically small.

Mei raised her eyebrows. "You speak French?"

"Oh, yes! I studied it in school." It was semi-true: She'd dropped French her senior year in high school, in a pathetic stab at her mother. Claire's enthusiasm for the language had ruined it for her.

"This is very surprising," Mei said.

"Really? I thought for sure I'd told you! My mother was a French teacher. I even had a French nanny when I was little." Aurélie, the

French nanny, had spoken perfect English, but Lindsey didn't mention this to Mei.

"It's a beautiful language. Maybe the most beautiful," Lindsey continued, shamelessly channeling her mother. "I would love a chance to speak it again!"

I sound like a jackass, she thought. *I sound just like her.*

"Okay. I will text you the details." Mei allowed herself a small smile. "He is a very special client. I know you will make him happy."

Traffic disaster, she texted Johnny. **I am SO LATE!**

Lindsey was riding in the back seat of Bill's car, staring out the tinted window at standstill traffic on Yan'an Expressway. Twilight had fallen. The elevated highway glowed an electric blue, lit from beneath with neon lights. In half an hour, they'd traveled two kilometers. At one time, being late wouldn't have worried her: In Shanghai, traffic was a fact of life. Now she was less confident. Mei had given her a second chance, and there wouldn't be a third one. She couldn't afford to have anything go wrong.

To calm herself, she popped in her earbuds. Long ago, at Wendy's suggestion, she'd made a playlist of songs with happy associations. Lindsey called it her Sunshine Mix.

I'm like a bird, I'll only fly away

The song reminded her of childhood, Saturday morning swimming lessons. For one golden summer, it had been a favorite of the teenage lifeguards at the Newton YMCA.

I'm like a bird, I'll only fly away
I don't know where my soul is
I don't know where my home is

Lindsey nodded along with the music, the girl singer with the scratch in her voice. She'd been young when she recorded the song;

now, like everyone else, she was sixteen years older. Where had she flown to? Had she ever found her home?

Lindsey stared out the window. Her birthday had clarified everything. Talking to her mother had reminded her of all the reasons she'd left. The humiliating wreckage of her love affair with Dean Farrell; the disappointed parents she both loved and hated—divorced now, another disaster she'd caused. Dean had a new girlfriend, four years younger than Lindsey. She'd been that easy to replace.

I'm like a bird, I want to fly away

Going back was impossible. For the moment anyway, working for Mei was her best option. Being Lily was a small price to pay for her freedom, the precious gift of owning her own life.

* * *

The client was staying at a hotel in Lujiazui, not far from the company apartment where, long ago, Lindsey had spent her stolen nights with Shen. It was a part of the city she now avoided—a cursed location like the Gate of a Hundred Pleasures, the haunted building where Rose Orchid was killed.

She arrived at the hotel forty minutes late. In the lobby she headed straight for the elevator, ignoring the leering doorman. It was clear from his expression that he knew exactly what she was.

The client's room was on the top floor. She knocked and waited what seemed like a long time. From inside the room she heard a clomping noise. Finally the door opened partway.

"*Bonsoir, mademoiselle.*" The man was old and cadaverously lean, wearing a white dinner jacket. He leaned heavily on an aluminum walker, the reason for the clomping. A black bow tie was knotted at his throat.

"*Bonsoir,*" she said gamely. "*Vous êtes Claude?*"

"*Oui.*" Claude opened the door and made a little bow. "*On se tutoie, bien sur.*"

Tu, the familiar form. *Of course,* Lindsey thought.

He ushered her inside. The penthouse suite was spacious and modern, with bare teak floors and a view of the Pudong skyline. She followed him to a low couch, slowing her gait to match his. On the coffee table were two empty glasses.

"*Quelquechose à boire?*" he asked. In a corner near the window was a minibar with several cut-glass decanters. The concert wouldn't start for two hours; they had plenty of time for an aperitif. "*Un petit sherry, peut-être?*"

She hadn't touched alcohol since New Year's Eve, the disastrous end of her love affair with Shen. But accepting was easier than refusing. The trick, she knew, was to speak as little as possible. She was an excellent mimic with an ear for rhythm. If she spoke in basic declarative sentences and avoided the subjunctive, she could sound more fluent than she was.

"*Oui, merci,*" she said.

Claude handed her a glass. Up close he looked even older. His jet-black hair was parted on one side. At the part she discerned a narrow strip of white.

The sherry was surprisingly delicious. Claude worked in pharmaceuticals, but music was his real passion. He had a particular fondness for Chinese opera. Had Lindsey ever been?

"*Ah, oui!*" she said, with more enthusiasm than she felt. Her one experience at the opera had been grueling. The play was five hours long, the music bombastic and discordant. She went to bed with a headache and took aspirin for two days straight.

Claude beamed. Chinese opera was an acquired taste—*un gout acquîs*—though sadly, few Westerners managed to acquire it. He came to Shanghai often. Perhaps they could go together sometime.

Lindsey nodded enthusiastically. A regular client was just what she needed, a sweet elderly suitor who enjoyed the opera. Whatever else he might ask of her—the intimate needs of a man who appeared to be two hundred years old—she very deliberately did not consider. Claude was a safe harbor, a client with whom there was no danger of falling in love.

She reached for her glass and found it empty.

"Encore?" Claude asked, reaching for the decanter.

"Oui, merci," she said.

As he filled her glass he talked about Jiang Qing, the fourth wife of Chairman Mao, who'd been an actress in the theatre. During the Cultural Revolution, Madame Mao had banned the Peking Opera, calling it a bourgeois entertainment. In its place, new plays were developed. The *yangbanxi* were, for a period of time, the only available entertainment for a nation of 800 million people: operas, ballets, and a symphony, all dealing with revolutionary themes. Class struggle, the triumph of the proletariat. The stories were predictable, but the music was marvelous. It was a pity that Lily had never seen one.

Would she like another drink?

Her glass, somehow, was empty again. Lindsey shook her head, feeling sleepy. The room was very warm, the heat running full blast. Claude's exegesis about Jiang Qing had taxed her vocabulary, reminding her that she didn't actually speak French.

He seemed to read her mind. *"Tu parles un français impeccable,"* he said. She had almost no American accent, a fact he found remarkable.

"Merci. C'est gentil," Lindsey said.

He asked about her parents, her family. Why he should want to know these things, she couldn't imagine, but the vocabulary was easy enough: *mon père, ma mère, ma petite soeur.*

"My mother speaks French," she told him. "And now I have met a French man. She will be very happy."

She was talking nonsense, but in French it sounded better.

"But I am not French," he said with a gummy smile. "I am Swiss."

It was the last thing she remembered.

* * *

Pain woke her, her left hand aching. *The door,* she thought. *My hand is caught in the door.*

She opened her eyes to a blinding light. The room was cold and very bright. She was lying on a bed, naked. Claude was standing over her, fully clothed, tying her hand to the bed frame.

When she tried to scream he grabbed her by the throat.

"*Soi pas stupide!*" he told her, spraying saliva. She was fine. Everything was fine.

Lindsey gasped, coughed, choked. A sour acid filled her mouth. *I'm going to puke,* she thought, and turned her head violently, wrenching free of his hand.

"*Malade,*" she rasped. "*Je suis malade.*"

She belched loudly, a burst of clear liquid. Claude shrank back as the vomit escaped her mouth. In a single movement she lurched out of bed, her legs slow and heavy, and lunged for the door.

The living room curtains were drawn, the floor littered with discarded clothing. A clomping noise in the bedroom, Claude shouting something in unintelligible French. Lindsey scooped up her dress, her purse and shoes, and ran naked into the hallway.

The corridor was empty and brightly lit. She struggled into the dress and zipped it halfway. Her arms and legs felt leaden. In the mirrored doors of the elevator her face was pale, her eyes wide and panicked, mascara smudged as though she'd been weeping. Her ears were loud with the pounding of her heart.

When the elevator doors opened, Lindsey split down the middle and disappeared.

The hotel lobby was silent. Behind the front desk the clerk was sleeping in his chair, a paperback book lying open on his chest. She crossed the lobby at top speed, her legs shaking. The revolving door felt impossibly heavy. She threw her whole weight against it and a moment later was free.

Outside, the temperature had dropped. The night was unusually clear, the sidewalk deserted. She crossed the street with her shoes in her hands, the asphalt cold beneath her feet. According to her phone, hours had passed. Somehow it was four in the morning.

When she called Bill the driver, the call went straight to voicemail. He had turned off his phone.

Lindsey shivered in the cold, hugging her bare arms around her. Her body felt strange to her, the lace dress rough against her nipples. She'd left her bra and underpants behind. Whatever Claude had put in her drink had knocked her out completely. She felt as though she'd been asleep for weeks.

"He was Swiss," Hester had said. "Or Swedish. One of those."

Hester had tried to warn her. Claude had left the girl from New Zealand tied to the bed frame. What else he'd done to her wasn't clear.

"A very special client." Of course, Mei had known exactly what would happen. Sending Lindsey to Claude was no accident. It was completely by design. Lindsey saw that she was being punished—for violating the terms of her employment, the nine illicit nights she'd spent with Shen. In Mei's eyes, Lindsey had embezzled from her employer, stolen valuable merchandise. She'd given Shen a body that no longer belonged to her, that wasn't hers to give.

When she popped in her earbuds, the song picked up exactly where it had left off.

I'm like a bird, I'll only fly away

She poked at her phone. According to the DiDi app, there were no cars in the neighborhood. One would arrive in eleven minutes. She requested the car, then sent a text message to Johnny.

Waiting 4 dd

Disaster night! Kill me now

Somewhere in the distance an engine was accelerating, tearing up the empty streets.

I'm like a bird, I'll only fly away

Lindsey fingered the tattoo on her shoulder. The sky seemed very close above her, the rabbit moon clearly visible. Grace still existed in the world—a little girl at summer camp, uninjured, unruined.

She tapped out another text.

Good luck in the talent show!
Send pix!

From behind she heard the roar of an engine, a squeal of brakes.

III

The Sound of Water

A cloud hangs over People's Park. The afternoon fug is a daily occurrence, climate plus mathematics: a low-pressure system over the Pacific; exhaust—mechanical and human—heating the heavens. (A million cars huffing at gridlocked intersections; thirty million inhabitants breathing in and out.) Beneath the park is a sprawling Metro station, the busiest stop on the largest subway system on the planet. Aboveground, grandmothers practice tai chi at an underwater pace.

In the central garden, the day's games are underway. Under a pavilion near the Lotus Pond, men square off across elephant chessboards. Silent spectators gather around them, like medical students observing surgery. Over each table is a haze of cigarette smoke.

On the south side of the pavilion, poker is played. The poker players are younger and more raucous. Both groups engage in aggressive spitting, competing in distance and volume. The poker players spit the loudest. The chess players spit the farthest.

At one of the poker tables, an outrageous bluff pays off handsomely. The men erupt in guffaws, scaring away the birds.

In the south garden a waltz is playing, buoyant and silvery. A portable stereo sits on the sidewalk. Elderly couples box-step around it, like planets orbiting the sun. They are dressed for a festive occasion—Western suits, silk cheongsams, the occasional dashing fedora. Husbands and wives, a few pairs of woman friends. There are never quite enough men.

On the lawn a family eats a picnic lunch: mother and father, sulky preteen daughter, incorrigible two-year-old son. The boy squeals at a punishing volume. He clamors to look at his sister's phone, sticks his fingers into her congee. He grabs a bun from her plate and jams the entire thing into his mouth. She loathes this child, product of the new policy—the son her parents wanted the first time, when they ended up with her instead. Her father is balding now, her mother graying. To see them pushing a stroller, talking baby talk, is simply embarrassing. She wishes, powerfully, that her brother had never been born.

Beneath a gazebo a Korean man sings operatically, accompanied by a teenager on accordion. A clean peach scent rises from the *osmanthus* trees like some rare perfume.

An old woman paces in circles, beating her back with a rubber mallet.

A young mother holds her baby over a fountain, a male infant in split pants. The boy urinates obediently, squealing with delight.

In the northwest garden, the marriage market is in full swing. A clothesline runs between two trees, photographs clipped to it like laundry. They are snapshots of eligible sons and daughters, approaching thirty and still unmarried—bare branches, leftover ladies. Cards are circulated, listing vital statistics, height, age, income. In urgent cases, assets are enumerated: real estate holdings; cars with year, make, and model; job titles; degrees earned.

In the rock garden near the Xishan Waterfall, the greenery is thicker, fresh eucalyptus, clumps of jacaranda. The waterfall smells of urinal cake. Men pace the perimeter in slow circles, smoking and watching a beautiful boy.

The boy lounges on a bench, plugged into headphones, nodding to some private music. He wears black tights and a clinging black T-shirt. His chest is as narrow as a child's. The T-shirt is printed with English words, in block letters like an optometrist's chart.

IS

NO REMEDY

OF

LOVE

The boy is the center of attention. Eyes closed, he pretends not to notice. Finally a man sits beside him and speaks in a low voice.

In the south garden the music ends, the dancers clap politely. Another song begins, the opening bars of the "Blue Danube Waltz." A solo dancer has joined the group, a stooped widower in a red ascot, his hair slicked back with some fragrant pomade. The widower dances grandly, with great sweeping movements, arms outstretched to embrace a woman who is no longer there.

*   *   *

Johnny sits at Lindsey's bedside, rubbing Tiger Balm into her feet. Visiting hours are technically over, but for him the student nurse makes an exception. On the wheeled table beside him is a vase of flowers, a small bouquet of irises he bought from a vendor in the street.

Lindsey's feet are not delicate. They're as wide as his own and nearly as long, and Lindsey hates them. "They're enormous," she once complained, another word she taught him. Johnny couldn't disagree.

The student nurse is shyly flirtatious. Some days she gives him an orange from Lindsey's lunch tray. Though the patient hasn't eaten in ten days, the trays keep coming. They sit untouched for several hours, while nourishment is fed into her veins through a tube.

Johnny rubs Lindsey's feet and remembers a night last autumn, unseasonably warm, when they went dancing. The rave was held illegally, in a pedestrian tunnel in a northern suburb, by two English deejays who called themselves Fu and Lu. Once a month, Fu and Lu threw parties at random spots throughout the city. The locations were kept secret until the last minute, the guests notified via text message. Johnny and Lindsey had never missed a single one.

The rave was mobbed, the tunnel packed with young people. Lindsey dragged him by the hand into the thick of the crowd. The booming sound system made thought impossible. A pulsing bass line throbbed like a communal heart. When three boys from Hong Kong offered them Ecstasy, Johnny and Lindsey each swallowed a tablet. Wordlessly they were absorbed into the group.

Dancing with Lindsey was a wonder. Dancing with Lindsey was Johnny's favorite thing in life. At all other times their communication was approximate; one or the other was always translating. On the dance floor they shared a native language, secret and proprietary. Their conversation was fluent, telepathic. Questions were asked and answered. There were running arguments and private jokes. They repeated and contradicted each other, mocked and flattered each other. They invented new moves as though plucking them from the air.

The rave in the tunnel went on for hours. The boys from Hong Kong disappeared without explanation, the music so loud it was impossible to speak. Johnny and Lindsey danced alone and together, they danced with boys, they danced with girls. Fu and Lu spun electro house, big room, hardstyle. In this way, lifetimes passed.

It was nearly dawn when the police arrived. Lindsey spotted them first, the blue van squealing to a stop at one end of the tunnel, uniformed men spilling out like bees from a hive. She grabbed Johnny's arm and pulled him in the opposite direction, toward the far end of the tunnel—where, a moment later, flashing blue lights came into view.

Lindsey kicked off her shoes and took off running, an enormous shoe in each hand. At the opening of the tunnel she swerved right, narrowly avoiding a police sedan. Johnny followed her foot-steps exactly. When a policeman shouted in their direction, Lindsey glanced over her shoulder. Her face was animated in a way Johnny would remember forever, a look of pure exhilaration and joy.

They learned, later, that arrests had been made, sixty revelers carted off to the police station and forcibly drug-tested. Fu and Lu were tried and sentenced. Only Lindsey and Johnny had escaped.

He rubs her enormous feet.

"I saw your parents," he tells her.

He'd been smoking in the hallway when the Western couple stepped off the elevator. He would have known them anywhere. The woman had Lindsey's curly hair and green eyes; she was Lindsey in miniature. The man was handsome and very tall, an older version of Curly Fu. Lighting his cigarette, Johnny was aware of the man's square shoulders, the smudge of stubble at his chin.

"Where does she work?" her father asked. "Some kind of language school?"

Johnny was stymied by these questions. Lying to his own parents was by now second nature, but it was quite another thing to lie to someone else's. Later, when Lindsey's father called to him in the street, running away was his first instinct. He hadn't run in many months, since the night of Fu and Lu.

When her father told him about the accident, Johnny was dumbstruck. His English deserted him; he was unable to formulate the most basic question. He was simply too stunned to speak.

On some level he'd been waiting for this—not *this,* exactly, but something. Worrying about Lindsey had become part of his daily life. Men can be unpredictable; Johnny knows this. Soon after coming to Shanghai, he went home with the wrong man. They met in a club and went back to a fancy apartment, where the man beat him badly. To this day he has no idea why. There were no warning signs, nothing strange in his behavior. Johnny limped home and told no one. He'd carried the secret for years, lodged inside him like a bullet, until he met Lindsey.

What he didn't tell her, has never told her: Each morning as he knocks at her door, he remembers the man's face.

She told him, once, that her clients called her Lily. Johnny found this significant, another way in which they were exactly alike. The man who beat him had never met Du Jun. The beating thus happened to someone else.

Her work didn't shock him. Last autumn, he'd left a dance club with a German tourist. When he woke the next morning in the man's hotel room, the German's luggage was gone, the room paid for. On the bedside table he'd left three thousand yuan.

The gesture was unambiguous. Only the sum was confusing. Johnny didn't know whether to be flattered or insulted. Three thousand yuan was a significant amount of money; but in another way, it wasn't so very much. It seemed to him that the German had made a valuation, a precise estimate of what his body was worth. He rode the subway home with a roll of bills in his pocket. He didn't want the money, but leaving it behind seemed a ludicrous gesture, at once proud and pointless.

"Nǐ hǎo?"

He turns. A woman is standing in the doorway. He smells her the same instant he sees her, a tender whiff of jasmine perfume. She is his mother's age, though she looks younger.

He studies her haircut with professional appreciation, her dark red lipstick. Stylish eyeglasses hang from a jeweled chain around her neck.

"Nǐ zài zhǎo rén ma?" he asks. *Are you looking for someone?*

The woman's eyes go from Lindsey to Johnny. She says that she is sorry. She has come to the wrong room.

In Shanghai the Litvaks settle into a routine. Each morning they meet in the hotel restaurant, where Aaron orders the full English breakfast. Claire drinks a cup of tea and watches him eat. The TV screen above the bar is tuned, always, to CNN International, news for travelers. Stock prices, weather reports. Aaron's eyes follow the crawl across the bottom of the screen.

Their daughter has been unconscious for eighteen days.

Their conversation is meager. Since the divorce they've become strangers to each other. It's as though the wreckage of their marriage has been swept into a pile in the middle of the breakfast table. They don't look at the pile or speak of it, but to Claire it glows brightly, a neat hillock of radioactive waste.

His company wears on her, his petty convictions, his stubbornness. Certain conversations they've simply stopped having. By unspoken agreement they avoid the subject of Lindsey's student loan. His insistence that she pay it off herself (How? *How?*) is a perfect example of his mulishness. On this point—on every point—Aaron is unbending: The payments are Lindsey's responsibility. Dropping out of college was her own terrible decision, and she'll have to face the consequences.

Claire understands the principle; of course she does. The principle isn't hard to grasp. Aaron can afford to pay off the loan; he can afford it many times over. But for the sake of the principle, he's willing to let Lindsey suffer. For the sake of the principle, she'll begin her adult life drowning in debt.

Nineteen days ago this seemed like a calamity, the worst thing that could possibly happen.

After breakfast they take a cab to the hospital. They sit with Lindsey for an hour or two, waiting for the doctor to appear. Claire pulls a chair close to the bed and listens to Lindsey's breathing, as she did in the dark time—the first, terrifying weeks of motherhood, when panic attacks woke her in the night, the mad certainty that her baby was dead or dying. Night after night she kept vigil in the nursery, watching the rise and fall of Lindsey's chest.

Her daughter kept breathing. Her daughter is still breathing.

"Come back," Claire whispers. "Come back, come back."

Since arriving in Shanghai it has become her mantra. Fifty, a hundred times a day, the words pass through her head like the crawl at the bottom of the TV screen.

Come back, come back, come back.

They last spoke on Lindsey's birthday. Since arriving in Shanghai, Claire has struggled to remember their conversation. Then, one morning at Lindsey's bedside, it comes back to her in a rush. They talked about Dean Farrell—his new teenage girlfriend, Trish filing for divorce. The call ended badly. Lindsey hung up on her and, when Claire called back, refused to pick up the phone. How could she possibly have forgotten this? Claire suspects she's still in shock, her mind acting in self-defense.

She managed, at last, to speak with Lindsey's doctor. The conversation was unsatisfying. Her team was watching Lindsey closely, the doctor promised in careful English. Head injuries were unpredictable. The principal danger was swelling of the brain.

Since then Claire has seen the doctor twice more. Both times she's offered the same explanation, in the same words exactly. It's possible they're the only English words she knows.

Lindsey has two nurses, a young one and a mean one. The young nurse is small and plump and speaks one word of English, "Hello"— pronounced, always, with a shy smile. The other nurse—skeletally thin, with a perma-frown and over-plucked eyebrows—says nothing. The mean one, Claire and Aaron call her, but maybe she isn't. Maybe that's just her face.

Come back, come back, come back.

Each day like all the others. Claire thinks of the absurdist plays she read long ago in her schoolgirl French, alienated strangers waiting for something to happen, terse, witty meditations on emptiness and despair.

There are no further sightings of Mr. Chen from the billing department.

*   *   *

"Still no word from the police," Aaron fumes.

They are loitering on the sidewalk outside the hospital, killing time while the nice nurse gives Lindsey her bath. The morning air is already humid. They stand in the shadow of the building to take advantage of the shade.

"I mean, what does it take to get action? Do they have laws here, a judicial system? It's fucking barbaric."

Claire says nothing. His obsession with the investigation is, to her, nonsensical—as if any amount of investigating will save their daughter's life. Each night in her hotel room, Claire combs through online medical sites, a pointless exercise. Without Google Search she is helpless. Whatever information exists on the Chinese internet is inaccessible to her.

Yesterday, in desperation, she left a long, rambling voicemail on Gabby Muir's cell phone. Later she felt foolish. Gabby is a primary care physician at a neighborhood clinic. That she'll know anything about brain injuries seems unlikely, but she is the only doctor Claire knows personally. She has no one else to ask.

Aaron has taken up smoking. He lights a match and cups it with one hand, unnecessarily. There is no breeze to speak of, no relief from the suffocating heat.

"She looks better today," Claire says. "Don't you think?"

"Better," he repeats, as if the word is unfamiliar, some arcane clinical term that requires explanation.

"Her coloring," Claire insists. "When we first saw her, she was as white as a sheet." Years of therapy have taught her to focus on the positive. It didn't come naturally to her and never will, but now, more than ever, it seems important to try.

"Maybe," Aaron says. "Honestly, it's hard to tell."

The area around the hospital is bustling, ambulances coming and going, delivery trucks idling at the curb. Aaron leans back against the brick wall of the building. The sidewalk is clogged with foot traffic, pedestrians in business attire, in worker's coveralls, in operating scrubs. A few wear robes and slippers—lucky patients who are still ambulatory, healthy or desperate enough to step outside for a smoke.

Aaron finds this remarkable.

He is full of such observations, a running commentary on the astonishing differences between the US and China. The massive crowds of pedestrians waiting at every intersection, waiting for the light to change. The surprising number of retarded adults navigating the streets on their own.

"What?" he says, seeing her frown. "I can't say 'retarded'?"

"Mentally challenged," Claire says.

Aaron continues, undeterred. Are the rates of retardation higher in China? Or are the retarded simply more likely to live at home and be part of society, rather than being institutionalized? Then again, maybe he's wrong; maybe the number is proportional. Maybe he's just seen so many goddamned people that, statistically speaking, a large number of retarded ones are bound to be part of the mix.

Claire thinks, *Please stop talking.*

A man pulling an IV pole asks Aaron for a light.

He reaches for his matches, still blathering. It isn't just the retarded; hasn't she noticed the large number of spinal deformities, the untreated cases of scoliosis and kyphosis? Healthy women in the prime of life with malformed bodies, bent sideways or with a dowager's hump.

"The way you'd look," he tells her, "if you'd been born here."

Claire flinches. Her scoliosis was detected in the seventh grade, a routine screening by the school nurse. She spent a miserable, pointless year of her adolescence in a Milwaukee brace. When that didn't work, she had surgery to straighten her spine.

"Right?" says Aaron.

He seems to be waiting for something. It takes her a moment to understand that she's supposed to be grateful, impressed that he remembered this fact, any fact, about her childhood. Claire who'd been his wife for twenty years.

He studies her, frowning, as though he truly doesn't understand—maybe he doesn't—that the words are hurtful.

"Oh, for Christ's sake. What's the matter?"

"Why do you remember that?" says Claire. "Of all the things to remember."

"Oh, here we go," Aaron says.

* * *

The days are endless. They sit at Lindsey's bedside until the mean nurse kicks them out. Then there's the question of how to fill the day, the eighteen hours until they can see their daughter again.

Back at the hotel, Aaron makes phone calls, attends virtual meetings. Claire rides the subway to nowhere in particular, eavesdropping on strangers' conversations. The language remains impenetrable. It closes her off like a brick wall, the deepest kind of loneliness. She has taken to smiling at babies, hoping the mothers and grandmothers will smile in return.

One afternoon she finds a cinema the concierge recommended, which shows Chinese films with English subtitles. As the lights dim, she feels a frisson of anticipation. She is desperate to disappear into a story, to think of something besides Lindsey on life support on this hostile planet, twelve thousand miles from home.

The film is a romantic comedy set in a bleak industrial town. The young hero is a handsome factory worker with disappointed parents. Their dreams for him hinge on admission to something called the Chemical Institute, but instead he blunders through a series of scut jobs at the factory—Electrical Team, Plumbing Team—and witnesses multiple industrial accidents. He gets drunk and sings karaoke and bikes around town in pursuit of the factory's resident doctor, a preternaturally beautiful, improbably young woman who rides her bicycle in long, flowing skirts. Though achingly lovely, the doctor is a bore and a scold. She rebuffs the hero's advances and urges him to make something of himself.

In the climactic scene, he sits for an exam.

*   *   *

As she's leaving the cinema, Claire's phone rings. She doesn't recognize the caller's number or even, at first, his voice. Though he and Aaron are in constant contact, Peter has never, in her memory, called her cell phone.

"Claire, it's Peter. I just talked to Gabby."

"Oh, *Peter*!" she says, dismayed. "I left her the most hysterical message. I must have sounded like a crazy person."

"She said you have concerns about Lindsey's doctor."

Claire thinks, *My daughter has been in a coma for nineteen days. Yes, Peter. I have concerns.*

"Well, she's very nice," she says tentatively. "It just doesn't seem like they're *doing* anything."

"Is there anything I can do for you?"

The question catches her off guard; she is unprepared for kindness. Claire nearly weeps.

"We need a second opinion." Even as she says it, she feels defeated. The language makes everything impossible. Getting a first opinion was hard enough.

Peter says, "Let me make some calls."

Claire exhales. Somehow this reassures her. Her daughter is still in a coma, but Peter will make some calls.

"Great," she says. "That would be great."

"What about health insurance?"

"She doesn't have any. Or if she does, we can't find any proof of it."

"She's what, twenty-one?"

"Twenty-two."

"Roger that. I'll have Zoe look into it." Beeping on the line, the world clamoring for Peter's attention. "I need to take that. More soon, Claire."

Peter Muir is a pompous ass, but in that moment she'd give him her kidney.

"Thank you, Peter," she whispers, but he's already hung up the phone.

* * *

Peter Muir is a pompous ass. Once, when Grace was five or six, they invited Peter and Gabby to a backyard barbecue. While Aaron manned the grill, Peter held court on the screened porch. On her way to the kitchen, Claire overheard him talking about Grace.

"She's a gorgeous kid. But you know, China is full of them. When Aaron and Claire were looking to adopt, I told them to check it out." His tone was self-congratulatory, as if Grace were some extravagant gift he'd chosen especially for them.

Later, after the guests had left, Claire vented to Aaron. "Can you imagine? Adopting Grace was apparently his idea."

Aaron looked startled. "He said that?"

"To a half-dozen people. He sounded like a complete jackass. You should have seen Miranda Hulford"—their next-door neighbor— "rolling her eyes."

"Huh," Aaron said.

Claire eyed him suspiciously.

"You know, we *did* talk about it. I can't remember who brought it up, but it's possible he gave me the idea. I can't say for sure," he added hastily. "But it's *possible*."

Claire stared at him, appalled.

"Honestly, what's the difference? Why should it even matter?" Aaron seemed bewildered. "She's our daughter, and she's doing great. And you've never been happier."

It's true: Grace is Claire's golden child. And yet—for reasons she'd be embarrassed to articulate—it *did* matter. Raising Grace is, to date, the only thing she hasn't failed at. Peter took credit for the best thing in her life. Of course, this was completely in character. He has a bottomless appetite for recognition, admiration, gratitude. His good works are always public: the annual fundraiser for Doctors Without Borders, the Muir Media Lab at Harvard Business School. Why be generous if no one can see you? Peter wants the whole world to marvel at his largesse.

Is there anything I can do for you?

Accepting Peter's help is like joining the Hare Krishnas: You are expected to praise and thank him for the rest of your days. It's a measure of Claire's desperation that she is now fully prepared to do this. If he finds a doctor who can save her daughter, she'll sing hosanna until she's hoarse.

At Camp Friendship, the first session ends with Family Day. The Meeting House is decked out with patriotic bunting. Hanging in the dining hall is a green-and-white banner: WELCOME, FRIENDSHIP FAMILIES! The soccer field becomes a parking lot for parents' SUVs.

Team Monadnock has packed its footlockers. Beds have been stripped, sheets and towels deposited in the laundry cart. Only Grace's bunk is still intact, covered with its green wool blanket.

The day begins with an awards ceremony, to recognize campers for their achievements and contributions. This takes a very long time. Each child is roasted and applauded, presented with a trophy or certificate. Grace and Kira share the award for Best Dancer. Parents shoot video and snap pictures. Finally the camp flag is lowered. Families stroll across the campus for a celebratory clambake on Friendship Green. Grace follows a little distance behind, the only camper without a parent. Even Austine's make a brief appearance, though they don't stay for the clambake. After the closing ceremony, her dad carries her footlocker to a battered Subaru hatchback. Like a defendant leaving the courthouse on *Law and Order,* Austine is hustled into the car.

Lunch is served buffet style. Grace waits in line to collect her basket of clams. At the counselors' table she eats in silence, studying her bunkmates. All seem slightly embarrassed by their parents. Isabelle's mother is enormously fat. Sophia has two fathers. Haley's dad arrived with a pretty brunette who could easily be Haley's sister but turns out to be his girlfriend. Kira has an identical twin and a nearly identical mother; all three have the same square jaw and pale eyebrows and lank blond hair. Basically, they are a family of clones. To grow up in such a family is, to Grace, unimaginable. It seems both terrible and wonderful—like being three people at once, or being no one at all.

On the front lawn Team Monadnock says their goodbyes. The girls exchange hugs and phone numbers, they pose for selfies. With Grace they are polite and careful, as though she is recovering from an illness. No one understands why she isn't going home.

* * *

It's nearly dusk when the last SUV leaves the soccer field. Grace lies in her bunk in the waning light, scrolling through her phone. Outside, a wind has kicked up. The empty cabin is a little spooky, the eleven bare mattresses. Spiky shadows creep across the wall, tree branches waving in the wind. The new campers won't arrive until Saturday. For two nights Grace will sleep in the cabin all by herself.

She scrolls and scrolls. In China it's already tomorrow. She tries to picture what her parents are doing at this very moment, but this is impossible to do.

Every few days her mother calls with an update, always at the worst possible moment—just before breakfast, or five minutes before Lights Out.

Her mother's updates are unsatisfying. Lindsey is resting or being examined by her doctor or taking a shower. Lindsey is getting better, but it's a slow process. Lindsey can't call or text Grace—phones aren't allowed in the hospital. Lindsey sends her love.

The phone calls end abruptly, leaving Grace with many questions.

Breakfast is at the same time every day. Can her mother seriously not remember?

Why is Lindsey so tired?

How is this possibly taking so long?

Aaron takes the stairs to the lobby. The last thing he needs is to run into Claire in the elevator. The woman is a human polygraph; she'll know immediately that he is up to something. He has never even attempted to lie to her.

He slips out of the hotel by a side door, like a philandering husband leaving a tryst.

This morning, after a week of radio silence, Mrs. Li left him a voice message: The detective will meet with him this afternoon. Claire, if she knew, would insist on coming along—a terrible idea. The visits to the hospital unglue her completely. For the rest of the day she's shaky, volatile. A calm, rational conversation with the detective would be impossible in her agitated state.

At the police station, a uniformed officer shows him to a windowless room in the basement. A young guy with patchy facial hair sits at a round table. Beside him is Mrs. Li, wearing the same yellow sweater.

Aaron has prepared a list of questions. The detective answers them readily: the address where the accident occurred, the anonymous stranger who reported it to police.

"Do we know what time it happened?" Aaron asks.

He waits for Mrs. Li to translate. The detective answers succinctly.

"Between three and five o'clock in the morning," says Mrs. Li. "It is impossible to say for certain. There were no witnesses."

"Wait, *what*?" Aaron finds this hard to credit. Since arriving in Shanghai, he's been surrounded by people. "How is that possible?"

Pudong—the detective explains through Mrs. Li—is Shanghai's financial district. Early on a Sunday morning, the streets would have been deserted.

"Well, what about her phone? She must have had a phone with her. Have you tried to trace it?" Aaron knows from television that this is possible. Again he waits for Mrs. Li to translate.

The detective's response is lengthy. When at last he finishes speaking, Mrs. Li turns to Aaron.

"Yes," she says. "Of course."

"That's all? What else did he say?"

Mrs. Li smiles, covering her mouth with her hand. "He says we have the same television shows in China."

Unprompted, the detective resumes talking. Once again, Aaron waits for Mrs. Li to translate.

"Whoever has your daughter's phone must have changed the SIM card," she says. "With a different SIM card, the phone can no longer be traced."

"Right," Aaron says, feeling stupid.

The detective looks at him with something like pity.

*　*　*

From the police station he sets out walking, the same route as last time. The neighborhood is now familiar. The bald doorman at the Wang Building seems to recognize him. Aaron takes the elevator to the sixteenth floor.

The hair salon is empty except for a woman sitting at one of the sinks, smoking a cigarette and staring at a cell phone.

"Do you speak English?" he asks.

She eyes him quizzically.

"She doesn't understand," says a male voice behind him.

Aaron turns. A man is standing in the doorway, the building manager with the missing teeth.

"Then maybe you can help me," he says. "There's a young man who works here. Can you tell her I need to speak with him?"

Sun relays this to the smoking woman and waits for her response.

"The boy is sick today," he tells Aaron. "He didn't come to work."

Getting to the park is harder than Johnny expected. The subway is alarmingly crowded. For half an hour he waits on the platform, watching packed trains flash past.

Finally, a train stops. When the doors open, he sees that it, too, is crammed wall-to-wall with bodies, though it isn't the usual commuter crowd. The 11 train is full of families, parents loaded down with backpacks and strollers, children wearing plastic Mickey Mouse ears. There is a feeling of holiday in the air. It seems impossible that another person can squeeze in, but Johnny takes a deep breath and steps aboard.

Crowds make him nervous.

At the brand-new station on Xiuyan Road, the train vomits out its passengers. Johnny is the last to exit. The edge of the crowd, he has learned, is the safest place to be.

His fear of crowds is a recent development. Eighteen months ago, he saw a girl die at his feet. She was his own age, maybe younger. It was hard to know for certain. Her face was crushed beyond recognition, stomped to a bloody pulp beneath strangers' shoes.

That night—Western New Year's Eve—he'd gone dancing. For the rest of their lives, he'll spend Chinese New Year with his parents and grandparents; to do otherwise would be unthinkable. But the Western holiday means nothing to them, and Johnny was free to roam the dance clubs of Shanghai and celebrate with whomever he wished.

The club was packed, but at the time this didn't alarm him. A crowded dance floor meant vitality, variety—a dizzying selection of faces and bodies, a churning sea of eligible men. At twenty minutes before midnight, the club emptied out into the street, to join the public celebration on the Bund.

Johnny was fifty meters away from where the commotion started. Someone was throwing money out of a third-floor window. This set off a scramble, children and even grown men rushing to grab all they could. It was discovered, later, that the money wasn't real; a nearby club had printed coupons to resemble US dollars. They were simply free-drink tickets, to be handed out to the New Year's crowd on the Bund.

The stampede made national news. Thirty-six people were trampled to death, twenty-six of them women. Johnny combed through the list of victims. Any one of them might have been the girl who died at his feet.

The story of the fake dollars is apocryphal, or maybe it isn't. The original source of the rumor was the Shanghai Police. The department's official account posted it that night on WeChat. Later the post was deleted, the statement retracted. The cause of the stampede remains shrouded in mystery. Eyewitnesses agree and disagree.

*   *   *

The park is busy but feels spacious, with extra-wide lanes to prevent crowding. Johnny waits in a series of queues.

The admission queue is endless. Employees in Mickey and Minnie costumes hand out bottled water. Grandmothers open their umbrellas to shelter from the sun. Johnny fingers the two tickets in his pocket. He bought them online for three thousand yuan, the exact sum the German had left for him on the bedside table. It seemed a fair price for the best birthday present in history, a day he and Lindsey would remember forever. But nothing—nothing—has turned out the way he planned.

He wanders alone through the Alice in Wonderland maze. He could have resold Lindsey's ticket, to recoup some of the cost, but found himself unable to do so. As recently as yesterday, he still hoped for a miracle. To sell her ticket would be to say it couldn't happen. Selling her ticket would mean he'd given up on her.

He joins the queue for the TRON Lightcycle roller coaster. Ahead of him stands a group of teenage girls, chattering excitedly. Behind him, a pack of boys follow them with darting glances, erupting periodically in bursts of braying laughter. It's exactly the way Johnny remembers his own adolescence: the nervous, halting dance of boy and girl, himself somewhere in the middle, observing and completely alone.

He joins the queue for Adventureland.

He joins the queue for Once Upon a Time, an animatronic display of all twelve Disney princesses. Johnny takes careful photos of each princess, from every possible angle, to show to Lindsey. He is the only male present without a daughter or granddaughter. Mothers watch him suspiciously, pulling their children close.

He joins the queue for Tomorrowland.

By dinnertime he's tired of standing in queues. He sits on a bench to watch the parade snake down Mickey Avenue, surrounded on all sides by families. Beside him a young mother and father hold a small boy overhead, so that he is sitting on both parents' shoulders. The boy wears mouse ears. He points to an employee in a Donald Duck costume and squeals with delight.

The boy's parents are Johnny's age, a fact he finds incredible. He can't imagine being either of them. He can only imagine being the child.

The Litvaks wait at the nurses' station. At the end of the corridor, Lindsey's door is closed. As promised, Peter Muir made some calls. At this moment, as a personal favor to him, a renowned British neurologist named Gordon Hughes is examining their daughter. What exactly such an examination entails, Claire truly doesn't want to know.

"He's old," Aaron says. "I'm surprised he's so old."

Dr. Hughes looks to be in his seventies, a fact Claire finds reassuring. Lindsey's Chinese doctor looks not much older than her patient. And yet, with a blind faith that now seems foolish, Claire and Aaron have entrusted her with their daughter's brain.

At the end of the hall, Lindsey's door opens. Dr. Hughes steps into the corridor, a tall, stooped man with a shock of white hair and an oddly twisted mouth. When he introduced himself that morning, he explained that he was recovering from Bell's Palsy: "I promise you," he said dryly, "this isn't my normal face."

Claire and Aaron stare at him expectantly.

"Mr. and Mrs. Litvak," he begins.

Neither corrects him. In this moment, the label is entirely accurate. In this moment, it is simply who they are.

"Your daughter's MRI shows a unilateral brainstem lesion. This is considered a grade 2 injury. The good news is that only one side is affected. The location of the lesion is also in our favor. A midbrain injury is associated with far worse outcomes." He pauses delicately.

"That said, it's concerning that she hasn't regained consciousness. Three weeks is a long time."

Yes, Claire thinks. *It's a very long time.*

The doctor talks about the unpredictability of head injuries, the importance of managing intracranial pressure. "At this point, I would have to say the principal danger is swelling of the brain."

The same words, again and again. It's like being trapped in a recurrent dream.

"Can we take her home?" Aaron asks. "Back to New York. Or Boston."

Dr. Hughes looks perplexed. "I can't think why you'd do that. Moving a comatose patient is no small thing."

"But would she get better care?"

"Not necessarily. From what I can tell, they've done a reasonable job of it. They did a CT scan immediately, which is good. I'd have preferred an MRI, but tomography still provides valuable data. And they're managing her pressure, which is everything. I can't say I'd have done anything differently. You want my advice? Don't move her. The risks far outweigh any possible benefit."

"Okay, but now what?" says Aaron. "A week from now, a month from now. What can we expect?"

"In terms of outcomes, there's a range of possibilities. With a grade 2 injury, many patients survive with no functional impairment."

"Many," Claire repeats. "How many?"

"A quarter. Maybe more. Young, healthy patients like your daughter have a real advantage."

"Okay," Claire says, nodding energetically. "That's good news."

"In many cases, with proper therapy, they're able to regain most of their former functioning. *Eventually,*" he adds, holding up a hand. "Eventually, over time."

"Most," says Aaron.

"Sorry?"

"You said 'most.' *Most* of their former functioning."

"Yes. Well. Your daughter may be altered."

"Altered how?" Aaron says.

"I'm sorry to be vague. These questions are very difficult to answer."

There is a silence.

"But some patients make a full recovery," Claire insists. "It's *possible*."

"Anything is possible." For the first time the doctor smiles. "Mrs. Litvak, the human brain is an amazing machine."

The smile is disconcerting. He smiles with the left side of his face.

* * *

Jing'an Temple is the size of a small airport. The day after their meeting with Dr. Hughes, the Litvaks take a guided tour.

The visit to the temple was Claire's idea. The conversation with the doctor made it necessary. She'd been so hell-bent on getting a second opinion that she hadn't thought beyond it. It hadn't occurred to her that the second opinion would differ so little from the first.

The temple is built around a central plaza, currently teeming with Chinese people. Vendors sell prayer beads, incense, gourds strung with red tassels. At either end of the plaza stands a massive fireplace, each containing—barely—a blazing fire. A fragrant cloud of woodsmoke hovers overhead.

The temple itself is seven stories high. Each level is lined with a carved marble balustrade. Along each balcony is a series of intricately carved wooden doors.

Claire and Aaron wait in line at the ticket counter. His lack of enthusiasm for the temple is expected and doesn't deter her. After twenty years of marriage, he is incapable of surprising her. His reflexive hostility to all things spiritual is as constant as the sun.

When they reach the front of the line, Aaron pulls out his wallet to pay for the tour. The way he handles the money makes her crazy. He empties his pockets and examines each coin carefully, unsure of its value. In the end he hands the cashier a crumpled hundred-yuan bill. He handles the money like what he is, a foreigner to whom it means nothing—scraps of paper assigned an arbitrary value, as worthless as a handful of gum wrappers.

Their tour guide is a young woman in heavy makeup—TERESA, according to her brass-plated name tag. Her English is correct and careful. She carries a bright red umbrella for protection from the sun.

She leads them across the plaza, weaving her way through the crowd. They step around a tour group in matching blue windbreakers, gathered around what looks like a giant iron teapot—thirty feet tall, topped with three pagoda roofs. Men toss coins high into the air, trying to land one inside.

Teresa explains that the temple dates to the third century, the Wu Kingdom. "It is even older than Shanghai. From the Three Kingdoms period of ancient China," she says. The original structure was built on the other side of the Huangpu River, where it stood for a thousand years before being moved to its current location.

"When did that happen?" Claire asks with an encouraging smile.

Oh, come on, Aaron thinks. As though she could possibly care when the temple was moved!

Teresa says, "One thousand two hundred sixteen."

"Wait, *what?*" Aaron says, smelling bullshit. "That can't possibly be right."

Teresa is discomfited.

"Maybe I have made a mistake. In the year one thousand two hundred sixteen," she repeats. "Exactly eight hundred year ago."

Aaron frowns. "It doesn't look that old."

"Yes. Well." Teresa clears her throat delicately. "During the Cultural Revolution the original structure was removed."

"Removed?" Aaron looks amused. "I think you mean demolished."

She nods vigorously. "Yes, demolished. In this place was a factory."

"A factory?"

"Of plastics." Teresa adjusts her umbrella. The sunlight bleeding through the fabric turns her cheeks a rosy pink. "The temple that you see today was rebuilt in 1983."

Aaron guffaws. "Our house is older than that. I have *shoes* older than that."

My *house*, Claire thinks. *It's my house now.*

In the divorce this was a point of contention. Aaron wanted to sell, but Claire was adamant: The house in Newton was Lindsey and Grace's childhood, the only home they'd ever known. Later, camped out in the ruins of her marriage, she wondered if she'd made a mistake.

They pass a swarm of people waiting in line to touch a rock—a large slab of jade, the approximate size of a garage door. There are signs in Chinese and a smaller one in English:

LUCKY JADE STONE. TOUCH THE STONE AND GOOD LUCK IS BESTOWED ON YOU. MAKE A WISH AND YOUR WISH COMES TRUE!

Please don't, Claire thinks, but of course Aaron reads the sign aloud.

The line moves quickly. An old woman presses her entire body against the jade—back, then front—as though trying to make an impression on the stone.

Teresa explains that they are standing in the Precious Hall of the Great Hero. There is also a Jade Buddha Hall, a Hall of the Three Saints, a Hall of Virtuous Works, and a Hall of Heavenly Kings.

"Kings and heroes," Claire says. "There's always a great hero, never a heroine. Aren't there any monuments to great women?"

"Oh, yes," says Teresa, looking pleased. "The Guan Yin Hall."

It is, Claire realizes, like cuing up a selection in a jukebox: Teresa explains the significance of Guan Yin. The statue of the goddess, made of camphor wood, is six meters tall and weighs five metric tons.

"It is said that when a believer falls, Guan Yin places him in the heart of a lotus," she adds.

Aaron closes one eye, his skeptical face—an expression Claire has, over the years, come to detest.

They climb the stairs to the second floor and enter a narrow room, its walls covered with bright red curtains. At one end is a simple altar: five Buddha statues, each larger than a man, sit on a long table. Before each cross-legged Buddha is a plate of apples, piled in the shape of a pyramid. The ceiling is hung with looping festoons of gold fabric. People wait in line to kneel on a red satin cushion. Prayers are offered. There is the sound of coins dropping.

They follow Teresa from room to room. Behind each set of doors is another altar, another pyramid of apples or peaches or oranges, another coin box. Throngs of Chinese—some wearing Mickey Mouse ears—wait their turn to kneel in prayer.

They enter a room whose walls are plastered with yellow paper tickets, each stapled to a photograph. In one corner, a man sits at a card table, selling the tickets. The worshippers have come prepared with snapshots of the afflicted: unemployable sons, barren daughters, cheating spouses. Babies born clubfooted or with a cleft palate, grandparents felled by cancer or dementia or stroke.

A little girl hands over a photo of a dog wearing a tutu. The man takes her money and staples the photo to a yellow ticket.

Claire rummages through her wallet. She has a hundred images of Lindsey saved to her phone but not a single physical photograph that could be attached to a ticket. She recalls Lindsey's small, tidy apartment—blank as a hotel room, her personal keepsakes, if she has any, stored on her laptop. In the digital age, precious family photos are simply data. All of human life has been reduced to a binary code.

When the tour is finished, Aaron falls into step with Teresa. "So these people are all tourists?"

"Yes," she says.

"Not all of them," Claire interjects hopefully. "Some are Buddhists, right?"

"It's possible," Teresa says, sounding doubtful. "I think mostly they take photos."

"From what I understand, the Chinese are atheists," Aaron informs her, as though he's an authority on the subject.

Teresa frowns. "I am not sure of this word."

"It means not religious. Not Buddhist, not anything."

Teresa nods vigorously. She doesn't seem offended, she seems relieved and grateful, that Aaron has supplied the precise right word.

"It's true," she says brightly. "We do not believe."

Aaron grins smugly, as though he has won an argument. Claire thinks, *What an asshole I married.* The realization brings her no satisfaction, no pleasure. If she married this asshole, what does that make her?

"Excuse me," she says. "I'll be back in a minute."

Aaron looks irritated. "Where are you going?"

"Five minutes. Just wait for me here."

She doubles back into the central plaza, where she pays five yuan for a bundle of incense and waits her turn at the fireplace. As she lights the incense, a breeze kicks up. The fire is suddenly very loud, like a flag snapping in a stiff wind.

Your daughter may be altered.

Claire thinks of her own mother, helpless as an infant after her final, massive stroke. Her sweet smile as Claire fed and washed her, brushed her teeth and hair.

She holds the incense to her forehead and does as the Chinese do, making three slow bows in each direction: north, south, east, west. The smoky air burns her throat. Tears in her eyes, ashes on the wind.

She has no one to pray to, so she prays to Lindsey.

Come back, come back, come back.

Next she crosses the plaza and waits in line at the Lucky Jade Stone. When her turn arrives, she presses her face to the stone.

On her way out of the temple she notices a coin box next to the Lucky Jade Stone. It was an honest mistake; she hadn't meant to steal any luck she hadn't paid for. She combs through her bag and feeds a handful of coins through the slot. Then she doubles back and touches the stone again.

* * *

When they leave the temple it's late afternoon, the heat suffocating. The air smells of incense and diesel exhaust. A string of identical tour buses idle at the curb.

As they cross the street, Aaron outlines a new theory: Shanghai has poor drainage. This explains the faint odor of sewage that lingers over the city. He stops at a sidewalk grate and inhales deeply. (Why? *Why?*)

"Do you smell that?" he demands, sniffing the air.

"Aaron, will you stop?"

He looks genuinely puzzled.

"Why do you choose to focus on this? Why do you want me to focus on it?"

"I'm just saying," Aaron just says.

At the corner he hails a cab back to the hotel, to make his phone calls or do whatever it is he does all day.

"I'll catch up with you later," Claire says.

She watches the cab pull away into sluggish traffic, Aaron's hand trailing out the open window in a half-hearted wave. All day long she's been dying to get rid of him. It's the way she felt every day during the final, bitter year of their marriage, when his mere presence was a provocation and her every emotion seemed to exist in response to him. And yet, when he finally left, she felt lost and empty. Then, as now, she'd been desperate to be alone—but why, exactly? What had she hoped to do with her solitude?

The answer was the same as it's always been: She had hoped to write.

Across the street is a small, crowded park—A SHANGHAI CIVILIZED PARK, according to a plaque affixed to a concrete wall. Claire walks the perimeter, studying the crowd. A group of elderly people perform calisthenics to a recording of a man counting, played at high volume from a boom box on the ground. She stops to watch a man doing water calligraphy on the sidewalk. Slowly, with extraordinary attention, he draws Chinese characters on the pavement with a long, wet brush.

Claire watches him, mesmerized. It seems, to her, a perverse exercise. The water evaporates quickly in the summer heat. By the time the man finishes drawing a character, the previous one has already begun to disappear.

To Claire this is unthinkable. In her mind, every word she's ever written is precious—each sentence produced under a cloud of anxiety, the lurking dread that it will be her last.

Forgetting where or who or what she is, she turns to the calligrapher. "What are you writing?"

She is desperate to know the answer. The answer, she suspects, could change her life.

The man smiles faintly, not understanding. He presses his hands together and briefly bows his head.

* * *

From the civilized park she walks eastward, periodically checking the street signs, a futile gesture. After eleven days in Shanghai, she still can't remember the name of anything or anyone. This is not, she suspects, a temporary condition. If she lived here a hundred years, she'd be unable to distinguish between Changde Road and Changle Road, Changning Road and Changping Road. The language makes her head hurt, the same few syllables in different combinations. There simply aren't enough words.

How does Lindsey do it?

(Come back, come back, come back.)

Her daughter is an extraordinary person. Many times each day, Claire is reminded of this fact. She used to believe that she and Lindsey were alike, but coming to China changed that. During their whirlwind trip to Chongqing, she was struck—and slightly unnerved—at the ways Lindsey resembled Aaron. She had his uncanny sense of direction, his ability to identify a problem and solve it in the fewest steps possible. Claire can solve problems too, but her solutions are complicated and (Aaron says) totally illogical, arrived at by some intuitive method she couldn't explain if she tried.

She takes the map from her bag and studies the alphabetical list of streets: Jianguo Road, Jianpu Road, Jiangxi Road, Jiangyin Road.

Her former mother-in-law, Judy Litvak, has a terrible sense of direction. Judy told her, once, that it came from her own mother, who'd been a Holocaust survivor. Claire nodded as though this made sense, but the logic escaped her. In her opinion, Judy's poor sense of direction was the result of her long marriage to Joe Litvak. Claire doesn't blame Judy, not really. She knows what it is to follow a man, how easy and even pleasant it can be to place herself in his hands. Like his dad, Aaron is a human compass. For years Claire followed him blindly, paying no attention to where she was going because she didn't have to. For most of their twenty-year marriage, she had no clear idea where she was.

Though she's always loved to drive, she decided early on that it wasn't worth the struggle. Aaron was a lousy passenger—restless and fidgety, an incorrigible back-seat driver. If Claire drove, they were both miserable, so she stopped doing it. It was easier for them both if she simply let him drive.

When she married Aaron, she became a passenger in her own life.

Long ago, on their honeymoon, their roles were briefly reversed. It was Claire who planned their extended road trip through the South of France, with multiple stops along the way. She wanted to show off for her new husband, impress him with her command of the language. It was the first and last time she felt in charge of anything.

Their last night in France, they attended a vespers service at a Cistercian abbey. It was a Sunday evening in summertime, just after a thunderstorm. The church's heavy doors were propped open, filling the nave with a crepuscular light. Outside, the last raindrops tapped at the ancient cobblestones, a gentle counterpoint to the monks' singing—the resonant male voices hushed and hollow, a sound like blowing across a bottle. When the service ended, they stepped out into the fragrant evening, the fields of lavender soaked in cool rain. For Claire it was a moment of transcendence, a feeling Aaron refused on principle—or was simply unable—to share.

She was struck by his incapacity for wonder.

For as long as she can remember, she has yearned to believe in *something*. Her childhood was vaguely Christian, but her longing is like water; it will take the shape of whatever container it's poured into. Marrying Aaron meant that no container was available. His smug secularity—insistent and somehow gleeful—shattered them all.

She would have converted to Judaism if he'd wanted her to, if he'd had the slightest interest. Jewish ritual moved her deeply. Yom Kippur, she felt, was a holiday the entire human race needed badly: to stop consuming and consider the consequences of its actions, for a single blessed day. In the first year of their marriage, at Claire's insistence, they fasted together. They sat through the lengthy service at an Orthodox shul in Brookline. "Never again," Aaron said afterward. At the time, she dismissed this—not understanding, yet, that Aaron never changed his mind about anything.

His atheism was airtight, unshakeable. Religion was pure human invention, the ancient magic of frightened cavemen—confused Neanderthals spooked by lightning, bargaining with the sun.

His skepticism was infectious; it made believing seem pathetic. Eventually Claire surrendered to it. Exhibiting a striking lack of foresight, she neglected to cultivate a relationship with God, to pray or fast or do any of the things a person would do if she actually believed. Now, in her hour of need, she feels unable to ask for blessings. God, if such a being exists, might find her prayers insulting, Claire who's never given him the time of day.

Come back, come back, come back.

Now her daughter is lying in a coma and she has no one to pray to, and this, too, is Aaron's fault.

At four in the afternoon, Pudong traffic is bumper to bumper. Aaron stands on a street corner, studying the intersection. All around him, engines are overheating. Cars and buses huff like steer in a cattle chute—mighty animals crowded nose to tail, about to become steaks.

He crosses the street to study the intersection from all angles. It's impossible to guess which direction the car was coming from. At this hour the cross streets are equally busy, with multiple lanes of standstill traffic. It occurs to him that the driver was probably drunk, a terrifying thought. In broad daylight, presumably sober, Shanghai drivers are lethal enough.

This is what he's thinking when he notices the Bank of China ATM across the street.

He crosses again, to study it more closely. The security camera is mounted a foot above his head—pointed, quite logically, at the sidewalk in front of the terminal, where a mugging is likeliest to occur. Aaron touches his finger to the lens and traces its sight line, closes one eye to study it. Assuming the camera hasn't moved in the past three weeks, any passing car would be recorded.

He goes inside. The Bank of China is about to close. The lobby is empty except for a woman running a vacuum cleaner across the carpet.

There are two tellers on duty, both female. Neither understands English. Aaron tries his nodding and pointing routine, but how the fuck do you pantomime "security camera"?

Finally a man approaches, a uniformed security guard.

"Great!" Aaron says. Miraculously, he managed to get his point across. This is exactly the person he needs to see.

"That camera out front," he tells the man. "How long do you keep the footage?" He explains about the accident, his daughter left for dead on the sidewalk. If Aaron's theory is correct, the security camera captured the whole thing.

The security guard leads him through the front door and locks it behind him.

Aaron knocks at the glass, incredulous. Then he reaches for his phone. He will explain the situation to Mrs. Li, and she will translate for him. She'll tell the security guard exactly what he needs.

As always, he reaches her voicemail.

"There's a security camera across the street," he tells the recording. "At the Bank of China." He is aware of his voice shaking. "The detective needs to look at that footage."

*   *   *

The Wang Building smells of its plumbing. Somewhere behind the walls, in the hidden entrails of the basement, a clogged pipe is leaking putrid water. The first floor smells of cigarette smoke, the second of nail varnish, the third of some perfumed lotion.

There is no fourth floor.

The fifth floor smells of nothing, the sixth, inexplicably, of Band-Aids.

Floor eleven smells of foreign cooking, unrecognizable spices, meat burned on the unauthorized charcoal grill a Turkish couple smuggled into their apartment.

Floor fourteen smells, ominously, of burning plastic—day after day, week after week. No one can determine the source of this smell.

Floor sixteen smells of hair spray, the stinging sulfur odor of permanent wave.

Day and night, in a high corner of the lobby, a security camera points at the door. It records the daily life of the Wang Building, its predictable rhythms, the comings and goings of its residents. The travelers loaded down with luggage: the businessmen with laptops bound for Modern Universe; the young Westerners with giant rucksacks, for the World Peace Guest House. The limping grandfather who comes each Tuesday morning to the New Me Acupuncture Clinic and leaves an hour later, still limping—still, regrettably, the same old him.

One Saturday night in June it captured Lindsey Litvak crossing the lobby, teetering on high heels, hair hanging down her back like a blanket of flame. She paused a moment in the open doorway. Then she stepped out of the frame.

* * *

The hospital is never quiet. There is a regular beeping somewhere nearby, a sound the comatose girl finds comforting. The sound is low and murmurous, like the dial tone of her mother's landline, receptive, expectant, at your service.

These are not human sounds. No birdsong here, no wind in the trees.

The primary danger is swelling of the brain.

From somewhere in the distance comes a more adamant beeping, pitched an octave higher. Shrill, insistent, a kind of electronic nagging— bad news delivered at top volume, alarming and alarmed. Somewhere a receptacle is overflowing or dangerously empty, vital signs spiking or plummeting. The beeping in the hallway is the sound of calamity, some electronic Cassandra crying for help.

Lindsey is alarmed.

She imagines she is lying in her own bed on the sixteenth floor of the Wang Building, caught in a dream she can't escape. It's a sensation she's felt before. Trapped in a burning building or chased by a mystery assailant, she realizes that she is dreaming and sometimes, through sheer physical effort, manages to open her eyes.

The student nurse pours herself a glass of water. The patient's eyelids are fluttering. She pours the water and watches closely, willing the girl's eyes to open.

The patient's eyelids flutter but stay closed.

Lindsey feels that she is lying in some deep place—the bottom of a well, maybe. Far, far above her is a white circle of daylight. She recognizes the sound of a glass filling, the unmistakable rise in pitch as the fluid reaches the top. It's a sound like no other, a sound from earliest childhood: her mother leaning over the tub at bath time, filling a jug to rinse Lindsey's hair. The sound fills her with longing.

It's the last thought she will ever have. More than anything in life, she wants to see her mother's face.

On the 165th day of the Year of the Monkey, the comatose girl takes her final breath. A red-haired girl stands in the doorway of the Wang Building. It is the next-to-last image ever taken of her. The final one, taken at the hospital, has already been deleted from the female officer's phone.

The penultimate image, and no one will ever see it. As he does each month, the doorman erases the security camera's hard drive. Lindsey Litvak freezes in the open doorway. A moment later she is gone.

Lindsey's apartment is filled with sunlight. In the kitchen, the jade plant looks desiccated. The floor is littered with its rubbery leaves. The last time Claire was in the apartment, it looked perfectly healthy. If she'd watered it then, she might have kept it alive.

She sits at the little table near the window, looking down at the street. Children are running, a group of girls in identical school uniforms, red kerchiefs tied at their necks.

When the worst happens, a certain calm descends.

She watches the girls running and remembers her lost year, the dark time after Lindsey's birth. The crippling sadness, the lethargy, the bleak anomie that made all of life seem effortful—eating, sleeping, breathing. To Claire it had come as a revelation: She could do all these things or none of them, and in the end, it wouldn't matter. She had glimpsed the terrible truth at the center of everything, her own powerlessness. Her wishes were immaterial. What would be, would be.

Now the feeling is back, with one difference. Postpartum, her brain hummed with anxiety. The world was rife with invisible enemies, malevolent spirits conspiring to harm her baby. This time she isn't anxious, because the worst has already happened. There is nothing left to fear.

When she came back from her afternoon walk, Aaron was waiting in the hotel lobby. She knew it the moment she saw his face.

What happened next—the cab ride to the hospital, the signing of papers—is too painful to recollect. She recalls only certain moments.

(Aaron's hands shaking as he lit a cigarette. His white shirtfront soaked translucent with her tears.) It was Aaron who spoke with the doctor and arranged for the cremation. Claire was present for these conversations. As far as she can recall, she didn't say a word.

After the hospital they sat in the hotel restaurant, the same table as always, staring at each other across their untouched plates. Aaron ordered a bottle of wine and then another, and in the end they went up to her room. What happened next was inevitable and necessary. Sex wasn't physically possible, and anyway, neither of them wanted it. They undressed and fell asleep clutching each other, as they had done long ago.

They had always slept naked—entwined, in the beginning; curled around each other like puppies huddled for warmth. Later, middle-age ailments (Aaron's bum knee and torn rotator cuff, Claire's carpal tunnel) made such contortions unimaginable. Sleeping together required special equipment—Aaron's knee brace, Claire's earplugs to muffle his snoring. Still they slept unclothed.

Last night, for the first time in many years, they once again slept naked—dead drunk, both of them, and flattened by grief. It is a wound from which neither will recover: the daughter they made together, the living miracle who was equal parts both of them, gone forever from the world.

In Aaron's arms she dreamed vividly. The whoosh of the air-conditioning became a mighty river rushing beneath her, his body a life raft. Claire held on for simple survival. There was nothing left in the universe, no shelter or comfort beyond the familiar shape and heat and smell of this body she knew better than her own.

Now Aaron is on a plane back to New York. In his carry-on bag is a cardboard carton, the size of a Kleenex box but significantly heavier, sealed with packing tape. What exactly they'll do with the contents isn't clear. When Claire returns from Shanghai, they'll drive together to New Hampshire. They will tell Grace that her sister is gone.

"Gone," she told Sun, the property manager. And then, the unforgivable words she hadn't yet spoken aloud and can never take back: "My daughter is dead."

He left her alone to clear out the apartment. When he closed the door, she noticed again the card affixed to its back, printed in both English and Chinese. KINDLY REMINDING FROM THE POLICE STATION. The Chinese characters are intricate and surprisingly beautiful, and she remembers the tattoo on Lindsey's shoulder. She'd meant to take a photo of it. She'll never know, now, what exactly it said.

She starts in the bathroom. Clearing out the medicine chest, she finds that she is unable to discard anything. There is nothing to do but send the toothbrush and face cream and cotton swabs back to Newton, Massachusetts. These homely objects have become precious to her, for the simple fact that Lindsey once touched them. It's entirely possible that Claire will keep them forever — evidence that her daughter once existed, sanctified relics like the bones of a saint.

The kitchen is mostly empty. The dead plant goes into the trash, along with the strange, meager groceries — cellophane bags of rice and seeds, some unrecognizable dried fruit. Claire doesn't bother with the few dishes. She chooses a single teacup and slips it into her purse.

The closet is empty. Claire stands there a moment, blinking back tears.

She charges down the hallway, takes the elevator to Sun's office. "Someone was in the apartment," she tells him. "My daughter's clothes are missing. Someone has taken her things."

"That's not possible," he says calmly. "No one has entered the apartment."

"Come and see for yourself."

She leads him back to the apartment, where she opens the closet door with a flourish.

Sun says, "Have you looked inside the bed?"

He drops to his knees and opens a deep drawer, concealed in the base of the platform. Inside are items Claire recognizes: a down coat, scuffed UGG boots, a pair of Nikes. There is a blue suitcase and a battered canvas rucksack. Long ago it was Claire's most prized possession, acquired during her junior year abroad.

The sight of the rucksack unglues her.

"Thank you," she whispers. "That's helpful. But there were dresses in the closet, shoes and dresses. Someone has taken them."

"That's not possible," Sun says again, getting to his feet.

"I am sorry for your daughter." He nods decisively—once, twice. Claire sees that his eyes are tearing. He steps into the hallway and closes the door behind him—still nodding, as if in complete agreement with himself.

* * *

Back in his office, Sun makes a phone call.

No one answers, so he leaves a message on the voicemail. "The mother was here. She asked about the dresses," he says, and hangs up the phone.

He gathers his jacket and briefcase, his mug of hot water. Seeing the girl's mother has left him shaken. He takes the service elevator to the basement, hoping to avoid another meeting. He fears that he will cry again.

Since his wife's death he cries at the slightest provocation—whether he is sad or happy, for any reason or none at all. The urge is illogical, wholly unpredictable. It makes him distrust himself. His crying reflex is a faulty mechanism, like the car alarms that have become popular. The slightest disturbance will set them shrieking: a gust of wind, a bird overhead.

When Mei asked him to let her into the girl's apartment, Sun asked no questions. When she left with an armload of dresses, he understood that they would be given to other girls.

In his pocket his phone vibrates, a voice message from Mei. **What did you tell her?**

Nothing, Sun replies.

Mei is a tough person. She reminds Sun of his grandmother, the toughest person he has ever known. For years, now, Mei has brought Western girls to live at the Modern Universe Service Apartments. They are exemplary tenants—quiet, tidy, and apparently well paid. At Mei's suggestion, Sun charges them double rent and keeps the extra for himself. How exactly they earn their money is none of his business, as long as they meet their customers elsewhere. The Wang Building is a respectable address.

The girls come and go. Mei brings them one at a time; she doesn't like for them to know one another. Why exactly, Sun has never asked.

Lindsey Litvak. To Sun she wasn't beautiful—too tall for a girl, her hair exceedingly strange. And yet she spoke his language with care and delicacy. She had a sweet smile.

Twenty-two years old. At that age, Sun knew nothing of the world. Foreign movies were forbidden then, music, magazines. Even in Shanghai, they were impossible to find.

He thinks of the girl's mother. Her grief moved him, though parental love is, to him, an abstraction. His own mother died when he was small. Some years later his father, an economist at the university, was sent down to the country for reeducation and eventually died there—of a congenital heart defect, the family was told. He was forty-one years old. The official explanation made no sense, and no one expected it to. By then such stories were common. There was no point in asking why.

After his father was sent down, their apartment was taken over by the local housing authority. Sun came home from school one day to find their furniture in the street. He went to live with his grandmother in the *lidong,* a narrow alley house carved up into tiny apartments. His grandmother's bed was in the kitchen. Sun slept on a mattress in the hall.

The *lidong* was lively. The corridors smelled, always, of neighbors' cooking. The alley was loud with children's games, dueling radios. He remembers it, now, as the happiest time of his life.

At fifteen he left school. At one time he'd been a good student, but the subjects he excelled at—languages, literature—were no longer taught. The classes given in their place seemed invented overnight: Revolutionary History, Mao Zedong Thought. By the time he left school, good students were an extinct species. It was no longer something one aspired to be.

He got a job in a factory that made aluminum windows. His future wife—he didn't yet know her—worked there too. When they married Sun was twenty-one, his wife five years older. A Christmas cake, his grandmother called her, too old for marriage; but Sun married her anyway.

They had no children. His wife had a condition that prevented it, a medical problem unrelated to being a Christmas cake. At the time he didn't care; their life together satisfied him completely. The window factory closed, and thanks to his proficiency in English, he was hired to manage the Modern Universe Service Apartments. Things went on this way for many years, until his wife was diagnosed with lung cancer, caused by his smoking. Eight months later, she was dead.

She had never smoked a cigarette in her life. Meanwhile Sun, who has smoked since age ten, is in perfect health. It's a diabolical punishment, a fate worse than cancer, to have caused the death of the woman he loved. Thinking of it fills him with despair, which makes him want to smoke.

Since her death, it is his only consolation. Their empty apartment is too quiet, so he sits on an old couch in the boiler room of the Wang Building, smoking. He brought an electric teakettle from home, a portable radio. The furnace is noisy, but he finds the sound soothing. The boiler room is warm and dry.

He thinks again of the girl's mother. Her anguish brought tears to his eyes. Sun wasn't a tough person. His wife had been tenderhearted, and their years together had made him soft. His grandmother, before she died, found this worrying. Her son had been a soft man too, and where had it gotten him? He had died in exile, killed by his own government. For a soft man, modern China is a dangerous place.

Dangerous, polluted, crowded, expensive. Sun lives in a Shanghai he no longer recognizes—a city where he can afford nothing, a city where he can barely breathe. In his lifetime, its population has quadrupled. The city is full of migrants from poor rural provinces, living in Shanghai without permission. The streets have been taken over by cars. When Sun was a boy, almost no one could afford one. Their downstairs neighbor in the *lidong* made a reasonable living pulling a rickshaw through the streets.

Now the rickshaws are mostly gone. The *lidong* itself is gone. Twenty years ago, the last residents were evicted. Some, like his grandmother, refused to leave. She'd lived in the *lidong* her entire life, through the Occupation and beyond, and intended to die there. The local housing authority seemed willing to help. First they cut off her water and electricity. Her elderly neighbor was beaten senseless by the demolition squad. In the end, the *lidong* was razed by bulldozers, another common story. The same thing was happening all over Shanghai.

In the weeks before the *lidong* was razed, Sun joined the protests. The housing police arrested him and knocked out his teeth. Eventually he was fitted with dentures, but the bottom plate hurt him. His gums bled, his jaw ached; but for years he wore it anyway, ashamed for his wife to see him without teeth. After her death he gave up and wore the top plate only, lived on noodles and congee, because what did it matter? He was an old widower, loved by no one. No one cared how he looked.

Sun's grandmother is dead now, his wife, his parents. He has no children or grandchildren. He is a human island, unconnected to any living person on Earth.

Long ago he had an aunt in the north—his mother's sister, dead now—and a cousin who'd been born blind. The boy was sent to Shanghai for schooling, where he was trained to give massages—a common occupation for the blind, who were said to have a highly developed sense of touch. (How anyone knew this for certain was unclear.) Sun's cousin lived in Shanghai for many years, at an apartment near the blind school. From the Wang Building, it was a twenty-minute walk.

After his wife died, Sun called the blind school and scheduled a treatment. The man who massaged him was his own age; according to his nameplate, his family name was Tan. As he manipulated Sun's legs and feet, Sun imagined introducing himself to his cousin. After thirty minutes the treatment ended, and Sun left without speaking. A year later he went back for another treatment and was told that his cousin had died.

Sun cried and cried.

He is crying now, smoking and crying. He feels gutted by the randomness of life. His cousin died without ever seeing the ocean, a sunset, a beautiful woman. His wife died of lung cancer without ever smoking a cigarette. Lindsey Litvak was dead at twenty-two—her life ended in the most senseless way possible, beneath the tires of a stranger's car.

So many cars.

To Sun, who never learned to drive and never wanted to, they are a nuisance—chronic, inescapable. He hears them every waking moment. Their exhaust contaminates every breath he takes.

He cries for Lindsey Litvak, now gone forever. That her dresses will be given to another girl shouldn't shock him. He is fifty-nine now, old enough to be her grandfather. Next year he will be required by law to retire. It's hard to imagine what he'll do with himself then.

Will he play cards in People's Park, will he take up ballroom dancing? What is left for him to do with his life?

Aaron rides to the airport in rush hour. Fittingly, the driver is the same one who picked him up at the airport, a lifetime ago. He stares out at bumper-to-bumper traffic on the ring road and feels an unhinged certainty that these are exactly the same cars, in exactly the same order, as he saw two weeks ago. In a kind of dream logic, he is retracing his steps.

On Thursday he came down to the lobby, still groggy from his afternoon nap, and a desk clerk in Mickey Mouse ears told him to call the hospital.

At the hospital he did not cry. He felt the warm weight of Claire sobbing against his chest, deep wrenching sobs that sounded biological, as though something inside her was being torn.

His dry eyes didn't surprise him. In all the years of their marriage, he couldn't recall shedding a single tear. When his father died, Claire—who'd been fond of Joe—cried oceans. Aaron felt that she was crying for both of them—as though, by some mysterious trick of hydraulics, his tears had been rerouted to flow through her. It seemed a natural division of labor, arrived at by tacit agreement: Claire did the work of crying, and Aaron did the work of comforting her.

In the hallway at the hospital, she again cried for both of them. When the young doctor took Claire's hands in her own, the very simplicity of the gesture nearly unglued him. Still, no tears came.

At the airport he attends to airport business. He prints his boarding pass and checks his bag. Though he is selected for additional screening, no one asks about the cardboard box, surprisingly heavy, that takes up most of his carry-on bag.

He boards with business class, places his bag in the overhead compartment, and straps himself in for the long flight to New York. As he gropes for his seat belt, his phone vibrates—a voice message from Mrs. Li.

She speaks slowly and carefully. The detective knows about the Bank of China security camera. When he contacted the bank, he was told that the footage had been erased. Mrs. Li repeats her phone number, in case Aaron has more questions for the detective. She is sorry not to have better news.

Aaron deletes the message immediately. He has no further need for Mrs. Li's phone number. None of it matters anymore.

He buckles his seat belt, thinking of his carry-on bag in the overhead compartment. The cardboard box weights three kilograms. Three kilograms is 6.6 pounds, exactly what Lindsey weighed when she was born.

As the plane lifts from the runway, he finds himself weeping.

Never in his life has he been so glad to leave a place. He and Claire rescued one daughter from this godforsaken country. In his shattered state, it seems to him that China has retaliated. For the offense of taking one of its daughters, they have been punished. China has taken one of theirs.

On Sunday Johnny dresses in his goodson costume and rides the ferry out to the island. On the upper deck he takes an orange from his backpack. For two days he has carried it with him everywhere.

On Friday, as usual, he ducked out of work at lunchtime and headed for the hospital. When he arrived at Lindsey's room, her bed was empty. The student nurse was changing the sheets. In its usual place on the wheeled table was an untouched lunch tray. In a voice just louder than a whisper, she explained that his friend had died. Then she gave him an orange from the tray.

On Saturday morning, as he was smoking a cigarette in the hallway with Anqi, Sun stepped out of the elevator with a woman. He led her down the hall to Lindsey's apartment, unlocked the door, and followed her inside.

Anqi made a clucking noise. "Can you believe it? That toothless old goat!"

She repeated a rumor Johnny had heard before: Sun was known to take women into the empty apartments and have sex with them. Probably he gave them money. He was an old man with no bottom teeth, too ugly to be fucked for free.

Johnny smoked and listened and didn't comment. He recognized the woman from Lindsey's hospital room, her dark red lipstick, eyeglasses hanging from a chain. Her fragrance lingered in the corridor, a sweet ghost of jasmine perfume.

Now he peels the orange and eats it, tossing the peel overboard.

*   *   *

At his parents' house, dishes are passed around the table. When the meal is finished, Johnny speaks.

"I have bad news," he says, choosing his words carefully. "There's been an accident."

When his voice breaks, he feels his father's displeasure like a storm passing over water. He tries again.

"Lin has died in hospital in America. She was struck by a car."

His round, talkative mother grasps him tightly. His slender, quiet father clasps both Johnny's hands in his.

Jun, truthful Jun. Even his lies have truth inside them. The truth is that he loved Lindsey and can never replace her. The truth is much, much larger than the lie.

*   *   *

The first week of each month, Shen comes to Shanghai.

Lying awake in the company apartment, he thinks of Lindsey. Months have passed since he blocked her number. At the time it seemed necessary. Her constant questions about his wife, her childish jealousy, had grown tiresome. No Chinese girl of her age would behave in this way.

The instant he blocked her number, peace filled him. He spent a quiet New Year's Day with his family. He built a kite with his son and taught him to fly it, in the same grassy field where he'd flown kites as a boy. The peaceful feeling lasted two weeks exactly, until he returned to Shenzhen.

After two weeks at his parents' house, the tiny apartment felt cluttered and stifling. Family life wore on him: his wife's nagging, his son's constant questions and occasional whining. Spoiled by his grandparents, the boy had become addicted to sweet treats and adult attention. And television! At his grandparents' house, he'd seen a TV program about the new Disney park and clamored to be taken there.

Shen came home from the office later and later, to ensure that both his wife and his son would be asleep when he arrived. In the quiet apartment he lay on the sofa listening to music on his headphones. He closed his eyes and dreamed of Shanghai.

In this way, months pass. In weak moments he imagines divorcing his wife and taking his son, leaving dull Shenzhen and making a new life with Lindsey in Shanghai. That his wife would never allow this is an inconvenient detail.

He unblocks Lindsey's number but doesn't call her. If they are meant to be together, she will find him. Whatever happens next will thus not be his fault.

The first week in July, he comes to Shanghai as usual, certain that he will see her. He has no idea where she lives—he never asked—but she knows exactly where to find him. In his daydreams she appears without warning at the company apartment. He wakes to her naked body—materialized as if by some magic, curled behind him in bed. Later he will understand it as a kind of temporary insanity, how firmly he had believed.

He looks for Lindsey in the crowded streets, the Metro stations, a karaoke bar where his colleague takes him. Finally he breaks down and calls her, but it's too late. Her number has been disconnected.

There is nothing left to do but phone her employer, the woman called Mei.

She seems surprised to hear from him. It's been several months, she points out. Is everything all right? Was he displeased by the girl she'd sent him?

Not at all, Shen says. Lily was perfect, a charming young lady. He would very much like to see her again.

Silence on the line.

"I'm sorry, that's not possible," Mei says coolly. "Lily is no longer with us. But we have many other young ladies you would enjoy meeting. Not Chinese-speaking. But we have many lovely Western girls."

"I'm sure they are lovely," he says. "But I would like to see Lily."

"Lily has left Shanghai." A pause. "She has gone back to America."

And suddenly it all makes sense: Lindsey has reconciled with her family, gone back to university. She has chosen a better life. Shen understands that her change of heart, just months after meeting him, was no accident. He himself was the catalyst. Meeting him has changed her life.

He believes this without question. In his heart he is glad. The next time he visits Shanghai, he takes his wife and son with him, to spend a long, expensive day at the Disney park. Thinking of Lindsey no longer pains him. It gives him joy to know that she lives and breathes in the world. He imagines her with an American husband, a blond-haired son and daughter like the Western children one sees in films.

He loves her enough to be happy for her. It is best, he thinks, it is best.

News of Lindsey Litvak's death travels widely. In the Wesleyan Class of '16 Facebook group, it is briefly a hot topic, though the chatter dies down quickly. Most of the class has no memory of her, this tall red-haired girl who dropped out after sophomore year.

But Hope Childress remembers. When Lindsey was a no-show at graduation, she was hurt and angry. She nursed a grudge for most of the summer. "I'm not calling her," she told anyone who'd listen. "She has my number. She can call me."

In September, Hope relents. But when she calls Lindsey's phone number, a recorded female speaks soothingly in Chinese. Hope calls again and makes a recording of the recording, to play for her landlady. (This leads to an awkward moment when Mrs. Kim explains that she is Korean, not Chinese.) In the end Hope calls Lindsey's mother in Massachusetts, who tells her that Lindsey is dead.

Her immediate reaction is disbelief. No one close to her has ever died. Hope's grandparents, unimaginably old, are still living. And now Lindsey—three months younger than Hope!—is gone, gone, gone.

It is Hope who posts the photo on the class Facebook page. It was taken at the end of freshman year—Hope and Lindsey in identical Wesleyan sweatshirts, happily drunk at an outdoor kegger, making peace signs for the camera.

RIP, Lizzer! she writes, inanely. **Gone but never forgotten. Your BFF, Hope**

Her classmates respond with a flurry of emojis: blue and purple

JENNIFER HAIGH

hearts, some of them broken; the sad face with the upside-down smile, shedding a single tear. These expressions of sympathy are, to Hope, unsatisfying, so she sends an email to Zach Dorn.

At school they barely knew each other, though she had a front-row seat for Zach and Lindsey's college romance. The night of their first hookup, Hope slept on a couch in the TV lounge, as was customary. The next morning she pressed Lindsey for details. From the outset, Hope's prognosis was pessimistic. Lindsey was a free spirit, and Zach's doglike devotion would bore her eventually. A year later, when Lindsey called from Beijing to announce their breakup, Hope felt vindicated. She'd been right about Zach all along.

Sorry to be the bearer of bad news, she writes to Zach. **I thought you'd want to know.** She pours out her heart to the screen and includes her phone number, in case he wants to talk.

He calls her a week later, apologizing for the slow reply. Now in law school in Indiana, he rarely checks his old Wesleyan address.

"Thanks for reaching out," he says. "But, you know, I already knew."

He heard the news from Lindsey's father. That summer, Mr. Litvak had called him out of the blue. "He wanted to know what she was doing in Shanghai. Like I'd have any clue about that." The call went on for half an hour, with Aaron doing most of the talking.

"He's a nice guy," Zach says. "I felt bad for him. But, you know, he seemed a little nuts."

This is the extent of Zach's analysis. In a few years he and Hope will meet in person, at a classmate's wedding, and share a drunken clinch both pretend to forget the next morning. In his arms Hope will think of Lindsey and cry a little, because her friend is dead and Zach is a terrible kisser. He kisses like what he is, a sweetly awkward overgrown boy.

On the fifteenth night of the seventh month of the lunar calendar, the gates of heaven and hell spring open. For this one night each year, the dead move freely between realms. If they wish, they can visit the living. On Ghost Night, Johnny's grandmother sets an extra place at the table, an empty chair where her dead mother can sit. She burns a joss paper house to shelter her mother in the afterlife. She burns a paper car, a paper television, and even a paper servant—luxuries her mother, who came of age in a different China, never experienced on this Earth.

Johnny never knew his great-grandmother, but as a young boy he assisted in the burning. At that time, death was just an idea—as abstract as success or wealth or happiness, but spookier and more romantic. As a teenager he devoured ghost stories. When he imagined the spirit of Rose Orchid hovering over the Gate of a Hundred Pleasures, it gave him an electric thrill.

In the Year of the Monkey, death becomes real to him. At the ferry terminal he buys a joss paper lantern in the shape of a lotus. Inside it he places Lindsey's birthday present, her ticket to Disneyland. Before leaving the island, he'll ignite the lantern and drop it into the water. He'll remember rainy afternoons, eating dumplings and watching cartoons, being children together. He'll imagine her dancing. He will say a prayer to Guan Yin, the mercy goddess. From the ferry he'll watch the lotus float out to sea.

Lindsey will have a light to guide her to wherever she's going, a place even farther than America. It's the only thing she needs now, the only thing Johnny can give her: a light to guide her home.

2031

IV

Red Thread

My sister never intended to leave me. I know this beyond all doubt. When she left our home in Newton, Massachusetts—forever, it turned out, though she couldn't have known that—she went to China. It's true that she moved twelve thousand miles away, but in her mind—so unlike my own, and yet I know it better than I know anyone's—she was moving closer to me.

The last time I saw her we were riding to the airport. I sat in the back seat between Lindsey and Zach, cuddled up close to my sister so that no part of me was touching him. Not because I found him repulsive—I didn't—but because I was angry. I blamed Zach for what was about to happen. I believed he was taking her away from us, which couldn't have been further from the truth. It was Lindsey who wanted to go to China. For Zach, Lindsey *was* China. Loving her was the great adventure of his life.

The airport was busy at that hour, the loading area outside the terminal crowded with cars. Dad parked at the curb, and the whole family got out to say goodbye. In front of Terminal E, International Departures, I hugged Lindsey for the last time.

"You can come visit," she said. "You think you don't want to, but trust me. You're going to change your mind."

They strapped on their backpacks—Zach a brand-new high-tech frame pack, Lindsey an old canvas rucksack—and headed for the terminal, pulling wheeled suitcases behind them like large, well-behaved dogs. As they approached the revolving door, a wave of panic came over me. To call it a premonition would be giving myself too much credit. I simply didn't want her to go.

"Lindsey, wait!"

She raced back and hugged me to her chest one last time.

"Don't worry," she whispered. "I'll be back."

But she never came back.

*   *   *

My sister was the hero of my childhood, the first person who ever loved me. The evidence is mounted in a family album—a photo of us together, taken by our mother at the orphanage in Chongqing. In the photo I am seven months old. Lindsey holds me high above her head—arms outstretched, her face lit with an expression of rapturous joy. As a child I misunderstood this image. I believed it to be a photo of my actual birth, Lindsey catching me as I fell from the sky.

In my mind it is the first photo ever taken of me, but this may not be true. Some months earlier, Aaron and Claire were sent two photos of a red and wrinkly infant that might have been me, or any of the hundreds of other girl babies waiting to be adopted at that massive state-run orphanage. The unwanted daughters were part of the ongoing trade deficit, yet another product made in China and exported to the West.

For the first seven months of my life, I was one of multitudes—the numberless discarded children of Chongqing, what was then the most populous city in the most populous country on the only planet known to be populated at all. But in that photo with Lindsey, I was no longer anonymous. I had been given a name, Grace Litvak. It was the day I became myself.

*   *   *

The summer she died, I began taking photographs. Exiled to summer camp for back-to-back sessions, I had simply run out of other things to do. For the first three weeks, I played tennis and rode horseback; I participated in all manner of organized fun. But by the second session, I'd had enough, and knowing my predicament—abandoned by my parents, my sister lying in a coma on the other side of the world— my counselor, Maya Schwartz, bent the rules in my favor. When the rest of Team Monadnock was sent into the woods with a map and a compass, I was allowed to spend the afternoon alone in the darkroom, an activity that appealed to me on every level. I am an introvert—a default setting programmed, perhaps, at that overcrowded human warehouse where I was stored for seven months. I wasn't a sedentary child; I simply preferred indoor activities—ballet class or dancing to music videos in front of a giant TV screen—to paddling a canoe. To me, a day at the beach felt like punishment. Even now, I can think of no more unpleasant sensation than sun on my skin.

There was another reason I hated the sun. Like many Chinese, I tan quickly and deeply. It takes only a single afternoon in the sun to turn my skin a golden brown. My schoolmates in the rich, lily-white Boston suburbs considered this a superpower, but it wasn't one I wanted. My adoptive family—a blond and two redheads—were congenitally pale, power users of high-SPF sunscreens. With a suntan I was even more conspicuously different. It was the last thing I wanted to be.

More than anything I wanted to be one of the swans, the blithe, confident girls who dominated my class at Pilgrims Country Day. Their place in the social hierarchy was uncontested. That they were exceptionally pretty wasn't a coincidence; even in childhood, the best predictor of female popularity is physical attractiveness. Every girl knows this. We are raised on Disney princesses; even our dolls are beautiful. From birth we're made to understand what's expected of us.

A few of the swans—Iris Farrell, Josie Upton, Caroline Sedgwick—were my close friends. The others tolerated me pleasantly enough. Though I was the only Asian girl at our lunch table, I never felt excluded. I was invited to birthday parties and bat mitzvahs. A casual observer would say I was part of the group, but I wasn't—would never be—a swan.

At camp I took pictures of deer and rabbits and glowing sunsets, but really, it was Lindsey I wanted to photograph. In family photos she is nearly as tall as Aaron. She has Claire's curly hair and sculpted cheekbones and green eyes flecked with gold. Her long, graceful neck is, to me, her most beautiful feature. She is, unmistakably, a swan.

*　　*　　*

The day I lost her I was working in the darkroom. Maya knocked at the door, slightly breathless; she'd jogged across campus to find me. "Your folks are here!" she called. She didn't know—no one had told her—that the next five minutes would change my life forever. There was nothing unusual in her voice, no trace of sympathy or solemnity or alarm.

I followed her to the director's office, a place no camper had ventured since the sexting scandal with Austine. This alone should have tipped me off, but at the time I thought nothing of it; I was simply excited to see my parents. Since Lindsey's accident I'd been homesick, queasy with anxiety. Now, at last, I was going home.

My parents were sitting in canvas camp chairs, opposite the big desk. The director was nowhere to be seen.

"Where's Lindsey?" I asked.

It was my mother who told me. I can't recall the exact words she used. I only remember feeling confused, unable to grasp the most basic facts.

"You just *left her* there?" I asked over and over again. In my fractured state, it was incomprehensible: They'd gone to China to get Lindsey and had come back without her.

Where's Lindsey?

I will ask this question for the rest of my life.

After her death, everything shifted. Without her, we became an insular family. She'd been the friendliest Litvak, the most adventurous and outgoing. For all her short life, she was curious and openhearted, alive to the possibilities of the world. From earliest childhood, I was the opposite: by habit and temperament and possibly genetics, cautious and reserved. Grief pushed or pulled me further in that direction. I learned at a young age that nothing lasts. To a cherished, somewhat spoiled child of twelve, it was a shattering discovery.

Claire and I had always been close, but when she came back from Shanghai we became inseparable. Unless I was at school or ballet class or a viola lesson, we were rarely more than ten feet apart. In the evenings we sat shoulder to shoulder on the couch, reading or watching television. We ate our meals at the little breakfast table in the kitchen. The dining room, with its big rectangular table, was like the set of a family sitcom long ago cancelled, a relic from another time.

In the months after Lindsey's death, I was prone to nightmares. The dreams were always the same: Lindsey and I were together in some busy place—a concert, an amusement park—and got separated in the crowd. Each time it happened, I woke gasping. I can still summon the feeling of panic, the horrible realization that I'd lost her all over again.

On those nights—there were many—I crept down the hall and slipped into Claire's bed. I have never slept so well, before or since, though a part of me felt guilty and embarrassed. I turned twelve that summer; I was nearly a teenager—old enough to know that sleeping with my mother was babyish and strange.

It was during that time that Aaron reappeared in my life. Since the divorce, I'd seen little of him. Under the custody agreement, we were supposed to spend alternating weekends together; but after he moved to New York, this was no longer possible. We saw each other over summer vacation, at birthdays and holidays—at most, every couple of months.

After Lindsey died, Dad rented a small, expensive apartment in Boston—the newly swanky Seaport District—where we would, in theory, spend our weekends together. In practice, it rarely happened. He looked for any excuse to come to the house in Newton—some household chore Mom couldn't manage without him, some unwieldy item to be moved or lifted, some appliance or gadget to be repaired, reprogrammed, or replaced.

It was thrilling to see him in the house again. Like many children of divorce, I harbored a secret fantasy that my parents would one day reconcile, so I watched them closely. I began a concerted, unsubtle campaign to get them back under the same roof.

Our house in Newton had three second-floor bedrooms: mine, Claire's, and Lindsey's, unchanged since she'd last slept there. On the ground floor was a pleasant guest room with its own bath, retro-fitted with grab bars and a sit-down shower for my grandma Alice, who'd lived with us for several months before she died. Since then it had been rarely used. Dad's rent in the Seaport was four thousand dollars a month—a needless expense, I told my mother. If she let him stay in Grandma's room, he could spend the whole weekend in the house with us.

"I don't think that's a good idea," she said.

One rainy night in December, Dad stopped by the house to look at the washing machine, which wasn't draining properly. While he labored in the basement, the rain turned to sleet, and it was agreed that he would spend the night. To me it felt like a holiday. For the first time in years, we ate together in the dining room—a special reunion episode of the cancelled family sitcom, now back by popular demand.

We lingered at the table for nearly two hours, laughing and reminiscing. We even talked about Lindsey, which is probably why, late that night, my nightmare returned.

As always, I crept down the hall to Mom's room. Unusually, the door was closed; when I tried the handle, I found it locked. On a hunch I padded downstairs to Grandma Alice's room. The door was open, the bed still made. From the window I could see Dad's car, still parked in the driveway.

I got back into my own bed and lay awake most of the night, filled with hope.

Of course, it never happened. Whatever transpired between my parents that night was not repeated, and they continued on their separate ways. In the spring Dad gave up his apartment in the Seaport. Then he gave up everything else. In the space of a few months, he quit his position at Neo, sold his New York apartment and bought a farmhouse in rural Vermont, where he lives to this day. I spent school breaks there, occasional weekends. Mom drove me to the train station and picked me up, but she never came along.

Her own transformation was less dramatic. It began with a home renovation project. Lindsey's old bedroom was large and sunny. Normally we kept the door closed, but sometimes, at night, I liked to sit beneath the glow-in-the-dark plastic stars she'd stuck to the ceiling, surrounded by her possessions—an old concert T-shirt she'd made into a pillow, her college textbooks gathering dust. A year after her death, I held the ladder while Claire peeled the stars from the ceiling. Together we covered the walls with cork panels, to muffle ambient sounds. Lindsey's room became Claire's writing studio, and from what I could tell, she spent most of her time there. When I came home from school at 3:30, she was often still at it. I could hear the quiet click of her typing behind the closed door.

* * *

Years passed. I applied and was accepted to Stirling College in Pennsylvania, the same school my parents had attended. I studied biology and contemplated medical school.

Early in my sophomore year, I became aware of a campus group called the Red Thread Girls. I learned about them completely by accident. In the basement of my dorm, a girl I vaguely recognized approached me as I was moving my wet laundry from washer to dryer.

"Were you adopted?" she asked. Her tone was accusing, as though I were guilty of some crime.

This girl, Carly Little, was in my Organic Chemistry class. When the TA took attendance on the first day, Carly had noticed that I, like she, was full-blooded Chinese—an Asian girl with the unlikely surname of Litvak.

She said, "I knew right away that you were one of us."

The Red Thread Girls met monthly, at the only dim sum place in town. I don't like dim sum, or fried food generally, so when Carly invited me I politely declined.

I made the mistake of telling my mother.

"Please go," Claire said.

It was unusual for her to phrase a request in this way. Usually she argued succinctly and aggressively, offering three or four bulletproof reasons why a certain course of action was the correct one. "Use your judgment," she'd say in conclusion, and nine times out of ten I did as she suggested—not to please her, necessarily, but because she was usually right.

This time was different. "Please go," she said. "This is something we could never give you." She didn't say what *this* was, but I knew what she meant: She and Dad couldn't be Chinese for me. They could only be who they were.

The dim sum place was an easy walk from campus. Including me and Carly, there were twelve Chinese girls, divided between two round tables.

The leader of the group was a senior named Emily MacDougal—possibly the whitest name I've ever heard, though her Chinese name, she told us, was Tianyi. She gave a brief presentation about interracial adoption, the tens of thousands of babies—nearly all of them girls—adopted from China and raised in the US. I can't remember the exact number, only that it peaked in 2005, the year Claire and Lindsey came to get me from the orphanage in Chongqing.

Hearing this affected me powerfully. I knew, of course, that I wasn't the first or only baby girl to be adopted from China. But it's one thing to know it and quite another to find yourself eating dim sum in a roomful of girls who are convinced they're exactly like you.

We took turns introducing ourselves: name, hometown, hobbies, and interests. It was impossible not to notice certain commonalities. Most of us had studied classical music. All but one had shoulder-length or long hair, gathered into a ponytail. Though our small liberal arts college was best known for the humanities, we'd all chosen majors in the sciences. For some reason this enraged me. I played the viola and was studying biology. As I listened to the others introduce themselves, I undid my ponytail.

The Red Thread Girls were extremely into being Chinese. The traditional dance classes I'd hated as a child were remembered fondly; a few of the girls, it turned out, had studied with the same teacher. About half of them had Chinese first names—some given to them by their adoptive parents, others self-applied.

I was the last to speak.

"What kind of name is Litvak?" asked Tianyi MacDougal.

"Polish. No, Lithuanian." I found myself fingering the scar on the back of my neck—a nervous tic, something I do when I'm uncomfortable. "My grandfather was one and my grandmother was the other. I always mix them up."

She shrugged as though the difference couldn't possibly matter. "What's your Chinese name?"

"I don't have one."

"Middle name?"

"Juanita," I said.

The meal was interminable, the appetizers—to me they all seemed like appetizers—served from little carts. On either side of me, Tianyi and Carly swapped humorous anecdotes about their Mandarin tutors. I followed the conversation like a tennis match, my head pivoting from side to side. Looking alike, it turned out, was not the same as being alike. I had nothing to say to any of these people.

Finally the meal ended. As we divided the check, I glanced around the room. For the first time in my life, I fit in completely; I looked like everyone else. It was a good feeling, so I whipped out my phone and took a photo to send to my mother.

My middle name is not Juanita.

As we left the restaurant, I studied the neck of the girl ahead of me, but there was no round white scar beneath her ponytail.

On the plus side, the dim sum was delicious. But the Red Thread Girls were not for me. For the rest of my time at Stirling, Carly continued to invite me to meetings, but I never went back. Tianyi's presentation had made me uneasy—the blanket condemnation of interracial adoptions, the aggrieved tone. What offended me was the assumption of commonality. Without knowing the first thing about me or my family, she was certain that I'd been morally wronged.

It was a facile conclusion—and in my case, a faulty one. I wasn't adopted by Westerners; I was chosen by Lindsey and Claire and

Aaron. I have never for a single moment wished I'd been left to grow up in an orphanage in China. Whatever its faults, my comfortable childhood isn't something I complain of. I had a sister who adored me. My parents loved me as much as any child could hope to be loved.

And yet the fact of being adopted is not insignificant. It isn't an exaggeration to say that it led directly to my choice of career. Adoptees understand better than anyone the allure of studying genetics. I can still remember my excitement at learning that I carried in my own cells a precise and knowable code that would solve the mystery of where I came from—a question that, in one way or another, has haunted my entire life.

My senior year, I sent a tube of my saliva to a company in Wisconsin. Later I was horrified by what I'd done—handing over my genetic code to a faceless corporation, to make use of in whatever way it wished. But at the time, this didn't occur to me. I was seduced by the promise of revelation, convinced that I would learn some profound truth about myself. Like most young people, I was narcissistic enough to believe that what I discovered would be fascinating. Six weeks later I learned that I was 100 percent Han Chinese—at the time, and still, the most common ethnicity on Earth.

After college I entered a PhD program at Stanford. Later I was awarded a postdoctoral fellowship at MIT, to work in the lab of Sebastian Graff. If you know anything at all about the field of genetics, that name will be familiar. By the time you read this, he is likely to have won the Nobel Prize. For a young scientist, the chance to work under a mind of this caliber is career making. I would have relocated to Mars if he'd asked me to. Instead, to my delight, the fellowship brought me back to Boston, a place dear to me not for any of its intrinsic qualities—to me it is just a city—but because it was near my parents, the two living people I truly loved.

I'd been working in the Graff Lab for a year when our paper was accepted for publication. Soon after, the team was invited to present it at an international conference, hosted by Fudan University in Shanghai. This was a rare opportunity. At the height of the COVID-19 epidemic, and for some years afterward, China's Zero-COVID policy made travel difficult. Even after effective vaccines were developed, visas were nearly impossible to get. But for a scientific luminary like Sebastian Graff, the bureaucratic seas parted. Our entire team was granted visas. In less than a month, I would be on a plane to Shanghai.

The night after I booked my ticket, for the first time in many years, I dreamed about my sister. Unlike my childhood nightmares, this dream wasn't sad or stressful, just nonsensical. It was brief but vivid: Lindsey sending me a series of text messages, inviting me to visit her upstairs.

*　　*　　*

A few months after Lindsey's death, three large boxes with Chinese postmarks were delivered to our house in Newton. I helped Claire carry them up to the attic, where they gathered dust for many years. She had no reason to open them; she'd packed them herself and knew exactly what they contained: toiletries, a single teacup, the jeans and UGG boots and canvas rucksack she'd found in the drawer beneath Lindsey's bed.

Atop the boxes sat Lindsey's old laptop. Claire had brought it back from Shanghai in her carry-on bag, and kept it for security reasons: Though Lindsey was dead, her identity could still be stolen, the necessary data accessed through the laptop. For a true hacker, it wouldn't be difficult; Dad's business partner, Peter Muir, had offered to put him in touch with one. This was in no way surprising; if Peter didn't know a hacker personally, he would certainly know someone who did. But my parents never took him up on the offer, and Lindsey's laptop sat untouched for many years.

A few weeks before my trip to Shanghai, I brought it down from the attic. Why I did so at that particular moment requires some explanation. My impending trip was one reason, but there were others. My personal life, at the time, was complicated. Grad school had been a period of questioning and change. I'd lost my virginity as an undergrad, an ill-advised hookup with a boy I barely knew. I felt no pleasure but was glad to have the experience behind me, like the tetanus shot I'd been required to have before registering for classes. Then, at Stanford, I fell in love with my best friend.

I'd had girl crushes before. As a small child, I loved Iris Farrell exclusively and fervently. At Camp Friendship, my bunkmate Austine figured in my first erotic dreams. At thirteen, I auditioned for a youth ballet production of *Swan Lake* and was mesmerized by the girl who danced the lead role. I can still remember her name, Nina Timilty—a name that trembles the way Nina did in her final scene, the last exquisite flutters of the dying swan.

My desire began, always, in covetousness. It was a small step from envy to attraction. I was drawn to girls, and later women, who possessed what was lacking in me.

(*Chinese girls are supposed to be small*. I carried that for years. I carry it still.)

I met Sarah in the lab, the best way to meet anyone. Watching a scientist work tells you exactly who she is. We fell deeply in love, though the relationship was never consummated. At the time she was still pretending to be straight, something I was no longer willing to do. I wasn't particularly worried about coming out to my parents, though I hadn't yet done so. Lindsey was the person I most wanted to tell.

I booted up her computer, or tried to. After sitting uncharged for many years, the battery was dead. Luckily, it was a cheap PC laptop, with a battery that slipped out easily. Finding a replacement wasn't difficult. The machine was by then woefully outdated, but there exists a mysterious demimonde of men (in my experience, they are all men) who deal in such relics on the internet. These men aren't rich and neither are their customers, which is why they buy this substandard equipment to begin with. The replacement battery cost me thirty dollars. I even got free shipping. Removing the old one and snapping in the new one took less than a minute.

From there it was a question of guessing Lindsey's password. It took me three tries. The winning guess was 021405—the day Lindsey and Claire came to get me from the orphanage in Chongqing, Valentine's Day 2005.

It is common, today, for pet owners to commemorate Gotcha Day, when their beloved dogs and cats were rescued from shelters. For human adoptees, the parallel is psychically uncomfortable; but Lindsey and I had made a joke of it. My Gotcha Day was our private holiday. Each year she showered me with small gifts—music downloads, Hello Kitty swag, my favorite macaroons. Without ever discussing it, we excluded our parents from our celebration. It was our holiday, not theirs. Aaron hadn't even been present that day at the orphanage, and Claire remembered the place unkindly. Her main contribution was taking that magical photo of me and Lindsey, capturing forever a moment I was too young to remember. If she had given me nothing else in life (and she has given me everything), it would be reason enough to love her.

When I keyed in my Gotcha Day, 021405, a Welcome screen appeared. The entire contents of Lindsey's laptop were now accessible to me.

* * *

Booting up Lindsey's computer was like gaining access to her brain, a condition of modern living. If I were to vanish tomorrow, my life could be reconstructed in much the same way.

My sister was a saver. As a child she kept valentines, birthday cards, seashells plucked from the beaches of Fort Lauderdale on our annual visit to Grandma Judy. Later she saved concert T-shirts, ticket stubs, yearbooks scrawled with messages from classmates at Pilgrims Country Day. *Good luck at Wesleyan! UR a star!!!*

In later years her keepsakes, like everyone's, were digital. On her hard drive I found Google and Word documents, thousands of emails, a massive collection of photos and videos. There were text messages in English and Chinese, downloaded from WhatsApp and WeChat; long exchanges with college friends whose names I vaguely remembered: Olivia, Caitlin, Kayla, Hope. These electronic artifacts were all that remained of my sister. We'd scattered her ashes from Peter Muir's sailboat, in the waters off Cape Cod.

It was hard to know where to begin. I sifted through the hard drive slowly and methodically. Though the collection was voluminous, it was also finite. To make it last, I found myself rationing the contents. It was as if, each day, I allowed myself a single bite of cake.

I started with the photos. Many had been taken in Beijing: Lindsey in the Forbidden City, walking along the Great Wall, eating a skewer of candied fruit in what I didn't, at the time, recognize as Wangfujing Street. There were a number of selfies taken with a beefy, round-faced blond guy I'd met only once — her college boyfriend, Zach Dorn.

In a folder labeled "INK," I found a series of photos taken in a tattoo shop. According to the date stamp, they were taken eight months after she left us for China — February 14, 2015, the first of many, many Gotcha Days Lindsey and I would spend apart.

In the first photo, she lies face down on what looks like a massage table. She is fully dressed, the sleeve of her T-shirt pushed up over her shoulder. Leaning over her is a young Chinese woman with tattooed arms. In another, Lindsey stands sideways, a square of paper stuck to her left shoulder, in the position where the tattoo would be placed. In the final photo, she shows off the finished product, a single Chinese character I—embarrassingly—didn't recognize.

When I showed the photo to Winston Lim—my closest colleague at the Graff Lab, and the only one who reads Chinese—he broke into a smile. "Grace, is this your girlfriend?"

At first I thought he was teasing me. I had recently come out at work, and Winston delighted in ribbing me.

Then he explained it. The character tattooed on Lindsey's shoulder was my Chinese name.

*   *   *

雅

When I was six years old, a Chinese graduate student tried to teach me to how to write it. That lesson—my first and last with the Mandarin tutor—ended in a crying tantrum, and I never studied Chinese again. Lindsey's tattoo was illegible to me, and yet I can't help feeling that I should have been able to identify it. That in some visceral, instinctive way, I should have recognized myself.

*   *   *

I read Lindsey's journal. I'm not ashamed to say that I read every word. If she were still alive, I would never have done this; I understand that those pages weren't meant for my eyes. But my sister was gone from the world and there was nothing else left of her. It was the last time I would ever hear her voice.

As I read, it was as though Lindsey were telling me the story of her time in Shanghai, what turned out to be the final year of her life.

Though we texted often and spoke regularly on the phone, I was a child still; there was a great deal she couldn't tell me. Even now, these revelations have the power to shock me. Even now, it seems too adult for me to understand.

First, her work for the escort service. Lindsey's journal gave me a rough understanding of the particulars. Like an old-school match-maker, Mei made the introductions personally. As far as I can tell there was no smartphone app, not even a website; for 2016, the business model seems jarringly analog. That the entire arrangement hinged on Lindsey's relationship with Mei is, to me, significant. I'm convinced that she would never have done this work at all if not for a chance meeting in that tourist bar in Shanghai.

Of the clients themselves, I know next to nothing. Lindsey's journal mentions them only in passing until the fall of 2015, when she met "Sean."

Sean, Shen. To me he is a mystery. Lindsey's hard drive contains only a single photo. He and Lindsey sit shoulder to shoulder in what looks like a movie theater, wearing 3D glasses. Shen has a square jaw, a wide smile. The rest of his face is obscured by the cardboard glasses—his right eye concealed by blue cellophane, left eye covered by red.

Despite this, I've spent more time studying this photo than any other on Lindsey's hard drive. For a while I fantasized about tracking him down, but eventually came to my senses. Shenzhen is a city of twelve million people, and I don't know his last name.

Shen, Mei, Johnny Du. Despite speaking not a single a word of Chinese, I imagined confronting them all, interrogating them. As though there were anything they could possibly tell me that would bring my sister back.

Of course, I never did this. Finding them would be as impossible as finding my birth mother, another hopeless quest I have far less interest in pursuing. China has more than a billion people, and only four thousand surnames. How many families in Shanghai—or even its nearby islands—are called Du?

What I learned about Lindsey's life in Shanghai was upsetting. Even more disturbing were the revelations about Dean Farrell.

For most of my childhood, Iris Farrell had been my best friend. Among little girls this is an honorific like no other; it confers all the singularity of "boyfriend" or "husband"—a kind of proto-monogamy, a precursor to adult love. If an analog exists among little boys, I've never heard of it. I suspect that this points to an innate difference between the sexes, or possibly in the way we are raised.

Mr. Farrell had been a presence my childhood, known and trusted. Apart from my own parents, he was the adult I interacted with most. Through elementary and middle school, Iris's house was my second home, the scene of countless playdates and slumber parties. Her mother was always at work, so it was her dad who took us to the playground, the swimming pool, to music lessons and ballet class.

I can still recall my misery on the evenings Lindsey spent babysitting: the pain of being excluded, the horrible knowledge that she and Iris were watching movies together, playing games and taking walks without me. To my young self, it felt like infidelity. I had been betrayed by the two people I loved most.

Lindsey was a senior in high school when I sensed the change in her. I was six years old, too young to grasp the reasons. I only knew that I no longer had her full attention. Clicking through the hard drive, I understood that it wasn't Iris who'd usurped me in her affections but Iris's father.

The text messages between Lindsey and Mr. Farrell—she downloaded and saved them to her hard drive—were painful to read. The early ones were businesslike: **Hi Lindsey, any chance you could sit**

with Iris tomorrow night? Sorry for short notice, Trish out of town.
Later their messages were more intimate, unmistakably flirtatious.
Mr. Farrell asked her to send photos—fully clothed at first, then
bikini shots and finally nudes. He even sent one of himself.

I didn't look at the photos Lindsey sent him. I'd seen her naked
plenty of times—we shared a bathroom, and she wasn't the sort
of person who'd cover up immediately when she stepped out of the
shower. I did, however, look at the photo Mr. Farrell sent to her. Why
I did this is hard to explain. To convince myself, maybe, that this
unimaginable thing had really happened. A part of me still hoped
that there'd been a mistake.

There had been no mistake.

The photo is shocking in every way. It shows a body that is fit and
athletic, but clearly a mature body—thickened around the middle,
his chest and belly covered with hair. His left hand holds his erect
penis—larger than the only one I've ever seen in person but modest
compared with what I or anyone could find in ten seconds on the
internet.

The worst part, to me, is that the body is headless. It is plausibly
Mr. Farrell's, what a person might guess he'd look like naked, but it's
impossible to say for sure. Of course, this was no accident; he had
a great deal to lose. Sending dick pics to a teenager may or may not
have been legal. To his wife the legality wouldn't have mattered. The
Court of Trish Farrell would have been—I am certainless forgiving
than Massachusetts law.

Bizarrely, the photo was taken in a room I recognized, the downstairs bathroom at the Farrells' old house in Newton. I thought of my
old bunkmate Austine, a twelve-year-old girl hiding out in a lavatory
stall to take naked pictures of herself. For a grown man to do this
seemed ridiculous and obscene.

The message thread ended abruptly.

Mom found my pills. I am in deep
shit. Call me!!

Hey, where are you? I keep getting
your vm

Why are you mad at me? I didn't do
anything.

What did she say to you? I will never
forgive her as long as I live

*　　*　　*

What I learned about Lindsey and Mr. Farrell was disturbing. It was also clarifying. Certain things began to make sense. The ways my sister changed after high school—her lethargy and reclusiveness, her unexplained anger toward our parents. She spent an entire summer locked in her bedroom, boycotting our annual family trip to the Cape. In September she went off to Wesleyan and pierced her nose. She chopped off her beautiful hair.

With Lindsey away at college, my family contracted. The noticeable coolness between my parents hardened into frost. In those years Dad traveled often for business, and most nights it was just me and Claire at the dinner table.

In the fall of Lindsey's sophomore year, my parents filed for divorce. How and why this happened was the great mystery of my childhood. Claire and Aaron offered distinctly different explanations, neither of which made any sense. My mother's was vague and somehow studied, as though she'd rehearsed it with a family therapist. Their marriage had worked for a long time, and then it stopped working. This wasn't unusual, Claire said, in a tone meant to be reassuring. It happened to many couples, gradually over time.

In her determination to say nothing bad about my father, she'd given me an explanation that was both unsatisfying and alarming. If love could stop "working" after twenty years, for no apparent reason, how could you ever trust it?

Aaron's answer was less careful. "Marriage is hard," he said. "Your mother is a good person. It was just too hard."

* * *

Disturbing, but also clarifying. Seven or eight years ago, during a summer break from Stirling, I was shopping at Whole Foods with my mother when Trish Farrell waved to us from across the produce section. To my astonishment, Claire pretended not to see her; she made a skillful U-turn with the grocery cart and headed toward the other side of the store. We didn't have time to stop and chat, she said, which surprised me. We weren't in any particular hurry.

At the time I didn't question it. Now I wonder: What did Trish know, and when did she know it? Is it possible that Claire never told her?

Someday I'll ask my mother these questions, and the answers will change nothing. Lindsey will still be gone.

* * *

As I clicked through Lindsey's hard drive, it was clear that she hadn't planned on dying. If she had, she would have left things in better order. Lindsey was that rare person who spends no time dying. After her final, massive stroke, our grandma Alice spent weeks in the ICU, months in a rehab center, and years in memory care, during which she did no further living. Lindsey died, as they say, in the prime of life. Until the moment an unknown driver ran her down in Shanghai, she was fully, vibrantly alive.

Sifting through the hard drive was an emotional experience. I felt waves of shock and sadness, anger and confusion, overwhelming tenderness and, finally, grief. I mourned the years we would never have together, the life my sister never got to live. Is it strange that I also felt gratitude? If Lindsey had been killed fifty years earlier, under identical circumstances—a fatal accident on the other side of the world—I would know nothing at all about her life.

Years ago, I saw a TV show about a forensic artist who, using the skeletal remains of an unidentified murder victim, sculpted a life-size replica of the woman's head. Clicking through Lindsey's hard drive, I thought often of this artist. Lindsey's photos and videos and text messages, and especially her journal, offered me a final, precious glimpse of her face.

*   *   *

The Fudan conference was held at the end of September. I'd attended similar meetings in the US and even internationally, but this was my first trip to Asia. What took me so long is a fair question, since I'd had several opportunities. Stirling College has a study-abroad program in Beijing—something my parents would have been happy to pay for if I'd shown the slightest interest. And the last time I heard from Carly Little, the Red Thread Girls were planning a group excursion to China, to visit the orphanages from which they'd been adopted. At the time, I had a plausible excuse—a summer job at a lab in Palo Alto—but the truth was more complicated. I wasn't yet ready to experience the place I'd come from, for reasons I couldn't have articulated even to myself.

Shanghai was an astonishment. It was also a trial—a series of psychic challenges that began the instant I stepped off the plane.

Riding the subway in rush hour was like nothing I'd ever experienced—the sheer density of humanity, the crush of strange bodies pressing in on all sides. I held my backpack close to my chest, as the locals did, and shoved my way into a train car. Accustomed to riding the rickety MBTA trains in Boston, I braced myself for the inevitable lurch forward and grabbed an overhead strap.

But there was no lurch. The train seemed to glide out of the station. As we raced along the track, I studied my fellow passengers, my bare arm next to all the other bare arms holding straps. Each had the same smooth, hairless skin, the same curve of wrist and forearm and elbow, and I had an absurd but terrifying thought: Each one of those arms looked like it could be attached to my body. For a fleeting, uncanny moment, I had a sense of having been made in a factory, rolled off a conveyor belt and loaded into a shipping container, like so many other Chinese goods.

It's hard to convey how powerfully this affected me. I was so panicked I could scarcely breathe. I got off at the next stop and made my way to street level, where I took several deep breaths.

So many people! That anyone would choose to live in that teeming city was, to me, incomprehensible. My whole life I'd felt physically different from those around me. Though it was sometimes painful, the feeling was so deeply familiar that I found it comforting. Being different felt *normal*—my default setting, intrinsic to who I was. But in China, my difference disappeared. Without it, I felt invisible. Wherever I looked, I saw young women of my age, dimensions, and general physiognomy. How could any one of us hope to distinguish ourselves, to be singular enough to be loved?

* * *

On my second morning in Shanghai, I sat in a café watching two Chinese men share a pastry. They didn't touch each other in any way, and yet it was clear that they were a couple. There was an intimacy in the way they passed the pastry between them—taking bites from the same end, unconcerned that it had touched the other's mouth.

At one time, I wouldn't have noticed them. Since earliest childhood, I have only enjoyed looking at women. Ironically, it was coming out that widened my focus. Now I wasn't just interested in women, I was interested in queerness—how queer people of all genders found and loved one another, how they made lives together in the world.

The men appeared to be in their thirties, handsome in distinctly different ways. One had a shaved head and gym muscles, biceps stretching the sleeves of his T-shirt. The other was slender, with an unusual haircut—long on top, shaved around the sides and back.

It was the haircut that got my attention. For a brief, insane moment, I was certain that I was looking at Johnny Du. Having a reasonable facility with statistics, I know how outlandish this sounds. But wishful thinking is a powerful force, and this was the way I wished to think of him, sharing a pastry with a man who looked at him with love.

* * *

In Shanghai I searched for my sister. I'd made a list of landmarks mentioned in her diary: a private venue called the Lotus Club, the pricy boutiques on Nanjing Road, the famous Peace Hotel on the Bund. I spent an entire morning walking the streets of the Jing'an section, hoping to find the automated stall where she'd bought her morning tea, the after-hours clubs where she and Johnny went dancing, the noodle shop where they watched the sun rise. I wanted to see where she'd lived her real life, the hours and days that had nothing to do with being an escort. The times when she was purely Lindsey, the person I loved and recognized.

I saw quickly that it was futile. The neighborhood—like much of the city—was loud with machine noise. All of Shanghai seemed to be under construction, nearly new buildings being razed and replaced with larger, grander ones. The Wang Building was gone without a trace. In its place stood a brand-new shopping mall.

That day—my second in Shanghai—the weather was stultifying. The humid air clung to my skin. In the afternoon the sky tore open, the most forceful rain I've experienced in my life. No one had told me that September was typhoon season, and I'd neglected to bring an umbrella—though I'm not sure it would have done any good. The volume of water was astonishing. Pedestrians huddled beneath awnings, in doorframes. Sidewalks flooded in a matter of minutes. The city was so relentlessly developed, the ground seamlessly covered in concrete, that there was nowhere for the rain to go.

I retraced my steps to Lindsey's address, rain pelting my bare arms, my sodden denim skirt clinging unpleasantly to my thighs.

The new shopping mall was quiet inside, the air perfumed and frigid. The central atrium was six stories tall, with a glass ceiling. I rode the elevator to the top. The sound of rain on the skylights was nearly deafening; it seemed as though the glass might shatter. The pooling water cast odd shadows. It was like being trapped inside a luxury submarine.

There was nothing to do but wait out the storm, so I browsed through a clothing store, an electronics store. I wandered into a boutique that sold cosmetics and costume jewelry and plastic knick-knacks, the sort of cheap bric-a-brac found in little girls' bedrooms: plush toys, beanbag chairs in candy colors, whimsical lamps shaped like rabbits and kittens and black-nosed pugs. Near the cash register was a display of mini umbrellas, patterned with tulips and polka dots in orange and neon pink.

The place was packed wall-to-wall with Chinese girls—teens and preteens chattering happily, shopping in groups of two or three. I watched them try on hats and heart-shaped sunglasses. They posed and took selfies. They sprayed one another with fruity perfume.

The girls were impossibly beautiful. Watching them, I felt exactly as I'd felt among the swans of Pilgrims Country Day: half lovestruck and half miserable; at once dazzled by their beauty and dismayed by my own ungainliness. Puberty delivered me even further from swanhood. My adult body is tallish and sturdy, with broad shoulders and muscular thighs and a wide, flat chest. I am strong and healthy, but no one has ever called me delicate. No one ever will.

As a teenager I blamed my ethnicity. Simply because I'd never seen one, I didn't believe a swan could be Chinese. At that shopping mall in Shanghai, I saw how wrong I'd been. These Chinese swans were the swanniest I'd seen anywhere—far out-swanning the beauties of Pilgrims Country Day. I hadn't been a swan in the lily-white Boston suburbs, and I wouldn't have been one in China either. I am not a swan anywhere.

Standing in line to pay for my umbrella, I thought of my sister, a swan of the first order. It's clear, now, that swanhood didn't serve her. It only served those around her. Dean Farrell, who took her innocence; the woman called Mei, who sold Lindsey's beauty and kept the profits. That she, too, was a woman somehow made it worse.

All things considered, I am lucky not to be a swan. Objectively, the outcomes are better. Even knowing this, I would happily become one if the chance presented itself.

Fortunately, it never will.

*   *   *

My last night in Shanghai, I was invited to dinner by an old family friend, Dad's longtime business partner. Aaron and Peter were still students when they founded NeoWonder, the company they ran together for twenty-five years.

When I was growing up, Peter and his wife, Gabby, were like glamorous relatives. Each year between Christmas and New Year's, they appeared on our doorstep bearing gifts: a bottle of scotch for my dad and, for the rest of us, a selection of small treasures Gabby had brought back from Africa, textiles and jewelry and, once, a complete set of miniature animals carved from wood.

Like family, only better. That they had no children of their own made them seem younger than Claire and Aaron. When they spoke to me, it wasn't in the rote, dutiful way of parents or teachers. Peter, especially, wanted to know what I thought. Which music did I like, which video games and TV shows, which brand of sneakers? To him I was a focus group of one, the sole spokesperson for an entire generation of future consumers, employees, collaborators, and what he called "thought leaders."

"It's your world, Grace," he liked to say. "When you're ready to take over, just say so. Until then, we're just minding the store."

During my years at Stanford, he often came to Silicon Valley on business. If he had a free evening, he'd treat me to an extravagant dinner at a new restaurant I hadn't yet heard of but soon would. For Peter it was a point of pride, discovering the next hot thing before anyone else did.

Those evenings were always enjoyable—an extended, adult version of our conversations at Christmas. If I sometimes felt I was being interviewed, that was part of the fun. As I rode the BART train into the city, I scrolled the day's headlines in preparation. Peter was interested in everything—sports, science, politics, popular culture. Whatever was happening in the world, he'd want to know my take.

Not long after I moved back to Boston to join the Graff Lab, Peter and Gabby divorced. My mother, I am sad to say, took a nasty pleasure in the news. She has always been cynical about Peter—his public devotion to Gabby, his shameless bragging about her work at Doctors

Without Borders. To me his pride seemed genuine, but Claire dismissed it as a performance. " 'Peter' rhymes with 'theater,' " she often said.

When she heard that Peter and Gabby were splitting up, she immediately assumed he'd been having an affair. " 'Peter' rhymes with 'cheater,' " she said with unconcealed delight.

After the divorce, Peter relocated to China, which made a certain kind of sense. Shanghai Disney was NeoWonder's largest client, heavily invested in its virtual reality products. The company needed a presence on the ground.

When I saw him in Shanghai, Peter had been living there for six months, in a rare detached house in the old French Concession. To me it is the most beautiful part of the city, with its colonial architecture and lovely tree-lined streets. It looks nothing at all like the rest of Shanghai, where sterile modern apartment complexes are the norm and trees are mostly relegated to public parks. Peter's house was set back from the road, behind a high wall of faded pink brick that looked older than anything I'd seen in Shanghai.

I rang the buzzer and waited. I hadn't seen him in more than a year. Our last dinner in San Francisco had ended awkwardly. As our handsome, unctuously charming gay waiter placed the check at Peter's elbow, he raised a practiced eyebrow. "Have a great night, kids!" he sang. And then, archly, to Peter: "You, sir, are a very lucky man."

It was an excruciating moment. Peter played it off, but his embarrassment was palpable. When he walked to me to the BART train, our goodbye hug was briefer than usual. We were careful not to linger.

I didn't know it then, but that was our final dinner together in San Francisco. That summer I was awarded a postdoc at the Graff Lab, and in August I moved back to Boston.

* * *

The gate swung open into a sunny courtyard, also paved with brick. Peter was waiting at the front door, wearing what looked like linen pajamas. When he hugged me they smelled expensive, a faint citrusy cologne.

"Grace! It's been forever. Come in, come in."

The house was cool inside, smelling of coffee. I remember a tall foyer with parquet floors, a curved staircase leading to the second floor.

I followed him into a bright living room, with french windows that opened out into a courtyard. I looked in vain for a shady spot to sit. On the only clear day I'd experienced in Shanghai, the room was sunny as a greenhouse, filled with large, healthy-looking green plants: a miniature lemon tree, a braided ficus. On a pedestal near the window was a blooming orchid, with paper-white blossoms bigger than my fist.

I complimented the house effusively. The furniture was antique and elegantly mismatched: a Louis XVI table, a chaise lounge covered in cream-colored brocade. In one corner was a demilune table set with liquor bottles and an ice bucket, an antique cabinet that held a small sink. It couldn't have been more different from Peter and Gabby's old place in Boston, a cavernous loft in the Leather District, decorated in what I'd always assumed was Peter's taste: spare, functional and aggressively modern, with bare floors and recessed lighting and not a curve in sight.

He offered me a gin and tonic. As he mixed our drinks, I filled him in on the recent developments in my life: my work at the Graff Lab, the paper we'd just published. The drinks were made British style, with lemon rather than lime. Oddly, Peter had mixed three of them. I wondered, but didn't ask, who the third drink was for.

We sat side by side on the settee, sipping very strong gin and tonics. The light, I remember, was spectacular, the sunset refracted by carbon emissions and industrial pollution. The western sky glowed a golden red.

"How's your dad?" Peter asked.

The question was startling: *He* was asking *me?* For most of my childhood, the day-to-day operation of NeoWonder had kept them in constant contact. If you'd asked me then, I'd have said they were closer than brothers. But after Dad left the company, their communication dwindled. There had been no rupture to speak of. They had simply grown apart.

"He seems good," I said. "I haven't talked to him in a couple of weeks." It wasn't for lack of trying. Dad had sworn off mobile phones years ago, so texting wasn't an option. The only way to reach him was via landline—itself a tricky business, since he spent most of his time outdoors.

"Me neither. What does he do all day?" Peter asked, with a trace of annoyance.

"He has a garden," I said. It wasn't the right word. The spring he moved to Vermont, he planted a few vegetables. The following year he tilled the entire backyard. When he planted more than he could eat, he left bags of tomatoes and cucumbers on neighbors' porches. When he planted more than the neighbors could eat, he sold the excess at the local farmers' market. At this point, he was running what would accurately be called a subsistence farm.

"Is he all right?" Peter asked. "Up there all alone. Honestly, I'd lose my freaking mind."

"He has a girlfriend." It seemed a strange term to apply to a woman my mother's age, but it's the word Aaron uses and I don't know a better one. Gitte—an exuberant Danish woman from the countryside of Jutland—owns the health-food store in town. They met when she began selling herbs from Aaron's garden. They spend the long

Vermont winters snowshoeing and cross-country skiing. After she moved into the farmhouse, he built her a sauna in the backyard.

When I explained this to Peter, he seemed mystified.

"Good for Aaron," he said with false heartiness. "Living his best life. I'm glad to hear it." And then, after a pause. "How's Claire?"

"Great," I said. "She's doing well."

Incredibly, it was true. In the months after she returned from Shanghai, I worried about her; I became, for a time, my mother's mother. I knew nothing, then, about her experience with postpartum depression—it wasn't the sort of thing you'd confide to a child—but I had always sensed her fragility. Both Lindsey's birth and Lindsey's death nearly destroyed her. I would be the daughter who kept her alive.

In the end it was Donald Trump who saved her. In November 2016, he was elected president, a national calamity that shook my mother out of her despair. Over the course of several months, she wrote dozens of Letters to the Editor, which she sent to the *New York Times,* the *Washington Post,* and the *Boston Globe.* The letters were stylish and brilliantly argued, and many were published. Her rage at the president functioned like electroconvulsive therapy, a targeted jolt to the brain.

In the final year of the Trump presidency, the COVID pandemic hit the US. When Pilgrims Country Day closed its doors, our unused dining room became my classroom. Upstairs, in Lindsey's old bedroom, Mom tapped away at her keyboard. That long somnolent first year of the pandemic, she wrote the first of her wildly successful children's books—published under her maiden name, Claire McDonald. Lydia, the heroine, is a gangly red-haired twelve-year-old with a preternatural gift for languages—a dead ringer for my sister at that age. Sequels followed. Soon there was a graphic novel, and most recently an animated TV series. Almost by accident, Claire has become a wealthy woman.

Soon after the first Lydia book was published, my mother remarried. I was the maid of honor at her wedding—a small ceremony at St. Patrick's, the Catholic parish to which she and Gerry belong. Surprising all who know her, she has become a churchgoer. Two or three times a week, she and Gerry ride their bicycles into Newton Centre to attend the morning mass.

Her embrace of Catholicism is, to me, confounding; I am my father's daughter, atheist to the core. Aaron, predictably, finds it ludicrous, and once or twice he's made the mistake of saying so. "Dad, stop it!" I told him sharply, and to his credit he did.

I won't let him laugh at her. Whatever he might think of her spiritual awakening, Claire is no longer suffering. Was it God who saved her or Gerry Duncan? Or was it—my personal theory—simply the act of writing? Each morning at her keyboard, she performs the miracle of resurrection. Day after day, year after year, she writes Lindsey back to life.

"How's the book doing?" Peter asked.

"Great. She texted me this morning. It's gone into a fifth printing," I said.

Peter gave an energetic thumbs-up. His feelings about my mother, and hers about him, have always been a mystery to me. I sense from both a strong antipathy toward the other, though Peter is better at hiding it. Claire is less decorous, or maybe just more honest.

"Fantastic!" he said. "Please tell her I said hello."

*　*　*

Up to this point, my visit with Peter had gone as expected: the questions about my parents, the polite show of interest in my work. I glanced at the clock. It was now 8 p.m. and there was no sign of dinner. I hadn't eaten since lunch, and I'm not much of a drinker. Peter's gin and tonic had gone straight to my head.

These were my thoughts when the doorbell rang.

"That must be Heather," Peter said. "She's always forgetting her keys."

He stepped briefly into the foyer, pressed a button to open the gate. From my vantage point on the settee I watched a woman cross the courtyard, a statuesque blonde in dark sunglasses. She looked like a celebrity hiding out from the paparazzi, her face half hidden by a cream-colored scarf.

In the time it took her to cross the courtyard, I learned that Peter had remarried. "Last weekend," he said, beaming. "We haven't had a chance to tell anyone stateside. You're the first to know."

His new wife made a dazzling entrance. "Sorry I'm late. Traffic was *disparate*," she said, unwinding the scarf from her throat. She radiated a kind of retro glamour, an air of Old Hollywood. Her shiny blond hair was twisted into a loose chignon. She looked completely at home in this room, at one with her surroundings. I understood, then, that this wasn't Peter's taste but hers.

Peter kissed her full on the mouth. She was tall, nearly his height, and if you squinted they looked right together. You might not notice that she was young enough to be his daughter.

"I made you a G and T," he said, handing her the third glass. "Grace is in town for a conference."

"Welcome, Grace. It's lovely to meet you." She spoke with a faint accent I couldn't place. She set down the drink and took my hand in both of hers, like an actress greeting an ardent fan.

From somewhere in the recesses of Peter's linen pajamas came a chirping noise. This struck me as slightly lewd, as though he were hiding a bird in his crotch. I found this so funny that I could barely contain my laughter—my first clue that drinking on an empty stomach had been a mistake.

He took a phone from his pocket and glanced at the screen. "Forgive me, Grace. This will only take a minute."

When he stepped out of the room, I felt a mild panic. To be left alone to make small talk with a stranger is an introvert's nightmare. I reached for my glass and drank deeply—remembering, too late, that mine was already empty. I had drunk from Heather's glass.

"Oh, I'm so sorry!" I said, mortified.

"No worries. You take that one. I'll mix another."

As she busied herself at the corner bar, I tried to think of something to say.

"Your plants look so healthy," I said, inanely. "You must have a green thumb."

"Oh, that's all Peter's doing. I take no credit." She squeezed a lemon slice into her drink. "Plants in the window bring money luck. That's what the Chinese say."

She sat on the sofa opposite me. "What brings you to Shanghai, Grace? What sort of conference?" Her voice was low and inviting—the sort of voice that made you want to talk about yourself. As she leaned toward me, I understood for the first time what is meant by the phrase "personal magnetism." The quality of her attention was striking. I could imagine this being extremely effective with men. Even I wasn't immune.

Emboldened by gin and the rapt attention of a beautiful woman, I talked about the paper my team had presented at Fudan. In more detail than she could possibly have wanted, I explained the diagnostic value of the genetic variant we'd discovered, its potential clinical implications. Heather, improbably, seemed fascinated by this. She made encouraging noises, asked leading questions. It was a bit like being interviewed for a talk show.

"Seeing Peter is a bonus," I said. "I had no idea he was living here." I explained that he was a family friend, that he and my father had started NeoWonder together.

"Oh, you're *Aaron*'s daughter!" She seemed pleased to make the connection. "Peter has told me so much about him. We were supposed to see him last summer in New York, but it didn't work out."

It being her first trip to the US, Peter had insisted on taking her to the top of the Empire State Building. Heather was afraid of heights, but as she looked down on the city at night, she felt strangely at home. New York was a place she'd known all her life, from an old American sitcom. An entire Australian generation had grown up on the reruns, which the TV networks broadcast in perpetuity throughout her childhood. The show was so familiar that for Heather—a lifelong insomniac—an episode of *Friends* was better than a sleeping pill. Even now, the song that played during the opening credits put her immediately to sleep.

I will admit, I found this story captivating. Mainly I liked watching her tell it. She had, I remember, a very beautiful mouth.

At last I thought of something to say.

"How did you and Peter meet?" I asked.

It was the sort of question Peter himself might ask. He'd once told me that all happy couples loved to tell their origin stories, and in the telling revealed essential truths about themselves.

Heather blinked.

"At work," she said briskly.

I waited for more, but there was no more. Still I persisted.

"Did you work on Shanghai Disney?" I knew from Dad that Peter had spent years wooing the park's developers. The resulting deal had made them both a bundle—the biggest contract in Neo's history, a lucrative collaboration that continues to this day.

"I was in the industry." Heather leaned in confidentially. "How are you enjoying Shanghai?"

The abrupt change of subject threw me slightly, and it took me a moment to formulate an answer. My accidental second drink had packed a wallop. I was half afraid to open my mouth.

"It's overwhelming," I said. My speech was a little mushy. "I've been wanting to come here for a long time. My sister used to live here."

"*Really?*" Heather seemed riveted, but I no longer trusted her enthusiasm. She would have feigned interest in whatever I happened to say. "Was she a student?"

"She worked for an escort service."

I hadn't planned to say it. In truth, I'd never said the words aloud, not even to myself. But this was my last night in Shanghai—Lindsey's final earthly address, the city where she'd lived and died—and I was feeling emotional. Telling the truth about her life felt brave and powerful, an act of solidarity and love.

Heather blinked rapidly. A spot of red appeared in each of her cheeks, like two symmetrical hives. My first thought was that she was having an anaphylactic reaction, and who could blame her? Most people are allergic to candor, the speaking of uncomfortable truths.

"Lindsey loved it here." Saying her name seemed important. "She was always telling me to come and visit."

Heather set down her empty glass. "Where is she now? Your sister. Did she go back to the US?"

"She died," I said.

Another uncomfortable silence.

"I'm sorry for your loss," Heather said smoothly. "How terrible. Did she get COVID?"

"No, it was before that." I explained that Lindsey had died in 2016, years before the pandemic struck. "She was hit by a car."

We were both relieved when Peter reappeared, ostentatiously powering down his mobile phone.

"Done!" he said, with great fanfare. "No more phone calls. As of right now I am officially *incommunicado*. Ladies, you have my full attention."

He sat next to Heather on the sofa and gave her shoulder a squeeze.

* * *

I will never forget the first time a Chinese person spoke to me in Mandarin. I had just landed at Pudong Airport and waited, with a full bladder, in a long line at Immigration Inspection. When I finally made it through, I made a beeline for the restroom, with such urgency that I didn't notice the yellow traffic cone placed at the entrance. A woman in a cleaner's uniform screamed at me in Chinese—telling me, probably, that the restroom was closed for cleaning.

I ducked my head in apology. Clearly she'd meant to scold me, but her words had the opposite effect. It's hard to express the exhilaration I felt. She had believed I was Chinese-Chinese! Winston Lim, my transgender coworker at the Graff Lab, describes feeling a similar elation the first time he passed as a man.

When the cleaning lady screamed at me, I felt honored, included. I also felt shame. I wasn't Chinese in any meaningful way; I felt unworthy of that distinction. I couldn't even understand what was being said to me. In that moment, I was filled with regret: for my childish refusal to study Chinese, my bratty resistance to the language tutor my parents had hired. They had offered me a gift of incalculable value—the chance to know my mother tongue—and I'd thrown it away with both hands.

My parents didn't understand—I've never told them—that I

found their gift wounding. Any acknowledgment of my Chineseness felt like a rejection, a cruel insistence on the ways I wasn't like them.

* * *

My evening with Peter and Heather ended uneventfully. Their cook, a young woman about my age, called us to the table. She had prepared Peking duck. Though I was still drunk, I meant it when I told her it was the most delicious meal of my life. After dinner Peter offered me another gin and tonic, which I politely declined. I had an early flight to Boston, and I hadn't finished packing. As we said our goodbyes in the courtyard, I felt overwhelming relief.

I've thought often of that night, the golden September evening in Shanghai. There was something surreal about that lovely old house in the French Concession, the tall, blond people sipping gin and tonics in their colonial mansion.

Plants in the window bring money luck. That's what the Chinese say. The Chinese, with their inscrutable ways: To Heather they were a different species entirely. In her eyes, we were two white girls having a chat.

The memory has lingered with me, for a compelling reason: It's the first time I can remember reacting as a Chinese person rather than as a white person. It was part of a gradual transformation that began my first day in Shanghai, with my panic attack on the subway. It continues to this day.

In Shanghai I was an outsider. Truly, I have never felt more American in all my life. Only after I returned to Boston did I understand that a shift had occurred. For the first time in my life, I also felt Chinese.

That winter I fell in love with someone I met, randomly, at a performance of the Boston Ballet—the woman who is now my wife, Angela Litvak-Chang. The ballet was *not Swan Lake* but a matinee performance of *The Nutcracker.* I see it every December, though it is a melancholic experience. The Boston Opera House is filled, always, with little girls—entire ballet classes of miniature bunheads, staring with rapt attention at the stage. I can remember being one of them. As a teenager, in a paroxysm of self-consciousness, I quit taking ballet; but somewhere inside me there still lives a twelve-year-old dancer who craves the dizzy joy of spinning bourrée turns, the heady sensation of flight.

It was the week before Christmas, downtown Boston decorated for the holiday. The performance was sold out, the theatre crowded. When I found my seat, Angela was already sitting in it, as though she'd been waiting for me all along.

The cheesy pop-psychology interpretation of our courtship—that falling in love with a Chinese woman allowed me love to myself, to recognize and celebrate my own non-Western beauty—is simplistic and insulting and also slightly true.

My wife looks nothing at all like the suburban princesses I grew up with, but she is definitely a swan. To my delight, she doesn't mind being photographed. Angela is beautiful in some of the ways Lindsey was—the long bones of her thighs and forearms, her slender, elegant neck—and in other ways that are entirely her own.

The defining characteristic of love, it seems to me, is specificity. To be seen accurately, in all our freakish particularity, to be loved for and despite it. That such a thing ever happens is as close as we get to a miracle.

It was my stepfather, Gerry Duncan, who married us. That he was no longer a priest didn't matter; in the Commonwealth of Massachusetts, anyone can marry anyone. In a voice trained to sing Gregorian chant, he delivered a sermon that was refreshingly secular, like a commencement address—a joyful sendoff into married life, a rapturous meditation on the infinite variability of love.

By the time he finished, both brides were in tears, though for different reasons. Angela told me later that she'd wept from pure joy, but my happiness was more complicated. During Gerry's sermon, I'd been watching my parents. Aaron and Claire sat in the front row, holding hands, something I hadn't witnessed since childhood—that brief golden time when we were like a family on television, a mother and father with two happy daughters, my sister radiantly, indelibly alive.

* * *

Lindsey will be young and beautiful forever. In her short life she was other things too, but no one could see them; her physical presence was so dazzling that it eclipsed all else. Lindsey didn't understand this. Her beauty was so new to her that she didn't wholly believe in it, or anticipate its effect on others. It was a dangerous power she never learned to control, and the danger was entirely to herself.

If she'd lived longer, her beauty would have faded. Maybe then the world would have seen the full truth of who she was: her curiosity and kindness and blazing intelligence, her loyalty and courage, her rare willingness to love. Her devotion to me is one of the happy mysteries of my life. Though I did nothing particular to deserve it, she loved me instantly and unconditionally. I understand how unusual this is. I know many sisters—blood-related, without our ten-year age difference—who feel nothing of the kind.

In our mother's novels, Lindsey's story continues. Claire will keep writing them until she herself is gone. For my sister, it's a strange kind of immortality: Lydia, the red-haired heroine, will be a child forever. I've read all the books, and it feels unkind to say so, but I find the stories tedious—far less compelling, to me, than the adult life Lindsey might have lived. I imagine her traveling the world, doing and discovering. Finding happiness, maybe, with a man who saw her clearly—the full complexity of the person she'd been all along, and the infinitely more interesting one she would have become.

Becoming, I've learned, is a lifelong process. My parents are sixty-five now, and still becoming. I am regularly astonished by their capacity for change. In her older age, Claire is generous in a way that once eluded her. In her face I see traces of the woman Lindsey might have grown into. My father's tenderness is sometimes startling. In all the years of my childhood, I can't remember him crying. When I visit him now, his eyes fill at my arrival, and again when we say goodbye.

Long ago, on the other side of the world, a driver misjudged a turn—an insignificant error, a meter's miscalculation. The rest is consequence. We live at the intersection of causality and chance.

At this writing, our short lives continue. The oblivious Earth spins in its orbit. The mechanism is impartial, constant as clockwork—a disinterested metronome, ticking off time.

ACKNOWLEDGMENTS

I began writing *Rabbit Moon* in 2016, when the Shanghai Writers' Association gave me time and space to write in that astonishing city. The months I spent there changed me profoundly. No place in the world has so inspired me to write.

I am indebted to the Maison Dora Maar, where I rediscovered these characters after a hiatus of some years, and to the Ernest and Mary Hemingway House in Ketchum, Idaho. It was a great honor to finish the manuscript in the master's final home.

Bill Clegg championed the book from the very beginning. Dan Pope, Laura Chen, Malachy Tallack and Helen Elaine Lee read the book at various stages and offered valuable insights. Dr. Yidi Wu read the final manuscript with extraordinary acuity and patience, and helped me make it better. I'm more grateful than I can say.

J.H.

ABOUT THE AUTHOR

Jennifer Haigh is the author of the short-story collection *News from Heaven* and six bestselling, critically acclaimed novels. Her first, *Mrs. Kimble,* won the PEN/Hemingway Award for Debut Fiction. Her latest, *Mercy Street,* won the Mark Twain American Voice in Literature Award. Published in eighteen languages, her fiction has been recognized by the Guggenheim Foundation, the Michener Foundation and the American Academy of Arts and Letters. She lives in Boston.